DON PENDLETON's

MACK BOLAN®

Sleepers

A GOLD EAGLE BOOK FROM
WORLDWIDE®

TORONTO • NEW YORK • LONDON
AMSTERDAM • PARIS • SYDNEY • HAMBURG
STOCKHOLM • ATHENS • TOKYO • MILAN
MADRID • WARSAW • BUDAPEST • AUCKLAND

First edition January 2003

ISBN 0-373-61488-8

Special thanks and acknowledgment to Mike Newton for his contribution to this work.

SLEEPERS

Printed in U.S.A.

"We'll get him. He's a human being like the rest of us."

"Don't be so sure. His dedication to the cause is all-consuming."

"That's exactly what I'm counting on," Bolan replied. Fanatics took themselves so seriously that they often made mistakes leading directly to their own downfall. From Rasputin to Hitler, Jim Jones to David Koresh, hard-core zealots had fumbled their way to self-destruction.

The bad news was that they nearly always took innocents with them into oblivion.

Bolan's mission was to minimize the body count and stop Jasha Seriozha before he could light a string of funeral pyres from coast to coast. So far, they were running behind, but the game wasn't over yet.

Not until he heard the final gun.

Other titles available in this series:

Blood Fever
Knockdown
Assault
Backlash
Siege
Blockade
Evil Kingdom
Counterblow
Hardline
Firepower
Storm Burst
Intercept
Lethal Impact
Deadfall
Onslaught
Battle Force
Rampage
Takedown
Death's Head
Hellground
Inferno
Ambush
Blood Strike
Killpoint
Vendetta
Stalk Line
Omega Game
Shock Tactic
Showdown
Precision Kill
Jungle Law
Dead Center
Tooth and Claw
Thermal Strike
Day of the Vulture
Flames of Wrath
High Aggression
Code of Bushido
Terror Spin
Judgment in Stone
Rage for Justice
Rebels and Hostiles
Ultimate Game
Blood Feud
Renegade Force
Retribution
Initiation
Cloud of Death
Termination Point
Hellfire Strike
Code of Conflict
Vengeance
Executive Action
Killsport
Conflagration
Storm Front
War Season
Evil Alliance
Scorched Earth
Deception
Destiny's Hour
Power of the Lance
A Dying Evil
Deep Treachery
War Load
Sworn Enemies
Dark Truth
Breakaway
Blood and Sand
Caged

Our history is every human history; a black and gory business, with more scoundrels than wise men at the lead, and more louts than both put together to cheer and follow.

—Philip Wylie,
Generation of Vipers, 1942

I won't repeat the great mistake of history. This time we finish it. This time we do it right and put the threat to sleep.

—Mack Bolan

For Yosef Ishran and Koby Mandell,
murdered by terrorists in Israel on May 9, 2001. *Shalom.*

PROLOGUE

April 4, Shelby County, Kentucky

Ardie Mathis loved caves. There was something about the dark, clammy world underground that set his pulse racing and made the small hairs bristle on his neck. It was a mixture of fear and excitement, recognizing the risks and still forcing himself to confront primal fears.

The fear of getting lost within a labyrinth where every passage looked the same.

The fear of being trapped belowground by a cave-in, crushed by falling rock or condemned to slow death from thirst and starvation.

The fear of being grounded if his parents found out.

Ardie Mathis was twelve years old, a budding spelunker whose father and mother dismissed his passion as a dangerous phase he'd outgrow, given guidance and time. They'd enrolled him in scouting to help him make friends and divert his "unhealthy" interest to more "normal" outdoor pursuits, but in the process they had missed the point.

Ardie had a hard time making friends. In fact, he was generally happier on his own than with peers.

And Ardie didn't want to be outdoors. He didn't care a thing about hunting or fishing or hiking in bright, sunny meadows.

He wanted to be underground.

It wasn't his fault, really. Ardie blamed it on Jules Verne and Mark Twain. Verne's *Journey to the Centre of the Earth* was Ardie's favorite novel, his paperback copy twice replaced in the past three years because he thumbed it to tatters. Twain's *Tom Sawyer* ran a fair second, if only for the part where Tom and Becky Thatcher elude Injun Joe in a perilous cavern.

Great stuff. And could Ardie help it if his parents chose to live within five miles of Tom Sawyer State Park? They should have known the temptation would be too great for their adventurous only child to resist.

What they don't know won't hurt me, Ardie thought, smiling as he began to check his gear. He had a flashlight and a plastic baggie filled with extra batteries, his Boy Scout knife with half a dozen useful blades, an old pair of his father's gloves, beef jerky, a canteen and two fat bags of trail mix.

He was good to go.

The cave was new to him. Ardie had found it two weeks earlier, exploring on the outskirts of the park, but this would be his first chance to explore it. It was Saturday, his father on duty at the Simpsonville fire station, his mother pulling a volunteer shift at the old folks' home in Todds Point.

Ardie was on his own until his mom got home at four o'clock, a sweet six hours and thirteen minutes down the road.

The entrance to the cave was on a southward-facing bluff above a riverbed. Ardie went in on hands and knees, knowing that he could wash his jeans before his mom got home and she would never know the difference.

He didn't need his flashlight for the first twenty feet or so, enough sunlight streaming past him through the cave's mouth to light his way. At first he worried that the lighted portion of the cave might be all there was, but then he encountered a wall of rock that seemed to be the terminus but found to his delight that the cave turned left at a ninety-degree angle, its stony floor descending at a gentle rate.

Too cool!

This had potential. If it panned out well enough, Ardie might look forward to several days of exploration when he had the time. And who could say he wouldn't have a truly great discovery on his hands?

Disappointment hit him like a slap in the face when his flashlight showed him a dead end some twenty-five or thirty feet beyond the left-hand turn. He almost groaned aloud, was ready to turn back before his flashlight picked out something in the farthest corner of the underground cul-de-sac.

Ardie's science teacher had told him once that there was no such thing as a straight line in nature. He wasn't sure he believed that—what about snowflakes and strata in rocks?—but he didn't believe Mother Nature had sculpted a square, boxlike object at the back of a cave fifty feet underground.

No way.

Which meant he'd found somebody's stash.

But stash of what?

Crawling toward the object, Ardie saw that it was wrapped in something resembling plastic, but thicker.

Prodding with his finger, he decided it was more like rubber-coated tarp. The thing was dusty, as if it had lain there undisturbed for years.

Where did the dust come from, inside a cave?

He thought about what might be underneath the wrapping. Something like a crate or chest, the way it felt. Rigid, unyielding to the touch. Someone had found the cave before him—maybe years before—and used it as a hiding place.

Again, for what?

He thought at once of drugs, like on the TV news, but quickly ruled it out. No one would hide a stash of dope that size for years when he could sell it and be a millionaire.

Some kind of loot, perhaps. Bank robbers could've pulled a job and stowed the money here, meaning to come back later when the heat died down, but they were caught instead and sent to prison. Maybe they were dead by now and took the secret to their graves.

It would be Ardie's secret now. He could forget about the drudgery of mowing lawns for pocket money. This could be his private bank and he—

Get real! What were the chances there would be cash inside?

Ask it another way—what were the odds that he'd find anything at all?

Ardie took out his pocketknife, opened the long blade and began to peel away the tarp. It had a greasy feel to it, beneath the layer of dust, that made him want to wash his hands.

Later for that.

There was a metal chest inside the tarp, dark green, reminding him of something from the Army-surplus store in town. There was a hasp and combination lock, but Ardie didn't have to beat the dial.

He simply had to use his head.

Folding the scout knife's cutting blade, he opened up another one and went to work with a miniature screwdriver, removing four small screws that held the hasp in place.

He raised the lid and blinked at what he saw. Some kind of radio, he thought it was. There was a pistol in a plastic bag, a funny-looking piece of pipe with threading on one end, and blocks of something that resembled clay.

On top of everything there was a plastic object that reminded Ardie of the little travel clock he took along on camping trips—except that this one counted backward.

...15...

Why was it doing that?

...13...

Why were those wires strung out between the clock and one of the clay blocks?

...11...

Ardie got it then, and panic overwhelmed him as he scrambled back the way he'd come, losing his knife and flashlight in the process. It was only fifty feet to daylight, but it seemed like fifty miles.

He made the turn, was through it with the sunlit entrance to the cave in view, when a thunderclap enveloped him and shot him out the cave's mouth like a bullet from a gun.

His last thought prior to impact was an image of his mother's smiling face.

May 11, North Las Vegas, Nevada

THE POSTMAN WHISTLED as he finished loading his truck. Bright and early Monday morning, eighty-two degrees in the shade, and he felt wonderful. It didn't faze him that his co-workers were bitching, some of them hungover from the weekend. That was normal. He had learned to live with it and had been in the same condition more than once himself.

But not this day.

This morning it was great to be alive.

The postman's name—as far as anybody knew—was Jacob Moss. It said so on his driver's license, on his Social Security card, on the three credit cards in his wallet and throughout his personnel file with the U.S. Postal Service.

There were nothing but exemplary reports in that file. Only kind words from his supervisors, testimonies to his dedication and efficiency. There were three letters of appreciation for his diligence from patrons on his route.

Jacob Moss had been carrier of the month nineteen times in his twenty years of service, an unprecedented honor in his zip code area. No matter that it made him sound a bit like Typhoid Mary when he spoke the words aloud.

It was an honor and he wore it proudly.

But the honors paled beside what he meant to accomplish that morning.

Finished with his loading, Moss stepped back to take a silent inventory. Six large bags of bundled mail, two dozen parcels and one duffel bag containing the items for his very special delivery.

The duffel bag hadn't been postmarked or inspected.

Moss had brought the bag from home. A little something extraspecial for this Day of Days.

Inside the duffel bag he had an AK-47 assault rifle loaded with a 100-round drum of 7.62 mm FMJ ammunition. A heavy bandolier of 30-round banana clips would keep the Kalashnikov rocking after he fired off his first hundred rounds. An assortment of antipersonnel and incendiary grenades had been included to spice up the show.

Moss was never satisfied with halfway measures.

He was "going postal" with a vengeance, doing it in style.

The Kevlar vest he wore beneath his powder-blue shirt wasn't the most comfortable item for a warm spring day in the desert, but it would extend his life span. It would let him get the most out of this Monday, when he needed to be at the top of his form.

This day—his last Monday—would be a true red-letter day.

Red for the cause he served and red for blood.

Moss turned up the radio loud as he pulled out of the parking lot and made his way through morning traffic to Las Vegas Boulevard. He turned north, putting behind him the famous strip with its lavish hotel-casinos.

For the first time in twenty years, Moss deviated from his normal route, in answer to a higher calling.

For the first time in two decades he felt free.

No one gave his postal truck a second glance as Moss drove north on Las Vegas Boulevard, following the traffic into north Las Vegas. There were no lavish gambling palaces in this suburb of the city some were pleased to call "Lost Wages." It could be any other slightly run-down desert town—long on thrift stores, coin laundries and mobile homes, short on glitz and glamour.

North Las Vegas didn't interest Moss this day. He had no business there. He drove on through, observing all the posted traffic regulations, watching for the sign that would direct him on to Nellis Air Force Base. He shifted in his seat, easing the pressure on the Colt Combat Commander semiauto pistol holstered at the small of his back.

He saw the Nellis turnoff coming up and signaled well ahead. Nothing out of the ordinary here. Business as usual, ladies and gentlemen. Your tax dollars at work.

The gate was down, same as it always was on his quarterly dry runs. Four times a year for twenty years, mapping demolition and new construction on the approach route, watching shops open and fold, names changing on the signs out front. Moss could've written a neighborhood history if he'd been so inclined.

No time for that now.

After this morning he *was* history.

An MP came out to meet him, clipboard in hand, side arm buttoned down in an awkward flap holster. Moss could have dropped him and plowed through the gate, but it would have blown his edge.

He wanted to be well inside before the shooting started, where he could inflict maximum damage in minimal time.

The MP didn't recognize him, but it made no difference. Who looked past a uniform? Moss knew from talking to the carriers who had the normal Nellis run that he should be passed through without a problem. All he had to do was sign his name, record the time and drive two hundred yards to the office building where mail was dropped off in bulk each morning, for later distribution around the base.

Most days it was a quick in-and-out.

This day it would be a one-way ride.

Moss signed the sheet with his true name, gave back the pen and clipboard, waited for the wooden gate to levitate. He drove through, navigating by the map he kept inside his head.

Forget about the mailroom.

He was heading for the hangars where they kept the fighters and their payloads. It was probably too much to hope that he would catch one of the Lockheed F-117A stealth aircraft on the ground, but he was sure to find plenty of other targets—maybe F-16 Fighting Falcons or General Dynamics F-111s, perhaps even an AV-8B Harrier II if he was very fortunate.

There would most certainly be men to kill, with all those lovely bombs and rockets.

Moss pulled up to the first hangar he saw and parked in its shade. He switched off the engine and left the key in the ignition.

Who cared if someone stole the truck?

Reaching behind the driver's seat, he unzipped the green duffel bag and removed his folding-stock Kalashnikov. Moss draped the bandolier over his head, across one shoulder, heavy with loaded magazines and grenades. Stepping from the truck, he removed the Colt from its SOB holster and slipped it inside the waistband of his pants, in front.

Ready.

Coming around the truck in shade, he met a fresh-faced airman just emerging from the hangar. Startled by the sight of Moss's armament, the young man froze.

"Mail call," Moss said, and gave him three rounds to the chest at point-blank range.

He stepped across the dead man's twitching legs and crossed the hangar's threshold. A dozen airmen and mechanics were immediately visible, none of them armed.

Why should they be?

It was peacetime and they were in the States.

"Mail call!" Moss said again, shouting this time to be heard over his own gunfire. "Come and get it!"

August 19, Dallas, Texas

THE CALL HAD BEEN a long time coming. After years—decades—of waiting, Jared Hatch had managed to convince himself that it would never come.

But he was wrong.

The meeting had been set for noon, his normal lunch hour, though Hatch had called in sick that day. He was supposed to meet the caller at a waffle house on Highway 67, east of Red Bird Airport. Tardiness wouldn't be tolerated.

Hatch had thought about refusing, trying to explain his change of mind and heart, but how did one explain a revelation that had crept up on him over twenty years, altering his thought processes one tiny synapse at a time? How could he make a perfect stranger understand?

Nobody's perfect, Hatch thought, swallowing a gust of nervous laughter.

He could joke about it the following day or the one after that, if he was still alive. Right now, survival was the top priority.

Hatch took the lockbox from its hiding place beneath the bedroom closet's floor, replaced the carpet there, then used his key. The lock was stiff—more than three years since he had opened it to check the contents of the box, but everything seemed fine.

Inside the box two pistols rested on a bed of felt. One was a .22-caliber Ruger Mark I target pistol, its seven-inch barrel fattened by a custom-made suppressor designed for use with subsonic rounds. The other was a Smith & Wesson Model 410 autoloader. It bore no suppressor and would be noisy as hell if Hatch started cranking off its ten .40-caliber rounds.

Which to take?

Make it both.

Hatch removed each pistol in turn from the box, verified that both were loaded and jacked a round into the chamber of each. That done, he set the Ruger's safety and gently lowered the Smith & Wesson's hammer. The larger pistol had a double-action first-shot capability that allowed him to carry it with the safety off. He had a shoulder holster for the Ruger, a belt holster for the Smith & Wesson. Neither one of them would show beneath the navy blazer he had bought a size too large, specifically to hide the guns.

He hoped that neither weapon would be needed, hoped the stranger would listen to reason, but instinct and training told him to be prepared for the worst. If there was trouble, he would use whatever force was necessary to protect himself.

When he was dressed and armed, Hatch made a final circuit of his small apartment, picking up his car keys, turning off the lights. It was a simple place and somewhat overpriced, but it was home.

Hatch was surprised to feel a sense of dread at leaving it behind.

The year-old Ford Escort started on the first try, and he drove west on Ledbetter Drive to intersect Highway 67, turning south on the interstate there and watching for the waffle house, its billboard looming on sixty-foot pylons. An off-ramp dropped him at the entrance to the parking lot.

The caller hadn't said what he was driving. Hatch was thirteen minutes early, so he sat and waited in the Escort, watching diners come and go. His contact was male and had promised to wear a red windbreaker; beyond that, Hatch was clueless. They were supposed to meet outside and go from there.

He sat and waited, checking his watch at compulsive ten-second intervals. Cars came and went in the lot, disgorging customers mostly in pairs or larger groups. The waffle house appeared to draw few solo diners at this time of day.

Hatch had begun to feel conspicuous, the odd man out, when he noticed a flicker of movement at the far-right periphery of his vision. Before he could turn, a sharp rapping on the passenger window made him jump. Hatch twisted in his seat and found a stranger staring at him through the window. Sandy hair combed straight back from an unremarkable face. The red nylon windbreaker covered a black polo shirt and gray slacks.

Hatch unlocked the door with a button on his armrest. A draft of cheap cologne preceded his contact into the Escort. The stranger looked him over for a moment. Hatch couldn't have said if his expression was a grimace or a blighted smile.

"You're very prompt, Comrade," the stranger said at last.

"You said it was important."

"Discipline is always critical."

"I was surprised to hear from you," Hatch said, "after so long a time."

"Surprised?" One of the sandy eyebrows arched.

"It seems superfluous. Today, I mean, with world conditions as they are."

"Why would you think that anything has changed, Comrade?"

The stranger's tone was reasonable and relaxed. Why, then, did Hatch feel suddenly as if the words were filled with menace?

"I assumed—"

"That you would be excused from duty? Why would you think that, *Comrade?*"

He stressed the title as a kind of warning, Hatch supposed. Could this man possibly be ignorant of all that had transpired in recent years? Was he insane?

"It has occurred to me that our priorities are different now," Hatch said.

"Fulfillment of your duty is the first priority." The stranger's grimace-smile had disappeared. "You took an oath, Comrade."

"Of course."

Hatch knew what he had to do. He shifted in the driver's seat, facing his contact more directly, freeing up the Ruger pistol slung beneath his left armpit. It would be awkward, trying to draw and fire within the confines of his vehicle, but it was better than stepping outside, fighting in the parking lot at high noon.

The stranger's face took on a sad expression, drooping at the corners of his mouth. "You disappoint me, Comrade. I was told you were a man who could be trusted."

"I've said I was surprised, that's all." Hatch slipped a hand inside his jacket, reaching for the silenced Ruger. "Would you like a cigarette?"

He heard a muffled *pop* and felt a wasplike sting beneath his right nipple.

"You don't smoke," the stranger said.

Hatch glanced down at his chest. There was no blood, but he was wounded. He could feel the numbness spreading rapidly. His empty right hand felt like lead, slipping into his lap.

"Ricin," the stranger said. "An extract from the castor-oil plant, if you recall your basic chemistry. Toxicity in concentrated doses is equivalent to the bite of a large cobra."

Hatch slumped in his seat, gasping for breath. His vision blurred, but he could see the snubby weapon his contact held. It resembled a sawed-off air pistol.

"You should have kept the faith," the stranger said. "Nothing changes. Nothing will ever change."

Hatch tried to answer him, refute those words, but his tongue and vocal cords seemed paralyzed. He was unconscious when the stranger left him, choking on his last breath moments later. As he slipped into oblivion, the stranger's last words echoed in his mind.

''Nothing changes. Nothing will ever change.''

CHAPTER ONE

Terre Haute, Indiana

Mack Bolan drove his rented Chevy Blazer past the federal prison at a steady fifty miles per hour, resisting the temptation to slow down and rubberneck. He'd seen the place before, but it was new to his companion. Passing by, she swiveled in her seat to watch the place until they were well past and headed south out of town on Highway 41.

"It doesn't look so bad," she said.

"It's bad enough," he promised her.

Terre Haute's lockup was the toughest in the federal system, a landlocked Alcatraz reserved for the worst of the worst. Lifers, who were rated dangerous even behind bars, were housed there in isolation so complete it was alleged by some to drive men mad. Terre Haute also housed the only federal death row in America, with a cast of dead men walking that included contract killers, terrorists and homicidal drug lords. Few of those who entered Terre Haute in chains would leave the place alive.

This day was an exception, and the Executioner was part of it. The plan hadn't been his, but he would make the best of it—and hope it didn't prove to be a catastrophic error.

Eight miles south of town he pulled into the parking lot of the Rustic Rest Motel. It had the first part right, at least, with some two dozen no-frills bungalows arranged in a squared-off C formation, butted up against a forest sprawling over several acres. The accommodations were distinctly rustic, but they didn't promise Bolan anything resembling rest.

He was here to work, not catch up on his beauty sleep or browse around the Antique Barn across the highway.

They had checked in as a couple to avoid suspicion, but the standard full-sized motel bed was undisturbed. After an early breakfast at the coffee shop a half mile farther south, they'd driven into Terre Haute and cased the prison twice, noting approaches and escape routes, eyeballing the place as if its looming walls might share some secret of whatever was transpiring on the other side.

Scoping the prison was more an academic exercise than anything else, as far as Bolan was concerned. He wasn't breaking in or helping anyone escape.

The prisoner he needed would be hand-delivered to his bungalow within the hour.

As for what came after that, Fate would decide.

His strategy could only carry them so far.

The woman slipped off her jacket when they were well inside the bungalow. It was a breezy autumn day outside, but the windbreaker was specifically intended to conceal the Gyurza P-9 semiauto pistol that she wore in a fast-draw shoulder rig.

The Russian Gyurza had an awesome reputation,

but was still untested in the West. Chambered for special 9 mm cored rounds, packing eighteen of same in its box magazine, the pistol could reportedly penetrate thirty layers of Kevlar and two 1.4 mm titanium plates at 100 meters, or 4 mm of steel armor at sixty meters. Nearly two inches shorter and 4.5 ounces lighter than Bolan's Beretta 93-R, it still threw slugs downrange at 1,362 feet per second, versus the Beretta's 1,230 feet per second.

He hoped Tasya Galenka could handle all that hardware if the need arose. By the time he found out otherwise, they might both be dead.

Her voice cut through his thoughts.

"You still don't like the plan," she said.

It wasn't a question, but she clearly expected some comment.

"I don't have to like it," Bolan said. "I just have to make it work."

"It bothers you to use Barnum."

"Is this a circus act? You're reading minds?"

"You make it obvious."

Why not? he thought. The notion of springing a lifer from maximum security and taking him out on a road trip ran hard against the grain for Bolan. This particular lifer made it that much worse.

"He could've told us what he knows and stayed inside where he belongs," Bolan replied.

"You don't think he can help us?" She made it a question this time, whether from true interest or a simple desire to prolong conversation Bolan couldn't say.

He cut it short. "We'll see when he gets here."

Another hour and seven minutes by his watch, one

minute less according to the cheap electric clock beside the bed. They would be getting Barnum ready now, a change of garb from prison orange to standard street clothes.

They would transport Barnum in a standard "unmarked" car, immediately recognizable as heat to any sharp-eyed felon by its whip antenna and its federal license plates. An armored truck would draw too much attention, but the guards would certainly be armed. Their cargo wasn't dangerous per se—not anymore, although the charges filed against him specified that he had caused at least eleven deaths.

Bolan would have been pleased to let him rot in peace at Terre Haute, but it had been determined further up the food chain that the prisoner could render critical support to Bolan's mission if they put him on a leash.

It would be Bolan's job to make him heel.

And if he failed, the federal lockup would be short one lifer. He wouldn't permit Barnum to slip the leash and disappear.

No way at all.

The woman peeled two sticks of gum and popped them both into her mouth, concentrating on the oral exercise until she found a rhythm. She switched on the television, surfed one time around the dial, stopping at a manic talk show. A studio audience was chanting while a pair of transvestites went head-to-head, making a sandwich of the program's host.

"Why do your citizens disgrace themselves this way?" the woman asked.

"They want their fifteen minutes," Bolan said.

"Explain, please."

"Andy Warhol said that in the future everyone will be famous for fifteen minutes. Some of these clowns took it to heart."

"Is fame so important to Americans?"

"To some, I guess."

She switched the TV off and turned to face him. "What is important to you?"

"Right now," he said, "this job."

"IF YOU ASK ME," Pete Travis said, "this whole thing stinks."

"Nobody asked you," Jack Finch replied. "They didn't ask me. They never ask."

"All I'm saying, it doesn't sit right."

"You're preaching to the choir. I don't like it any better than you do."

"We're supposed to bring pricks in, not let them go."

"I hear you, champ."

Finch felt cumbersome and bloated with the Kevlar vest beneath his suit, the powder-blue dress shirt a size too large and slightly rumpled. Body armor was for jumping fugitives, transporting witnesses or prisoners to court when they were likely to be shot in transit or rescued by accomplices still at large.

The Kevlar didn't seem to fit a job like this.

Of course, there'd never been a job like this before, as far as Finch knew.

So here he was with Travis, killing time in the reception area of maximum security. Their side arms had been checked on entering the prison; their heavy firepower—an Uzi and a 12-gauge Remington—was waiting in the car outside. They stood and sweated in their suits and Kevlar, waiting for the lifer they'd been ordered to transport.

And drop his sorry ass at a motel.

Ours not to reason why, Finch told himself, trying to relax under the scrutiny of a burly guard behind glass. The prison atmosphere made Finch uneasy, despite his frequent visits to federal lockups from coast to coast. He could feel the weight of the place bearing down on him, threatening to squeeze out a confession to some half-forgotten sin.

A door clanged in the middle distance, and he saw their lifer moving through a locked-off sally port, flanked by two guards. They were halfway to the reception area, having cleared one heavy door and waited for it to slam shut behind them before the next one was open.

Hurry up and wait in stir.

Proceed toward freedom one door at a time.

The lifer wore a brown suit that was more or less his size, straight off the rack at bargain rates. His shoes and socks were black, a major fashion felony. The chain around his waist was stainless steel—ditto the handcuffs on his wrists, connected to the belly chain by half a dozen polished links that kept his hands around groin level.

It was lifer chic, no shackles on his legs, but Finch didn't think the prick would try to run away.

He had already cut his deal. The chains were temporary.

He was on his way.

The closer door rolled open, then slid shut once more behind the two guards and their prisoner. The guards had dark frowns on their book-end faces, clearly angered at giving up their charge to men they'd never seen before, acting on orders they would never fully understand.

One of them had a clipboard with a ballpoint pen attached to it by string. He shoved the board at Finch, not quite touching him.

"Sign on the dotted line and he's all yours."

Finch was signing when the second guard spoke up.

"You want to tell us what this deal is all about?"

Finch finished, passed the clipboard back and said, "If I knew that, I'd have my feet up on a desk in Washington."

"It's like that, huh?" The guard was clearly skeptical.

Finch ignored the question, replying with one of his own. "You have keys for the cuffs and belly chain?"

The first guard switched hands with his clipboard, digging in a pocket of his slacks. "The cuffs are standard. Here's the padlock key."

Finch palmed it and put it in the inside pocket of his suit coat.

"Right," he said. "We're out of here."

He gripped the prisoner's left elbow with his right hand and propelled him toward the exit, Travis falling into step on the lifer's right and holding his other arm. They set a brisk pace toward the door, tracked by three pairs of hostile eyes. The booth guard made them wait five seconds before he keyed the lock and let them out into a corridor that reeked of Lysol and fresh paint. They stopped once more, to claim their guns, then hit the bricks.

Outside, the autumn sun provided more light than warmth, a breeze ruffling Finch's hair where it had thinned on top. He steered their prisoner toward a standard-issue Crown Victoria, dusty brown with black-wall tires, twin antennae sprouting from the trunk and black-on-white federal tags.

You might as well paint U.S. Marshal's Service on the doors, Finch thought. Anyone who didn't recognize the Crown Vic as a cop car had one eye closed and the other out of focus.

Never mind.

As disconcerting as their mission was, it still qualified as a milk run. Pick up the inmate at Point A and drop him at Point B, eight miles away. The lifer's crimes, though once the stuff of florid headlines, had been long since swept aside by other scandals, other felonies.

Old news. Nobody cared.

Except the victims, maybe, and the loved ones they had left behind.

The victims were deceased, though, and their grieving kin had no idea the man responsible for so much bloodshed was about to take a walk.

He'd cut a deal with Uncle Sam. It wouldn't clear the slate, but it would help.

Enough to let him make parole?

Finch hoped not, but it was out of his hands. This day he was nothing more than an overqualified delivery boy.

They put the lifer in back, secured the doors and took their seats in front of the Plexiglas screen, Travis behind the steering wheel.

"You ready?" Finch asked him.

"As I'll ever be," Travis replied.

"Okay. Let's get it done."

MAJOR TASYA GALENKA was tired of waiting. She had spent the past week in American hotel rooms, mostly killing time, and she was sick to death of it. Watching her strange companion, the American who called himself Mike Belasko, she wondered how he could accept the tedium with such apparent ease.

Police work and espionage, as she well knew, were fields that required patience. She had learned that much from the beginning of her service with the KGB, reborn as the Foreign Intelligence Service—SVR—when Russia discarded communism in 1991. Galenka had been a five-year veteran of the service when that political earthquake shook Russia to its very foundations, and she had remained in service—rising through the ranks on equal parts of cunning and merit—because she loved her country and believed it needed protection.

Sometimes, in fact, the SVR had to protect Mother Russia from herself.

It was a strange sensation, working in America. Her first time on U.S. soil, Galenka noted some of the problems trumpeted by *Pravda* in the old days, but she also saw much to admire. Much to covet. Her fellow countrymen were embarked on a course of action that would bring Russia closer to the West—closer, perhaps, to American standards of living—but there were snares along that path that had to be removed by skillful hands.

Galenka hoped her American colleague was equal to the task. He seemed competent enough on the surface, but they had barely met before embarking on the drive to Terre Haute. The real test would come later, when they took delivery of the prisoner and went to work.

Galenka hoped the tall man wouldn't disappoint her.

If he did, it might cost both of them their lives.

As for the world…

She didn't want to think about that possibility. An agent who anticipated failure at the outset of a mission often failed, in fact, a victim of his or her own low expectations.

Tasya Galenka had a personal stake in this mission.

Failure meant never going home.

Nervous and hating it, she toyed with the remote control but didn't turn the television on again. Must-see TV held no allure for her. There was enough grim drama in her life already, and canned laughter couldn't raise her spirits.

How much longer?

A glance at her watch told Galenka that barely two minutes had passed since the last time she'd checked. Dammit! She would've guessed a quarter of an hour had passed, at least, and the delivery was late.

She lit a cigarette to calm herself, drew the smoke deeply into her lungs. The American took no notice of her, thumbing through a tabloid newspaper that had been waiting for them in the room. Its headlines blared scandal and debauchery. Another Hollywood divorce. Another movie star arrested with narcotics. Senatorial sex games.

All of that held no interest for Major Galenka. The puerile American obsession with sex and scandal was one export she hoped her countrymen might shun. There were enough distractions in post-Communist Russia already, with runaway inflation, widespread poverty, product shortages, street crime, political upheavals, rampant racism and near universal corruption.

She shifted in her uncomfortable chair, reaching inside her windbreaker to adjust her shoulder holster. The weight of the Gyurza pistol and its two spare magazines reminded Galenka—as if any reminder were necessary—that her mission had life-or-death stakes.

There was no point in hoping that she wouldn't have to kill before the job was done. Wet work was preordained and unavoidable.

The only question now was when it would begin and how many would die—by her hand or Belasko's, maybe at the hands of those they hunted.

Galenka wasn't afraid of bloodshed. She had killed three persons in her sixteen years of service with the KGB and SVR. Two of them were Ukrainian drug smugglers who preferred death to arrest and trial. The third had been a triggerman for a Chechen crime syndicate, dispatched to kill Galenka after she arrested an important member of the "family."

All three were dead because they'd underestimated her, supposing it would be an easy thing to kill a woman who stood barely five foot four in stocking feet and weighed 130 pounds.

They had been wrong, but it was close with the Chechen. Galenka bore puckered scars front and back, from where his single shot had pierced her abdomen, passing within a millimeter of her left kidney.

She remembered the pain and the slow work of recovery.

And she had vowed never to hesitate again before she pulled the trigger on an enemy.

Not even one whom she had loved in better days.

"It won't be long now," Bolan said.

Galenka analyzed his comment, looking for an insult—possibly a hidden reference to her nerves—but there was nothing she could isolate.

"You think he will cooperate?" she asked.

"He's chasing clemency. I wouldn't bet on a reduced sentence no matter what he does, but if he tries a double cross he's history."

She wondered if Belasko had some private grudge against the prisoner, or if he simply held all traitors in contempt. Galenka sensed that he wouldn't mind using force against the prisoner if it should be required.

Neither would she.

Their mission was of critical importance. It transcended individual concerns and dwarfed specific lives.

Galenka would do anything required of her in order to succeed.

She hoped her own life wasn't calculated in the final price.

"HERE WE GO."

Adrik Dyakonov cocked his Model 81 Skorpion machine pistol and held the compact weapon in his lap, below the line of sight for any passing motorists. His driver, Dimitry Petrov, gunned the stolen Oldsmobile Cutlass Supreme to a legal fifty-five miles per hour, tailing the nondescript car that carried their target.

The third man on the team, Stanislov Babin, leaned forward and asked, "Are you sure it's him this time?"

"I'm sure," Dyakonov said, anger taut in his voice.

There had been two false starts this morning, beige prison vans departing from the Terre Haute facility on sundry errands, but this time Dyakonov had glimpsed the target through a pane of tinted window glass.

More to the point, he'd watched the lawmen arrive and enter the prison in their brown four-door sedan, no passenger visible in the cage behind the driver's seat. When they emerged twenty-five minutes later, the cage was occupied.

Who else could it be?

Dyakonov's orders were simple: kill the prisoner and anyone who tried to protect him. Deal with witnesses as necessary. He had received half of the contract payment up front—a tidy fifteen thousand U.S. dollars—and he meant to earn the rest as soon as the two lawmen reached their destination.

It was easy money, getting paid to do what turned him on when done free, and he wouldn't have tried to cheat his client on the contract.

Not after he met the man and caught a glimpse of what was lurking in the darkness just behind his eyes.

It would be easier to kill the U.S. Marshals and their prisoner, along with anyone else who happened to get in the way.

Babin was ready in the back seat with his AKMS assault rifle, humming softly to himself the way he often did before a kill. It was a disconcerting habit at first notice, but Dyakonov had worked enough contracts with Babin by now that he found the tuneless music calming to his nerves.

Three men, one vehicle.

They could have pulled alongside the brown sedan and strafed it from the driver's side, but their client was interested in learning where the prisoner was taken, who was waiting for him outside prison walls. Dyakonov had been instructed to purchase a Polaroid camera and snap photos of anyone he managed to kill on the reception committee.

Photographs were no problem.

For thirty thousand U.S. dollars he would happily have bagged their heads.

How many others were privileged to mix lucrative business with pleasure?

"Where in hell are they going?" Babin asked from the back seat.

"That's what we're trying to find out," Dyakonov reminded him.

To Petrov, he said, "More speed! You're losing them!"

"I'm losing no one," Petrov retorted. "You want a speeding ticket from highway patrol, it's fine with me."

"Do what I tell you."

Adrik Dyakonov wasn't afraid of the American highway patrol. He had no fear of any badge or uniform. In Russia he had killed militia officers who tried to lock him up, and he had done the same to a police detective in Chicago, last Christmas Eve.

Police were easy. Those in the United States were

easiest of all, with their elaborate rules and regulations governing each move they made. Obtain search warrants. Spell the names precisely. Read each prisoner his civil rights and furnish lawyers who made sport of the police at trial.

It was a joke.

American police were unprepared for someone like Adrik Dyakonov. They hadn't touched him yet, in seven years of operating stateside. He believed they never would.

"Who is this convict, anyway?" Babin asked.

"I already told you once, I didn't ask. The client wants him dead. The client pays in cash."

"It makes me wonder, though," Babin went on. "He must be someone special, if policemen come to rescue him from prison."

"It's no rescue," Dyakonov replied. "They take him to his death."

"But they're not knowing this. It makes me wonder."

"Think about the money, then. Wonder what you will buy with your five thousand."

It was only fair, as lead contractor on the team, for Dyakonov to keep the lion's share of the reward. Babin and Petrov didn't mind, or if they did, they were intelligent enough to keep their mouths shut.

"Turning," Petrov said.

Dyakonov could see that for himself, the flashing signal light in front of them. He watched the brown sedan pull off into the parking lot of a roadside motel.

"Drive past and circle back," he ordered Petrov. "Hurry!"

Petrov gunned the Oldsmobile, racing fifty yards

down the highway before he cranked the steering wheel hard left and put them through a tire-roasting U-turn. An oncoming truck blew its air horn in a long, wailing blast. Petrov jabbed his left hand out the open driver's window, middle finger raised defiantly. He cursed nonstop in Russian as he swung the Olds into the driveway of the Rustic Rest Motel.

The lawmen were already out of their vehicle, one of them helping a man in handcuffs emerge from the back seat. Both looked up as the Olds hit the parking lot, tires smoking in a skid.

Dyakonov lurched forward, unrestrained by a seat belt, as the car jerked to a halt. An outstretched hand kept him from kissing the dashboard, a curse torn from his lips as he fumbled with the inside handle of his door.

Behind him, Babin was out of the car and firing with his AKMS, peppering the unmarked police car with short bursts. Dyakonov shoved his door open and lunged for the pavement as all hell broke loose.

BOLAN WAS ON HIS FEET and reaching for the doorknob when the shooting started. He had heard the Feds pull in, confirmed it with a quick glance through the window, nodding once to his companion as he reached the door. The squeal of tires outside had put his guard up, but the sound of automatic weapons in the parking lot still took him by surprise.

He hadn't thought the killing would begin this early in the game.

Bolan drew his Beretta 93-R as he opened the door, ducking through in a crouch. A black Oldsmobile was parked fifteen or twenty feet behind the federal Crown

Victoria, doors open on both sides as three gunmen blazed away with automatic weapons.

The Crown Vic was taking hits, its rear window imploding as Bolan ran forward and knelt at the grille, momentarily shielded from incoming rounds by the sedan's engine block. He heard Galenka drop beside him, on his right.

To his left, one of the U.S. Marshals glared at Bolan and his weapon, blinking fresh blood from a scalp wound out of his right eye.

"Who the hell are you?" he demanded.

"Your contacts," Bolan told him. "Can the ID wait?"

"ID can kiss my ass," the marshal snapped. "If we get out of this—"

A spray of bullets cut the observation short. One round ripped through the marshal's cheek and lifted him enough to let another drill his throat. He went down in a spray of blood and stayed there, one leg twisted under him while the other briefly drummed blacktop.

Bolan moved up to take his place behind the Crown Vic's open door. It wasn't much in terms of cover, but he had no shot at all unless he made the shift. He thumbed the fire-selector switch on his Beretta down for 3-round bursts and waited for an opening.

Across the Crown Vic, on the driver's side, the second marshal called out, "Jack! Where are you, Jack?"

"He's down," Bolan said. "Watch yourself."

"I'm watching, pal!"

The marshal squeezed off two rounds from his Smith & Wesson autoloader, ducking behind his open door. It wasn't good enough, though, as a burst from a Kalashnikov punched through the sheet metal and knocked him sprawling.

Bolan framed the rifleman in his Beretta's sights and fired a 3-round burst before he had a chance to duck and cover. He was instantly rewarded as the shooter's head exploded with a crimson halo and the dead man toppled over backward, his finger clenched around the AK's trigger, firing at the clouds.

One down and two to go.

His Russian sidekick nailed the second, taking out the Oldsmobile's driver with a quick double tap from her Gyurza semiauto. The P-9's souped-up 9 mm rounds sounded more like Colt .45s at close range, cored projectiles slicing through the open driver's door like wad cutters through cardboard, finding flesh and bone.

That left one shooter, but he wasn't going down without a fight. The gunman strafed them with some kind of machine pistol, knocking shiny divots in the Crown Victoria's paint job, then retrieved his fallen comrade's AK to lay down heavier fire.

Where was the prisoner?

Back seat.

He had been climbing out, assisted by one of his escorts, when the shooting started. Whether the marshal had shoved him back inside the sedan or he had jumped back on his own, the door had slammed behind him, pinning him inside the cage.

It was as safe a place to be as anywhere, right now.

There was a lull in firing, punctuated by the clatter of an empty magazine somewhere in front of Bolan. Number three reloading the Kalashnikov.

Bolan picked out another sound, as well. What was it?

Something like a dripping faucet, but that made no sense. A punctured radiator, maybe, or—

The smell of gasoline reached Bolan's nostrils and he knew. The Crown Vic's fuel tank had been punctured. It was dribbling gas onto the pavement, reeking combustible fumes. A bullet spark or muzzle-flash could set it off and fry the prisoner before they ever had a chance to question him.

Bolan cared nothing for the man inside the car, but he couldn't afford to let him take his secrets to a fiery grave. The killing would've been for nothing then, and they would watch their chances for success go up in smoke while he was screaming through the final seconds of his wasted life.

Not yet.

The soldier lunged forward as the AK opened up again, spraying the Crown Vic's trunk and left rear fender, flattening the tire back there. Tasya Galenka cranked off three more booming rounds that drove the shooter briefly under cover.

Bolan reached the Crown Vic's right rear door and yanked it open to reveal a pale face streaked with fear sweat.

"Barnum?"

The prisoner responded with a blink and jerky nod.

"It's time to go."

Barnum shook his head emphatically. "I'm fine right here," he said.

"You smell that gasoline? You're one spark short of going up in smoke, and I can't spare you yet."

With that, he grabbed the convict's collar and

dragged him bodily out of the car. Barnum grunted as he hit the pavement, then got his legs working to help. They were both hunkered down behind the driver's door when the AK opened up again.

"You call this safe?" Barnum asked.

"Safe's a matter of degree," Bolan replied. "Stay here."

"Where the hell would I go?"

Bolan ignored the question, moving back toward the rear of the bullet-riddled Crown Victoria. He triggered two short bursts at the Olds, then rushed it, making for the passenger side. The shooter heard him coming and tried to nail him, but Galenka popped off two more slammers from her pistol and drove the rifleman back under cover.

Bolan reached the cover of the Olds and kept moving. The punctured door in front of him stood open, one last barrier before he had a clear shot at his target across the driver's seat. A spray of AK rounds took out the windshield from inside, too high to threaten him.

He cleared the door and met the shooter swiveling to face him. Bolan's Beretta stuttered twice, putting six rounds in the ten-ring from a range of six or seven feet. The impact lifted his target, driving the gunman backward, and Galenka made it official with a head shot that lifted his scalp like a cheap toupee in a windstorm.

Collapsing, the shooter still managed to fire one more burst from his assault rifle, strafing the rear of the car parked before him. Bolan heard a *whoosh* as something caught, and flames boiled up around the Crown Vic's trunk.

He doubled back, knowing he'd be too late for Barnum if the gas tank blew. Galenka got there first and dragged the handcuffed prisoner away, propelling him toward the shelter of their bungalow.

Bolan veered off course, sprinting for daylight. He was thirty feet and gaining from the Crown Vic when it blew, the shock wave dropping him facedown on blacktop.

"Are you all right?"

Galenka sounded miles away, the buzz in Bolan's ringing ears receding slowly as he rose and put his gun away.

"I'll live."

The prisoner was cutting glances back and forth between the burning car and Bolan. "That's a little close for comfort," he acknowledged in a shaky voice. "You saved my life."

"Don't take it personally," Bolan said. "I've never had much use for traitors, but you're all we've got right now."

CHAPTER TWO

Washington, D.C.

Hal Brognola took the call from Stony Man and switched on his office television, channel surfing until he came to CNN. They had a live report in progress from a motel parking lot in Vigo County, Indiana. A sign dubbed it the Rustic Rest Motel.

From where Brognola sat, it looked more like the Alamo.

Two shot-up cars were situated center stage, one of them torched, still smoldering. The bungalow behind the burned-out vehicle had taken bullet hits, as well, the windows shattered, tacky curtains flapping in the breeze.

The blond reporter needed one hand for her microphone, which left her one short to defend her hair and gaping, low-cut blouse against the gusts of wind that played with both. The big Fed focused on her words and thereby missed the best part of the show.

"...at least five now confirmed dead in what local authorities are calling Vigo County's worst known homicide in thirty years."

"Compared to what?" Brognola muttered at the screen. "Worst unknown homicide?"

"Two of the dead, we're told, are members of the U.S. Marshal's Service assigned to transport a prisoner from the federal prison at Terre Haute, eight miles up the road, to an as yet undisclosed destination. Prison administrators have declined to comment on where the officers were taking the prisoner or why they would have stopped here, at the Rustic Rest Motel."

Behind the blonde, two grim-faced men moved toward the bullet-riddled cars. In case their bearing didn't tip the audience, the windbreakers that billowed out behind them were emblazoned with foot-high letters: FBI.

"Three other victims of the shooting remain unidentified," the blonde stated, "but investigators on the scene acknowledge that the prisoner transported by the two slain federal officers is not among them. State and federal authorities refuse to speculate on whether he escaped or was abducted from his escorts by more gunmen still at large."

A prison mug shot filled the screen, giving the blonde a break. Her voice-over told Hal what he already knew.

"The missing prisoner is Burke Charles Barnum, formerly a lieutenant colonel with the U.S. Army assigned to intelligence work at the Pentagon. Barnum is forty-six years old and had seventeen years of military service behind him when he was convicted of espionage in 1995. Jurors in that case convicted Barnum of selling military secrets to Russian agents over a nine-year period before his arrest. He received a life sentence without parole when prosecutors demonstrated that several American agents exposed by Barnum either vanished or were killed in Eastern Europe before the end of the cold war in 1991."

The mug shot showed a bland face under thinning sandy hair. No one who passed him on the street would think about him twice, unless he wore the military uniform he had disgraced.

The blonde came back. Her hair was more or less in place, but no one had informed her that a button on her green blouse had worked loose, exposing lace and creamy cleavage.

Log those ratings points, Brognola thought.

"We're still waiting for an official statement at the scene," the blonde went on, "but it appears from what we've seen that gunmen in the second car behind me, here—" she half turned toward a battle-scarred Oldsmobile, showing more cleavage "—attacked the U.S. Marshals in their unmarked vehicle.

"Before our interview was interrupted by authorities, the motel's manager informed us that a man and woman now reported missing rented cabin number 7 this morning, about three hours before the shooting incident. They registered as Mr. and Mrs. Sam Dysart, a name now described by investigators as a possible alias. The Indiana license number listed on their registration card at the motel does not exist, according to the state Bureau of Motor Vehicles.

"Missing prisoner Burke Barnum was assigned to federal maximum security at Terre Haute because his crimes were considered particularly heinous, resulting in loss of multiple lives. Other infamous inmates confined to the prison have included Timothy—"

Brognola switched off the television. He'd seen enough to know what happened in the motel parking lot—up to a point, at least. Someone had trailed the marshals and their prisoner from Terre Haute, watching and waiting for a chance to strike the first time they pulled off the highway. He could even name the man responsible for the attack, with some degree of certainty.

Not that it did him any good.

The big Fed knew the bastard's name, but not where he was hiding. If he'd known the address, he could've ended it before the butcher's bill grew any longer.

No such luck.

The bloody game had started six months earlier, and no one could predict with any certainty when it would end.

Six months and half a dozen terrorist attacks on U.S. soil, each with an escalating toll of wasted human lives. They ranged from coast to coast, most recently from Newport News, Virginia, where a shipyard worker with fourteen years on the job had run amok for no apparent reason, spraying co-workers with autofire from an AK-47, killing nine and wounding seven, taking time amid the massacre to lob grenades at several ships in dry dock.

Russian frag grenades and a Kalashnikov.

It started adding up when Brognola found out that each of the attacks involved some kind of Russian army-surplus gear, none of it new. The riddle started getting scary when background investigation of the various unlikely terrorists revealed that none of them apparently existed prior to 1984 or '85.

Their paperwork went back to birth, no problem there, except that it was fake. In each of the five cases investigated by the FBI, the shooter's birth certificate belonged to someone else—specifically, to an infant who died within six months of birth at random points across the country. Someone with a fair amount of time and cash on hand had scoured the nation for those premature obituaries, then requested duplicate birth certificates in the names of applicants who had "lost" their originals. With birth certificates in hand, the rest fell quickly into place—passports, Social Security numbers, driver's licenses, high-school and college transcripts.

Stolen lives.

No, make that manufactured lives.

The first case tore it, when they fit the puzzle pieces into place. A young spelunker in Kentucky had been turned into a human cannonball after he found a buried stash of military gear. There wasn't much for lab technicians to examine when the smoke cleared and a local sheriff's team dug out the hillside with a backhoe, but the bits and pieces finally identified came from an AK-47 and a Russian military two-way radio. Soil-residue analysis identified the blasting agent as RDX plastic explosive manufactured in the Soviet bloc.

Three questions remained unanswered in that case: who had buried the stash, when and why?

Brognola now had a handle on *why,* thanks to the marathon confession of a Soviet defector who had come across in 1990, an ironic thirteen months before the Russian regime he was fleeing collapsed, rotted away from the inside.

The turncoat had described a long-term KGB campaign involving sleepers planted in the States, complete with hidden caches of communications gear and arms, programmed to spend their lives on standby for the moment when a coded call came through from Mother Russia to proclaim a day of reckoning with the U.S.

That call had never come. The Soviet state had self-destructed and the KGB was no more, at least in theory.

But what if someone from the bad old days still had a list of names and codes?

The turncoat, sunning in Miami Beach, had been contacted and supplied three names, fanatic black-ops veterans of the KGB.

One suspect had been executed in September 1991 for his part in a conspiracy to topple Boris Yeltsin's government by force.

A second candidate had eighteen years remaining on his thirty-year prison sentence, dished out for participation in the same abortive coup.

That left one name, and when he heard it Brognola had wasted no time summoning the Executioner.

But where was Bolan now?

Where were his Russian sidekick and the missing traitor who had been entrusted to their care?

Goddammit!

He scooped up the telephone and started making calls.

Clay County, Illinois

"YOU'RE ON TV by now," Bolan advised his backseat passenger. "*America's Most Wanted* by tonight. We can't afford to show you off."

"That's great," Barnum replied. "Just great. They let me out of prison to become a fugitive and get my head blown off."

"They let you out to do a job," Bolan corrected him. "It's recess time, not graduation day. We're still on track."

"Oh, really? You call this on track? The Feds'll think I set it up back there. They'll slap me with another stack of murder charges, if the Reds don't kill me first."

"There are no Reds," Galenka said, half turned toward Barnum in the Blazer's shotgun seat.

"Tell that to Seriozha when you see him—if you live that long."

Galenka blinked at mention of the name and said, "I will."

Bolan had the Blazer pointed west on Highway 50, open farmland gliding past as he maintained the posted legal speed. He had engaged the childproof locks on Barnum's doors, in case the traitor thought of bailing out. The Blazer's tinted windows screened Barnum's newly notorious profile from passing motorists or highway patrolmen.

None of which would help if they were stopped for any reason prior to finding cover for the night.

There had been time before they fled the Rustic Rest Motel to turn one lifeless marshal's pockets inside out and palm the keys to Barnum's chains. Galenka had removed them on the drive south to Vincennes, where they had crossed the Wabash River into Illinois. The crossing insulated them a bit from the ungodly heat they'd left behind—but only for the time it took news hawks to catch the squeal and get their act together.

Barnum's disappearance would be front-page news in every paper from New York to California by the following morning. Half the country's TV stations would be airing his mug shots within an hour, and the rest would pick it up by six o'clock. The crew at CNN would run it every hour on the hour, with whatever updates they could scrounge. He would have so much ink and air, a posting to the FBI's Most Wanted list would be superfluous.

Which meant that Bolan had to keep him out of sight, if possible.

And he was right, of course, that threw the plan off track, at least to some extent.

Barnum's release on loan to Bolan and Galenka had been orchestrated as a covert operation. The traitor had gained some weight and lost some hair since he was put away in 1995; if no one in the free world knew he was at large, the odds against coincidental recognition would be astronomical.

Now everybody knew, and they were screwed if Barnum showed his face.

His current face, at least.

"I need a good-sized town," he told Galenka. "Someplace large enough to have an outlet for theatrical supplies."

She smiled at that and fished a map out of the Blazer's glove compartment. Barnum chimed in from the back seat with a strained, "Say what?"

"We need to change your look," Bolan replied, "and we can't wait around for you to grow a beard or heal from plastic surgery."

"You're kidding, right?"

"The answer's makeup. Nothing Boris Karloff, but a decent makeover. We don't want Groucho glasses and a rubber nose, so scrub the small-town gag shops."

"Makeup, Jesus." Barnum shook his head. "What do you think that will accomplish?"

"If we're lucky," Bolan said, "it might keep you alive until the job's done—or at least until you've done your part."

"Oh, right."

The traitor lapsed back into silence while Galenka scanned her map. "Decatur's sixty miles due north," she reported. "A little farther on is Springfield, the state capital. Due west is East St. Louis and—"

"St. Louis just across the Mississippi," Bolan finished for her. "West it is."

They drove for several silent miles before the traitor said, "I don't think this will work."

"Look on the bright side," Bolan told him. "You're a dead man if it doesn't."

"That's the bright side?"

"Pretty much."

"Terrific."

"Some would say it's still a better chance than you deserve."

"But suddenly I'm useful," Barnum said.

"If you're alive. And if you know the man we're looking for."

"I know him. If you doubted that, I'd still be back at Terre Haute."

"That brings us back to breathing. Someone obviously wants you dead."

"You mean someone besides the Company, the NSA and all my old friends in G-2?" The convict's laugh was strained. "Tell them to take a number."

"They already have a number—yours."

Barnum's reflection in the rearview mirror stared back at the Executioner with narrowed eyes. "You think those guns at the motel were Seriozha's?"

"You tell me," Bolan replied.

"If that's true, we're already screwed. It means somebody on the inside tipped him off that I was getting out. It means he knows *you* know. He's taking countermeasures."

"What's a mole or two between comrades?"

"Nothing much," Barnum said. "Just the difference between success and failure. Make that life and death."

"I understood you volunteered."

"To help, all right? Not spend my last few hours in a shooting gallery."

"You want me to, I'll turn around and take you back right now."

"And testify in my defense when Justice charges me with murdering two federal officers?"

"No testimony," Bolan said. "We don't exist."

"Uh-huh. I recognize the lady's accent," Barnum said, "but what are you?"

"What difference does it make?"

"I like to have some idea who I'm dealing with."

"My job gets harder if you're dead. Leave it at that, for now."

"Okay. You may as well keep driving, then. Check out that makeup shop. A nice Bill Cosby look might get me through the weekend in one piece—or maybe something in a Cameron Diaz."

"I'll see what I can do. Meanwhile, you might try something else."

"What's that?"

"Go back to the beginning and get it off your chest."

"While I've still got a chance, you mean?"

"There's that."

HE HAD A POINT. The motel shootout had unnerved him worse than anything since his arrest in 1995. It was worse than standing up in court and hearing "Life without parole" come from the judge's lips.

There was no threat of rape or murder in his isolation cell at Terre Haute. He had three squares a day and would survive indefinitely, until he lost his mind from loneliness or some disease stopped by to punch his ticket.

In the free world, though, he was a moving target on an endless firing range.

"From the beginning, huh?"

"Have you got something else to do?" the driver asked.

"Like getting killed, you mean?" Barnum forced a smile and shook his head. "I haven't thought about the way it started in a while, that's all."

How *had* it started? What were these two looking for, besides the obvious?

Barnum had no illusion that they wished to analyze or understand him. The female escort was Russian intelligence, maybe one of those who had perused the information he sold to her government over the years. As for the driver, Barnum thought he would've cheerfully pulled off the highway, put a bullet into Barnum's head and left him there without a backward glance.

He was the rock-ribbed patriotic type.

I used to be like that.

"I'll spare you all the childhood psychobabble," Barnum said. "We weren't *The Brady Bunch,* but it wasn't V. C. Andrews, either. Two parents, one older brother, high school and puberty—the usual."

Barnum watched the flat country scroll past his window for a silent mile before he spoke again, addressing himself to the driver.

"You're wondering what turned me, right? Your partner already knows. She's been there, on the other side. It's funny about treason. When you get down to the root of it, there's no great secret. Benedict Arnold was pissed off because he got passed over for promotion in the Continental Army. Aldrich Ames had a high-maintenance wife with expensive tastes. Simple."

"So what's your excuse?" Bolan asked.

"The root of all evil," Barnum answered. "Put me down with Aldrich. It's the money, honey. Not to please the wife, though. We'd already split by then. I wanted more for me."

Reflected eyes regarded him with loathing from the rearview mirror.

"Have I disappointed you? Would it help if I spun tales about a father in the Navy, gone for months or years on end, and how it made me want revenge against the military? I can spin a fable if you want me to, but it would be a crock of shit.''

''The money.''

''In a nutshell,'' Barnum said, ''I can't even plead poverty—although a looey-colonel's salary hasn't exactly kept up with inflation through the years. I wanted more, that's all.''

''You've justified it to yourself,'' Bolan stated.

''We all do that,'' Barnum replied. ''One day I looked around the Pentagon and realized the cold war was a joke. More to the point, it was a cash cow for defense contractors, field-grade officers and so-called patriots in government. Ninety percent of what you saw on television or read in the newspapers about missile gaps and falling dominoes was bogus. The Russians had a hard enough time feeding themselves without trying to capture the world, and one thing they fed their people on a daily basis was the same kind of propaganda we cranked out. Moscow had *Pravda,* Washington has the First Amendment. Hooray for democracy.''

''How long have you rehearsed that spiel?''

''I've been refining it since I was picked up by the FBI in '95, and it's still true. You think it's accidental that the major newspapers and TV networks are owned by international conglomerates? The masthead on the *New York Times* reads 'All the news that's fit to print.' It should read 'All the news that fits our agenda.'''

''And with all this greed around, you just decided to cash in?''

''Why not? Defense spending has been America's

number-one gravy train for the past sixty years. Who'd notice one more modest piglet at the trough?"

Cold eyes held Barnum's in the mirror. "You weren't screwing the treasury on contract overruns. You sold out agents in the field and got them killed."

Barnum couldn't deny it. He'd been charged at trial with contributing directly to the deaths of three American covert agents in Europe. Five others were missing and presumed dead, their names deleted from the federal indictment for lack of evidence.

He hadn't known the dead men, never saw their faces until photographs were offered at his trial. They'd come to him in dreams sometimes, for two or three years after he was sent to Terre Haute, but Barnum had seen nothing of them for a while.

He hoped they were at rest.

"I can't undo what's done," he said, letting the hard edge of his voice relax a bit. "If I serve forty years or get my ass shot off this afternoon, they'll still be gone. It does no good if I apologize and gnash my teeth. But this..."

He let the comment trail away. Barnum hadn't attended church, except for funerals and weddings, since he joined the Army at nineteen and did his turn at Officer Candidate School. He was uncomfortable with the concept of redemption, but he didn't have a better term for what he hoped to gain by giving up Seriozha.

"What are you hoping for?" Bolan asked.

"Beats me. I can't undo the past, okay? But maybe I can still break even on the future. If you want soul-searching, I'm fresh out."

He'd thought Seriozha was dead or in prison, along

with the other hard-liners who'd shot their wad against Yeltsin back in 1991. The coup had been a desperate, almost pathetic attempt to resuscitate Russian communism and put the old guard back in power. Some coup leaders had gone to the wall for their trouble; hundreds more were shipped off to the gulag with sentences of twenty years and up.

Seriozha should've been among them, but he'd always had the devil's luck. Come Judgment Day—if there was such a thing—he'd probably slip out a back door somebody forgot to lock and find a neutral corner for himself in purgatory.

He glance back at the rearview, but the driver's eyes were on the road. "You've read my file, I guess," he said.

"Extracts."

"So you'll know I met Seriozha while he was attached to the Russian embassy in Washington. Some diplomatic cocktail bash, I think it was. He was a major in the KGB, but they'd disguised him as an auditor sent out to balance their accounts. Somebody had a sense of humor at Dzerzhinsky Square, I guess. The FBI was busy watching all those so-called cultural attachés, trailing them to strip joints and massage parlors. Old Jasha slipped under the radar and they never had a clue."

"He bought you, just like that," Bolan said.

"I didn't give it up on the first date, but close enough," Barnum replied. "He told me money was no object, and I liked the sound of that. It's funny when you think about it. Money's still no object, and I haven't had to spend a cent in seven years."

"What can you tell us about Seriozha?"

"Anything you want to know," Barnum said. "But maybe your comrade should start. She knows him better than I do."

TASYA GALENKA HAD BEEN waiting for the other shoe to drop. She wasn't sure if Barnum would remember their first meeting, seven years before he was arrested. It had been in Paris, spring of 1988. She'd been with Seriozha then, in every sense.

"I thought you'd have forgotten me," she said. "I was a blonde then."

"Not a very good one," Barnum told her. "Always check the roots, hon."

She ignored Belasko's sidelong glance. He knew enough about her background work with Jasha Seriozha to surmise a personal connection, but he didn't know how personal it had become in those last months, before the world turned upside down for true believers in Moscow.

"What's this?" Belasko asked.

"No biggee," Barnum said. "Another boozer at the embassy in Paris. I think spies spend half their lives at cocktail parties."

"No one mentioned that you knew each other."

"We don't," Barnum replied. "Ships passing in the night, you know? Seriozha introduced us, but I'm better with faces than names."

"No matter," Galenka said. "I was undercover then."

"And under *covers* with old Jasha, would be my guess, from the way he treated you."

Galenka felt a flush of color rising in her cheeks.

"My knowledge of the subject qualified me for this mission," she replied.

"I'll bet."

"Can it," Bolan ordered.

She heard the smile in Barnum's voice. "You didn't know they were an item, right? More secrets. Wonders never cease."

"Right now," Bolan said, frowning, "I want to hear your version of the play that brought us here."

"Why not?" Barnum replied. "You have to understand I was peripheral, at best. My thing was mostly pushing paper, but in 1986 or '87 Seriozha started asking questions. Were the FBI or G-2 sniffing any Russian sleepers in the States? I couldn't answer for the feebs, of course, but G-2 never caught a whiff."

"Sleepers." Bolan's stony face was starting to relax a bit.

"You know, deep cover. So far underground they wouldn't raise a mother's eyebrow. There were rumors of hypnosis, so the sleepers wouldn't even know who they were working for."

"Hypnosis?"

"Like that movie, back when I was still in junior high. Charles Bronson and Lee Remick chase some bald guy all over the country. You ask me, it was a crock. The sleepers always know. They're just real good at keeping a low profile, waiting for the word."

"Which word is that?" Belasko asked.

He knew the answer from their common briefing, but Galenka recognized his need to milk the prisoner for information, make him prove his worth.

"The doomsday word," Barnum replied. "You

have to bear in mind that while the Russians never really had a prayer of capturing the world, they *did* have nukes enough to blow it up. We would've helped, of course. One missile in the air, and both sides would pile on with everything they had. Still might, I guess—but now we're friendly with the Russians and pissed off with the Chinese. The President says we should throw a few gazillion dollars at the Pentagon to keep Beijing in line. It's always something, right?"

"Sleepers," Bolan prompted, refusing to be sidetracked.

"Sleepers, right." Barnum stared out the window, speaking to the ghost of his reflection in the tinted glass. "From what I gathered, certain hard-core types at KGB thought they could shift the odds in any final confrontation if they planted moles around the countryside and left them there for the duration. Every sleeper was supposed to have a stash of arms and commo gear, whatever's needed for diversionary sabotage and random acts of terror. If someone in Moscow sees nuclear light at the end of the tunnel, they send the word and we've got chaos on the home front, made to order."

"They never thought the system would break down," Bolan said.

"Who did, really? Ronnie Reagan? Forget about it. He spent eight years reading cue cards on his way to the old actor's home. Bush Senior? Please! He could barely find Noriega in Panama City. The Russians did it to themselves, and they didn't even see it coming. No offense, lady."

"None taken," Galenka replied, tight-lipped.

He was correct, of course. Russian communism hadn't been destroyed by any effort of the West. It had imploded, rotting from within.

She'd been a part of that but had survived the turnaround. Others weren't as fortunate.

And some fought on, believing they could challenge history, turn back the march of time.

"And Seriozha knows the codes," Bolan stated, not making it a question. This they knew already, from the start.

"That's why we're here," Barnum replied.

"But *you* don't know the sleepers."

"Not a chance. The flow of information ran one-way when I was on the payroll. What I know about the doomsday plan, I've gleaned from conversations and the questions I've been asked by various interrogators through the years. They think they're pretty slick, but if you really listen, half the time they'll give themselves away."

"Sorry," Bolan said. "It doesn't track. If all you did was pocket Seriozha's money in exchange for documents and pick up bits of idle conversation over time, you wouldn't be here now. More to the point, he wouldn't want you dead."

"Who says he does?"

"I don't have time for games. Those shooters back at the hotel weren't CIA or FBI. They damn sure weren't G-2."

"All right. Who were they, then?"

"They smelled like Russian Mafia to me."

"And you'd know Russian Mafia because...?"

"I've dealt with them before."

"That's comforting."

"Your comfort's no concern of mine," Bolan retorted. "You've brought heat down on us before we're even up and running. If you want to see it through, convince me that you're worth the risk."

Barnum considered that for half a mile or so before he said, "Okay, you're right. I wanted this gig for a shot at commutation or reduction of my sentence. Maybe it's a pipe dream, but it's all I've got."

"Wrong answer. That's your motive, not your value."

"I was in G-2 the whole time I was feeding paper to the East," Barnum replied. "Military intelligence, okay? We're barred by law from operating inside the U.S., but so what? It's never stopped the CIA or anybody else from running operations anytime they feel like it."

"You ran a check on Seriozha?"

"Bottom line, I wasn't comfortable with him holding my life in his hands while I had nothing. Call it a quest for parity. I tracked him where I could, playing connect-the-dots. For an accountant shackled to the embassy, he got around pretty good—like coast to coast. He'd touch base here and there. Official business for the most part, but a few of his connections were...unusual."

"Such as?"

"Joe Average, teaching school or fixing cars in Our Town, U.S.A."

"Potential sleepers."

"In a word."

"And when the incidents began in April—"

"I missed April and May," Barnum said, interrupting. "The first name I recognized was Thomas

Yeargin. Shot the hell out of an L.A. shopping mall in June. Cops put him down. Then Ed Spencer two weeks ago, in Virginia."

"Two for five," Belasko said.

"Nobody's perfect, right? The thing is, I've got more."

"More names?"

"And then some. Addresses, phone numbers—all dated, of course, but it's better than nothing. I wasn't satisfied to follow him around. We pulled a black-bag job and found a list."

"You have this list?" Galenka asked him.

"Right up here." The traitor smiled at her and tapped his temple with an index finger. "Photographic memory, you know? Of course, it won't be easy to retrieve if I get ventilated by an AK slug."

"You didn't bargain this at trial," Bolan pointed out.

"For what? The KGB was history by then. For all I knew, Seriozha was, too. The Army had a dead-bang case. They didn't want to hear about some crazy conspiracy."

"But Seriozha's back," Bolan stated.

"Looks like." Barnum went back to frowning at his image in the tinted glass. "Between me and the ex-blonde here, you've got a chance to bag him, though—if you can guarantee I stay alive."

CHAPTER THREE

Atlanta, Georgia

Jasha Seriozha was furious. He raged at the dead men on his television screen, wishing he could resurrect them for the simple, atavistic joy of killing them again.

Bastards! Pathetic idiots!

Their mission had been simple: trail a car and kill the occupants at their first opportunity. They were supposed to be professionals, trained killers who had learned their trade with Spetsnaz and carried it into private practice.

There should have been no problem.

Instead of a clean kill, though, Seriozha was treated to hourly updates on the target's escape and continued evasion of authorities.

Five men were dead, yet the one Seriozha meant to kill—the one whose death was imperative—had slipped through his fingers and fled. He was free now, somewhere at large in the land.

Seriozha despaired of finding Barnum. He would surely hide, if he wasn't already doing so. More infamous now than he'd been at his trial in 1995, the traitor had no choice but to avoid contact with the authorities at any cost.

Two dead U.S. Marshals insured that manhunters would take no chances with the fugitive. Barnum faced a near certain death sentence if convicted as an accomplice in those murders, and who would believe he wasn't? A small army of FBI agents had already been mobilized to run him down, each member of the team a potential executioner.

There was nothing Seriozha could do to help them find Barnum. Television was the altar where most of them worshiped, and he trusted it to bring down the fugitive, one way or another.

In the meantime, how should he proceed?

There was no question in his mind of giving up. It was unthinkable. He hadn't spent the best part of his working life on Project Trojan Horse to simply shrug it off and watch the plan unravel like a cheap sweater.

The question foremost in his mind was could Barnum stop him?

Answer—not alone.

In order to defeat the plan, Barnum would have to share his information with authorities and mobilize resistance. But the men and women Barnum needed to achieve that goal were now his mortal enemies, hunting a traitor who had managed to escape from life imprisonment and killed two federal agents in the process.

It was almost perfect.

If he couldn't kill Barnum, at least Seriozha had rendered him impotent.

The shooters he had used might be identified in time, but they couldn't be linked to Seriozha. Not in time, at least. For now, the fact that Russian gunmen had been killed while liberating Barnum made the fugitive that much more odious, a kind of double traitor to his country.

There was speculation on TV about more gunmen still at large, perhaps conveying Barnum to a safehouse and arranging for his flight from the United States. So much the better, then, if nervous federal agents overtook him and he made a sudden move.

Shot while resisting arrest.

It had a nice sound, albeit less satisfying than if Seriozha's men had done the job he'd paid them for.

He didn't fully understand the various, sometimes contradictory media reports on Barnum's escape. Some hinted that a pair of guests from the motel were being sought for questioning, either as witnesses or suspects in the shooting. Seriozha didn't know who they were and he had no means of finding out, but nagging doubts had crept into his mind.

Barnum was scheduled for a court appearance. Why, then, had his escorts stopped at a small-town motel?

What was he missing?

Seriozha had a sudden fear that Barnum may have tricked him somehow, anticipating the murder attempt.

Impossible!

Or was it?

If the FBI was privy to his plan, or any part of it, what could he do?

Press on and damn the cost.

The Americans didn't frighten him now, if indeed they ever had. They'd grown softer since the cold war ended in apparent victory for global capital. These days they went to war with tiny Third World nations to arrest drug smugglers or slap the wrists of fundamentalist zealots. At home they squabbled endlessly over abortion, prayer in schools and the endangered-species list.

If Seriozha had his way, Americans would all be an endangered species soon.

What could they do that would dissuade him now?

Nothing.

Six months ago, his doctor had informed him that he had a year or less to live. The cigarettes he'd chain-smoked from age nine were killing him. It was too late for surgery, and drugs would only slow the process while leaving him bedridden, a pathetic shadow of himself.

Seriozha had decided to make his death count for something. He would strike a last blow for the cause he'd always served, the cause that had deserted him when traitors seized the helm of government in Moscow.

He couldn't revive the Soviet Union or restore its lost empire, but he *could* insure that Russia's enemies didn't enjoy their place as leaders of the new world order.

He could take some of the bastards with him, proving even as he died that some things never changed.

Some struggles were forever.

And if Barnum tried against all odds to stop him, Seriozha would be pleased to snuff his life out like a candle flame.

Atlanta was the next step in his plan.

He had conceived the scheme himself, though others who outranked him in the KGB had taken credit for it at the time. It was *his* brainchild, devious and cruel. He'd overseen the details of its execution and stood ready for the order to proceed.

He was still waiting when the Russian revolution was betrayed from within, loyal comrades driven from their posts by men who wanted nothing more than to become the enemy their fathers had despised. He'd known the coup of August 1991 was doomed to fail because the loyalists lacked resolve. He had escaped to Switzerland and started planning for the day when he would have his sweet revenge.

Such things took time—and money. Seriozha found no shortage of employers in the next decade, rulers of nations rich in oil or other natural resources who were anxious to modernize their security apparatus and launch new inquisitions for the twenty-first century. Some coveted nuclear arms, and Seriozha also had influence in that area.

It was the grand, delicious irony of capitalism triumphant: everything and everyone, without exception, was for sale.

At last, just when he was ready and his bank accounts were fat enough, Seriozha had been startled by the grim news from his doctor. At first he had been close to screaming in frustration, but his mood had swiftly changed.

He'd left the doctor's office laughing, and the doctor much confused.

Who better to destroy the new world order than a dead man walking?

It was perfect.

The Americans believed themselves triumphant;

their doddering leaders all had dislocated shoulders from patting themselves on the back.

The Soviet Union was dead!

Long live modern Russia, the capitalist clone!

They didn't know a cold war ghost was coming back to haunt them, watch them squirm and die.

The reckoning, long overdue, had already begun.

Jasha Seriozha lit a cigarette and smiled through the haze of smoke.

His children waited for him.

It was time to play.

CHAD FLEMING STOOD in the neon-streaked darkness and tried to remember his name. Not the one on his Georgia driver's license and American Express card, but the name he'd been given at birth, almost forty years ago.

There were months—even years—when his birth name never crossed his mind. On those occasions when it did, he sometimes had to stop and ask himself which of his two identities was real, which was the fantasy constructed to deceive his enemies.

The mask he wore each day was now a living part of him. Sometimes he thought that if he pulled it off, his bleeding flesh would go with the disguise, leaving a lifeless skeleton behind.

At last he had resigned himself to carry on forever with the mask in place, believing that the call would never come.

But he was wrong.

Two days ago, a ringing telephone had changed his life. A voice barely remembered had pronounced the name he'd hidden from the world at large for two-thirds of his life.

Cheslav Fedorenka.

In a heartbeat he was changed, transformed.

Reborn.

It still amazed him, how the residue of decades could be shaken off so easily. A few words spoken on the telephone that could have been a magic spell, considering their impact.

"The time has come, Cheslav."

He didn't have to ask which time the caller meant. There could be only one—the moment he had waited for, living the lie that was his daily life.

Now that the wait was over, Fedorenka told himself he could've waited for another twenty years, remaining ever faithful to the cause. He could've died with the mask on, taking the secret to his grave.

But that wouldn't be necessary now.

He had been chosen, finally, and privileged with a chance to serve.

The rendezvous had been arranged and he was early, taking care to scrutinize the street his handler had selected. It wasn't the kind of neighborhood that made Atlantans proud. It wasn't featured in chamber of commerce brochures, though many tourists sought it out. They came in search of pleasures normally forbidden, lured by the knowledge that whatever they desired could be procured for a price.

The prostitutes had tired of hassling him, deciding he was neither customer nor cop. Having processed that information, they proceeded to ignore him—outwardly, at least. Fedorenka assumed that some of them had memorized his Nissan's license number, but he didn't care.

The plates were new that morning, stolen at an East Point shopping mall, and by midnight they'd be rusting at the bottom of the Chattahoochee River.

Rust in peace.

He smiled and checked his watch against the dashboard clock. Six minutes left.

His handler would be punctual.

It was the mark of a professional.

He had retrieved his tools last night from the Cobb County swampland he had purchased on arrival in Atlanta, back when Jimmy Carter occupied the White House. Over time he had been offered several times the price he'd paid for seven boggy acres, but he'd always turned the would-be buyers down.

I have my reasons, he would say, and smile. It's sentimental. Call me crazy. Sharing laughter at his own expense, a simpleminded Georgia cracker who would rather raise mosquitoes than put easy money in his pocket.

Now the last laugh would be his.

He sat and watched the hookers working, male and female, with a few who might go either way. It was a slow night on the boulevard, but they still had their share of customers. Straight johns, sick tricks, rough trade—they trolled in luxury sedans and rented compacts, vans and vintage pickup trucks. They came with cash in hand, to meet a primal need.

It all comes down to this, he thought.

Fedorenka had seen the news broadcasts from Russia during recent years, the Moscow neighborhood where he was born now serving customers identical in most respects to these.

It sickened him.

There had been prostitutes under the old regime, as well, he realized, but they had been contained, employed to serve the state like everybody else.

It was a different world.

Would anything he did after this night divert the course of history? Could Russia recapture the sense of purpose it had nurtured under communism, or had the flame been forever extinguished?

Was it too late to matter?

Such questions were beyond him. Fedorenka shrugged them off and waited for his handler to appear.

He was a soldier with a mission to complete, and that was all that mattered. He didn't care that the new breed of rulers in Moscow had either forgotten he existed or had never known to start with. They were traitors to the revolution—misguided at best, corrupt and avaricious at worst.

He had a job to do, but passing time made it more difficult. There were things he needed to discuss with his handler, unforeseen obstacles that had to be overcome.

For all the prescience of his mission, those who'd planned it couldn't see the future in precise detail. They hadn't known how Russia—or America—would change in twenty years. Who could've predicted the Internet, Reaganomics or perestroika?

In the final analysis, his mission remained unchanged. It didn't matter if the political world had tilted on its axis. If anything, his country needed him now more than ever, in its hour of darkness.

He wouldn't fail.

With thirty seconds left to spare, Fedorenka saw his handler walking toward him, on the far side of the boulevard. The hustlers did their best, but he ignored them, brushing past without acknowledgment that they existed.

Singleness of purpose was his watchword.

Dedication was the central focus of his life.

How had this man survived the upheavals in Moscow? Where had he been through the long years since the revolution was betrayed, and why had he returned now, to set the wheels of judgment in motion?

No matter.

Fedorenka didn't care, any more than his handler would care about the daily details of his mock life since he was established as a sleeper in Atlanta.

Nothing mattered now except the struggle, more specifically, his role in what was preordained.

The day of reckoning had finally arrived.

He flashed the Nissan's headlights once and watched his handler cross the street, jaywalking in the middle of the block. Hookers on this side of the boulevard had seen him brush their sisters off and wasted no time trying to entice him.

They had other sheep to fleece, and it was only half-past ten o'clock, the best part of the evening still ahead.

Fedorenka experienced a moment of misgivings, wondering if he should take the automatic pistol from its place beneath the driver's seat and tuck it underneath his jacket, but the feeling quickly passed.

His handler was the one person he trusted in a world gone mad. Without that trust, he might as well have used the pistol on himself.

He had switched off the Nissan's dome light for this meeting, so it wouldn't show his handler's face to any passersby as he slipped into the car. It was a small precaution, likely wasted, but soldiers survived on their attention to detail.

"Cheslav."

He remembered the smell of tobacco the man carried with him, as if they'd last met yesterday.

"Major."

"Let us drive while we talk."

He drove and listened, smiling in the dim reflection of the dashboard's light.

Malden, Missouri

"I'D FEEL MUCH BETTER if we had the list," Bolan said.

Barnum smiled. "You *have* the list. I told you that. It's safe and sound as long as I'm alive."

"Because you have a photographic memory."

"They call it something else these days, but that's the bottom line."

They'd found a cheap motel and rented two rooms for the sake of appearances, fearing the grizzled manager might balk at thoughts of a ménage à trois under his sagging roof. Barnum had stayed in the car, out of sight, and kept his face averted from the motel office as he ducked into the room he'd share with Bolan.

Television news was dominated by the tale of his

escape. It had eclipsed another budget battle in the U.S. Senate and the White House nomination of a former Christian Coalition leader to sit on the Fifth Circuit federal court of appeals.

"We could save time," Bolan said, "if you put the list on paper."

"You think so? How's that?"

"We could arrest them," Galenka commented, chiming in for the first time since she had joined them in the shabby motel room.

"Based on what? Because a fugitive from justice drops a name?" There was a touch of bitterness in Barnum's smile. "Sure, I can hear it now. The FBI director tells his troops, 'Pick up John Smith in Baltimore, ASAP! Burke Barnum says he's dirty!' That'll get a warrant for you every time."

"Forget arrests," Bolan said. "We can neutralize them."

"Ah. We're talking hit list now. I'm already doing life as an accessory to murder, they'll have warrants on me by tomorrow for the marshals back in Terre Haute—maybe the shooters, too, if they use the felony murder rule—and now you want me to help you kill fifteen or twenty more? So you can do what, snipe some guy while he's dumping his garbage or mowing his lawn?"

Fifteen or twenty.

Bolan hadn't thought there'd be so many. But why not? Seriozha'd had years to plan his operations, years more to put the sleepers in place. Seen in that light, they were lucky it wasn't 120.

"They're enemy troops," Bolan said.

"With one difference. They're harmless until Seriozha triggers them."

"Which I'm assuming he can do long distance?"

"He could, but he won't," Barnum said.

"Why not?"

The traitor caught Galenka watching him and said, "You want to tell him, or shall I?"

"He may be right," Galenka stated. "Seriozha is—or was—a gamesman. He'd establish rules for any *conspiratsia* he planned and follow them in scrupulous detail. He saw it as a challenge to himself, besting the enemy."

"You're switching tenses," Bolan said. "That was another time, when he had backing from the KGB. He's freelance now, as far as we can tell. What makes you think he won't change tactics?"

"Knowledge of the man," she said, avoiding Bolan's eyes as she replied. "He may act in desperation if cornered, to have the last word, but otherwise he'll do whatever's necessary to maintain a scheduled sequence of events."

"You're sure?"

"I'd stake my life on it."

"You did that when you joined the team," Bolan reminded her.

"There's something else," Barnum said.

"What?"

"The personal touch. He wants to leave his mark on America, physically and psychologically. He has a better shot at that prolonging the attacks, stringing them out."

"More reason to neutralize the sleepers," Bolan said.

"You think? Maybe my eyesight's going, but I don't see any SWAT teams standing by. If they're around, we could've used their help this afternoon. If not, how many can the two of you take out before you piss him off and make things worse?"

Bolan stared hard at Barnum. "You're supposed to be the answer man," he said, "but all I hear from you are questions and objections."

"You're in luck, then. Because I have the answer for you."

"Spit it out."

"I already told you, I've got his list of sleepers."

"So?"

"So, it isn't just a list of players. It's a game plan. Get it? Seriozha's using them in sequence."

"Hold on. You told us earlier you missed the first two incidents."

"I missed the news reports," Barnum corrected him. "When the G-men showed up to chat, they filled me in on the others and I recognized Jacob Moss from the list. He should've been number one, but the kid in Kentucky threw it off. You know that was an accidental detonation, right? Kentucky should've been thirteenth on the list."

"It's thin," Bolan said.

"Is it? Then ask the FBI and Dallas PD about Jared Hatch. He should've been number three, but instead, Ed Spencer did his thing in Newport News. I told your buddies and they checked it out. Hatch was murdered in Dallas on August 19."

"Meaning what?"

"Best guess? He got cold feet and tried to quit on

Seriozha. Sleepers don't have much in terms of a retirement plan."

"Okay," Bolan said. "If you know that, you must know the Kentucky sleeper's name."

"Sure do, for all the help it is. My guess would be she's in the wind by now."

"A woman?" Galenka sounded skeptical.

"You surprise me, Comrade. Sexism, coming from one of KGB's finest? Why not a woman, Major?"

"Why not prove it?" Bolan countered.

"Fine. She calls herself Ardelia Grant, or did, at least, before the kid blew up her stash. She had a place on Benson Valley Road, outside Frankfort."

"What was her target?"

"Sorry. Seriozha didn't list the targets with the sleepers, but you've got a range of possibilities. Frankfort's the state capital, which gives you the governor and all the state officials you could ask for. There are three universities and three major airports within a half-hour's drive, not to mention Fort Knox, Abe Lincoln's childhood home, the Patton Museum—"

"Enough. I get the picture," Bolan said.

"I'm glad, because the next mole on the list lives in Atlanta. Shall we talk military bases? America's busiest airport? The good old Omni Coliseum?"

"Let's have the name."

"I'll tell you in Atlanta. We should try to catch an early flight."

Bolan stepped into Barnum's space.

"Get something straight," he said. "We're not playing *Let's Make a Deal.*"

Barnum stood his ground, despite a further loss of

color from the face that hadn't held a tan for seven years.

"The deal's already made," he said. "You need me to find Seriozha, I need you to stay alive. From where I stand, that makes us even."

"Wrong. We only need you if your information's good and puts us closer to the target. Any time—the *first* time—I have reason to believe you're scamming us, all bets are off. And you won't have to worry about murder charges back in Terre Haute. We understand each other?"

"Five by five," Barnum replied. "You want to make the airline reservations, or shall I? I can't be sure, but I believe my AmEx card's expired."

Washington, D.C.

SOME DAYS BROGNOLA thought the only kind of news that still existed in the world was bad news, most of it addressed to him and being hand-delivered with a bill for postage due. It was a paranoid idea, but what the hell?

A bumper sticker that he'd seen last week in traffic nailed it: Even Paranoids Have Enemies.

So true, he thought.

Ardelia Grant.

He'd heard the name for the first time in his life an hour ago, and it haunted him already.

Stony Man had taken Bolan's call from somewhere in Missouri. Bolan's team was on the move and headed for Atlanta, hoping for a solid contact there before the next incident went down. Their tracker was cooperating to a point, but milking it to help himself.

Can't fault the bastard there.

Whatever Burke Barnum had done in the past, he was still one of their last, best hopes for nailing Jasha Seriozha and his troop of sleepers before they wreaked untold havoc from coast to coast.

The other hope resided in Tasya Galenka, Bolan's temporary ally, whose prior relationship with Seriozha had been euphemistically described as "both professional and personal." Brognola had a fair idea of what *that* meant, and he frankly didn't care if she'd ridden Seriozha bareback to a photo finish in the Kentucky Derby, as long as she could help bring him down when it counted.

And soon.

Brognola had a nagging sense that they were running out of time.

They had certainly missed their chance with Ardelia Grant—or whatever her name was—that morning, at least for the moment. He had dropped a word to contacts at the Hoover Building, and an FBI Hostage Rescue Team had raided her old Kentucky home that very night. The federal warrant alleged illicit possession of automatic weapons or destructive devices, and for all Brognola knew it could even be true.

Not that it mattered, since the bird had flown.

Ms. Grant—whoever she was in real life—had taken an emergency leave of absence from her eighteen-year secretarial job at Kentucky State University back on May 14, claiming her elderly mother had suffered a stroke in North Carolina and needed full-time care for the duration. There'd been no communication from her since, but the FBI's resident agent in Wilmington reported that the ailing mother in question—listed under next of kin in Grant's personnel file as Mrs. Edna Sotheby Grant—was no longer a resident of the Tarheel State. She'd died in February 1957, in the same car crash that killed her six-month-old daughter, Ardelia.

In retrospect, the big Fed understood the timing of the fugitive's departure. She had chilled out through the brief furor produced by the discovery of her arms cache in April, knowing the bits and pieces of hardware that survived the RDX blast could never be traced to her doorstep.

She was free and clear, perhaps even a little relieved.

Until May 14, when she suddenly fled to provide bedside care for her mythical mother.

Why then?

Three days before her flight, mail carrier Jacob Moss had run amok at Nellis Air Force Base, in north Las Vegas. His shooting spree had been front-page news nationwide, although its true significance went unrecognized.

By the media, at least.

Had Ardelia Grant known, or guessed, somehow, that the Nevada incident was Seriozha's opening shot in the States? Brognola doubted it. Seriozha wouldn't jeopardize his operation by letting the sleepers meet and mingle. He was far too savvy for that.

What, then?

How had Grant put two and two together, deciding it was time to get the hell out of Dodge?

Contact.

It was the only answer that made sense. Seriozha was reaching out to his moles beforehand, confirming their survival and continued dedication after decades of inactivity, years after the Soviet system and their reason for staying in place had ceased to exist.

When the call came, what would Grant have thought? Would she have told Seriozha that her gear had been destroyed accidentally, and by a child at that? Would he believe the story if she tried?

Exit running, and not without reason.

If Burke Barnum's information was correct, Jared Hatch had been executed in Dallas for trying to break his contract with Seriozha. Maybe he assumed the collapse of the USSR rendered the plan null and void, or maybe he'd simply found something he liked in the States. Either way, he'd been cut from the team with extreme prejudice, right around the time he should have been moving on his unknown target.

Justice had circulated a description of Ardelia Grant nationwide, all very discreet and hush-hush. She was forty-six years old, according to her stolen birth certificate; five foot five, 150 pounds, brown hair and eyes to match. She wore prescription lenses to correct a slight astigmatism. The photo on her driver's license showed an average, no-nonsense woman who had neither the time nor inclination to smile for a camera.

The quiet APB called her armed and dangerous.

Brognola thought they might have added "running for her life."

But running where?

There was an outside chance she'd run *to* Seriozha, rather than away from him. She might request a meeting and explain the trick of fate that had disarmed her. It wasn't her fault the kid had come along; their buried caches had been booby-trapped for just that reason, to destroy incriminating evidence.

Disloyalty had been Jared Hatch's crime in Dallas, if Brognola read the scanty evidence correctly. The elusive Ms. Grant might be a hard-core loyalist after all these years. She might try to ingratiate herself with Seriozha, serve him in some other way—perhaps even lash out at her original targets, if he could replace the lost hardware.

It was enough to keep Kentucky lawmen on their toes for now, operating under a gag order that specified immediate dismissal without appeal for any officer who leaked their local panic to the media.

Brognola hoped the warning had been stern enough.

Meanwhile, Atlanta was the next potential killing ground on tap. Barnum was playing cagey, refusing to give up the name in advance, and Bolan was reluctant to sweat him at that juncture.

Strictly speaking, the traitor had little or nothing to lose. He had been serving life without parole, no realistic hope of ever setting foot outside the Terre Haute facility again, when he was plucked from the slow-baking oven of prison and dropped into the crackling skillet of Bolan's mission. Capital murder charges were in the pipe for the two marshals killed in Indiana, and Brognola had refrained from interfering on that score to give Bolan a bit more leverage on their pigeon, for what it was worth.

Maybe nothing.

Barnum was playing it his way, but only to a point.

And in the meantime, they had two wild cards at large.

Correction. Make that fifteen or twenty, based on the turncoat lieutenant colonel's ballpark estimate.

Brognola wondered if Bolan's team could intercept Seriozha before the Russian put his other homicidal pawns into play. One more was too many; the whole bloody list could send the mission spinning out of the big Fed's control.

If it wasn't already, he thought, scowling at the notion.

Bad news.

Some days is it was enough to make you wish there was no news at all.

CHAPTER FOUR

Atlanta, Georgia

The disguise wasn't bad, overall. Galenka had helped Barnum apply his new face overnight, getting used to the beard and mustache in his natural color, tinted contacts that gave him blue eyes and horn-rimmed spectacles with plain glass lenses that evoked a bookish air. Put it together with a new tweed-hat-and-jacket combo, and they had a college professor straight out of central casting.

Bolan still didn't feel like testing Barnum's new face on a crowded commercial flight, and since their made-over sidekick lacked the photo ID required to board an airliner in any case, they settled on a private charter company flying out of Kennett, Missouri. One-way tickets to Atlanta with no waiting and no questions asked cost Bolan five hundred dollars apiece.

The flight was no-frills, their reception in Atlanta likewise. Instead of entering the busy terminal along a jetway, they deplaned on tarmac and helped unload their own gun-heavy luggage. A fancified golf cart was waiting—ten dollars extra—for the hundred-yard run to a rental-car agency where Bolan had a beige Buick Skylark on hold. He showed the clerk his Belasko ID with plastic to match and they closed the deal in less than five minutes.

Another five and they were seated in the car, Bolan and Galenka rearmed, Barnum fidgeting behind his professorial face. He rode the shotgun seat at Bolan's side, Galenka seated behind him and ready to take any appropriate action if Barnum should try to bail out.

"All right," Bolan said. "We're in Atlanta, on the ground. Let's have the name and address."

"This thing itches," Barnum told him, poking at the beard.

"It could be worse. The name."

"Chad Fleming's what he calls himself," Barnum replied. "Last time I checked, he had a house on Lindbergh Drive and lived alone. He was working for the athletic department at Emory University, some kind of coach wanna-be."

Galenka had a road atlas open on her lap, tracing streets with a finger. "I have Lindbergh Drive," she said. "Go north on Highway 75 through downtown, then catch the Northeast Expressway above Piedmont Park."

"What about Emory?" Bolan asked.

"It's right...here." She jabbed the map emphatically. "Two or three miles southeast of Fleming's home. It's near...."

Bolan waited, then glanced up to find her eyes locked on his in the rearview mirror.

"It's near what?" he prompted her.

"The Centers for Disease Control."

Bolan felt a sudden chill. "The CDC?"

"They're on the same street here," Galenka said. "Also a children's hospital, all within a mile."

The Centers for Disease Control.

Ebola. Anthrax. AIDS. Bubonic plague. Smallpox.

New bugs and viruses that hadn't been named yet.

Had the CDC even existed when Seriozha was planting his moles, back in the late 1970s and early 1980s? Bolan didn't know, and he wasn't sure it mattered. They didn't know yet if Seriozha's deadly pawn were programmed to attack specific targets—like Nellis Air Force Base in Las Vegas—or if they enjoyed a measure of free will, simply ordered to wreak as much havoc as possible before they were killed or captured.

If a specific target was assigned fifteen or twenty years ago, what then? Anything could happen in two decades. A target could be renovated, demolished or relocated. Was each sleeper committed to blitzing a particular address, or was the plan more complex?

Too many questions—too few answers.

And too little time.

"He should be home at this hour," Galenka said.

The Buick's dashboard clock showed 6:19 a.m. It seemed unlikely that a college gym teacher would start working much before nine, but Bolan knew nothing of Emory's class schedule. For all he knew, Chad Fleming might be an insomniac workaholic, volunteering for early-morning duties.

Or he might already have gone underground.

More questions. Still no answers.

It was simple logic to try the house first, catch him napping if they could, or sitting down to breakfast with the television on for company. Unarmed was even better, but he wouldn't count on it—especially if Seriozha had already been in touch.

Fleming might know a way of contacting the Russian, setting up a meet.

He might not want to share.

There were ways around that kind of impasse, but they'd need the guy alive to check it out. The top priority was stopping him by any means available, before he carried out his unknown mission.

Bolan caught the interstate and goosed the Buick up to seventy, making fair time with the pre-rush-hour traffic. They would circumvent downtown Atlanta this way, missing the worst of its snarl.

"How far?" he asked Galenka.

"Seven miles to the expressway, then perhaps another two for Lindbergh Drive."

Call it three or four minutes, with the highway interchange and off-ramp, slower speeds mandated on the surface streets.

Not long.

Too long?

Bolan went grim and concentrated on the traffic flow.

CHESLAV FEDORENKA POSED before his full-length bedroom mirror, examining himself with a critical eye. His grooming was adequate; some women might even have called his face handsome, but Fedorenka was more concerned with his clothing.

He didn't want the weapons underneath to be too obvious.

The Czech CZ-75 pistol was easy, worn with an

inside-the-pants holster at the small of his back, where the full cut of his sport coat would conceal it perfectly. The rig would be a bit uncomfortable while driving, but Fedorenka could endure a bit of minor bruising for the cause.

There might be worse in store for him than that, this morning, but he didn't care.

At last, his duty called.

The AKS assault rifle was more problematic. It measured twenty-six inches with the metal stock folded and weighed almost nine pounds with a 30-round magazine in place. He'd thought of sawing off the barrel, right back to the rifle's gas piston, but finally balked at giving up the front sight.

He might well be called upon to fire precision semiauto shots before this day was done.

The AKS hadn't come with a shoulder sling, so he was forced to improvise. He used a leather belt, punched new holes with an ice pick and devised a sling that held the rifle snuggled in his right armpit, its muzzle falling just below his hip. The sport coat wouldn't cover it, so Fedorenka chose a lightweight raincoat from his closet to complete the ensemble.

It was dark and cool enough outside for the raincoat to pass without comment, at least for the few moments he required it to cover his secret. After that, it wouldn't matter whether strangers looked askance at him or not.

Any gawkers who crossed his path would be dead.

His extra ammunition and explosives went into the leather gym bag he normally carried to work, emblazoned with Emory's logo in the school's colors. He packed the bag with a dozen spare magazines for the Kalashnikov, antipersonnel grenades and seven blocks of RDX plastique with timers already implanted.

A big bang was coming, and it had nothing to do with astronomy.

He hefted the gym bag, testing it, and decided it wouldn't slow him enough to matter. Surprise was the key. His first—and worst—hurdle would be the security guards. The two he was sure of were both armed with pistols and pepper spray. Once they were dead, the rest should be relatively easy. There were various security points to breach, but the AKS and grenades would clear his way nicely.

The target switch had been his own idea, and he was pleased that his handler approved it. Approved it enthusiastically, at that, praising him for his dedication and initiative.

It was a virtual suicide mission, after all, with long odds against his escape once the first shot was fired. Not hopeless, exactly, but between the nature of his target and the probable police response, Fedorenka assumed he would be trapped at the scene when the RDX charges went off.

So be it.

If his handler's plan was successful, most of the world's population would soon be annihilated anyway.

He would simply beat the rush.

Checking his pockets, Fedorenka satisfied himself that he had everything he needed. He wouldn't require a map to find the Centers for Disease Control, located less than half a mile north of the Emory campus, where he spent more than forty hours a week for the past sixteen years.

He could find it with his eyes closed, had the outer layout memorized.

It wouldn't be a snap, by any means, but it was doable.

He said goodbye to his condominium, pausing on his way out the door to take a stack of unpaid bills and drop them in the trash.

He felt suddenly free, like a man reborn.

The feeling lasted from his doorstep to the sidewalk, where his Nissan Maxima sat waiting at the curb. Fedorenka opened the right-hand door and placed his loaded gym bag carefully on the passenger seat. He was walking around to the driver's side, hugging the awkward weight of the AKS against his ribs, when he heard the engine noise of a car racing up behind him.

Fedorenka turned to find a beige sedan speeding toward him, southbound on Lindbergh Drive. He pressed himself against the Nissan, trusting the overwrought driver to pass him with room to spare, but instead the crazy bastard hit his brakes, tires smoking to a halt at midblock.

Doors flew open on both sides of the car and Fedorenka recognized his error.

The driver wasn't crazy.

He was simply running late.

Pistols drawn, the driver leaned out his open door, while a female back-seat passenger emerged on the left. That left one in the car, a nerdy-looking bearded type who gaped at Fedorenka in fear or fascination.

There was no time to determine which it was. No

time for anything, in fact, as he swung his AKS rifle into action and sprayed the beige sedan with automatic fire.

TASYA GALENKA DUCKED the spray of bullets as their target opened fire from thirty feet away. She heard the telltale rattling sound of a Kalashnikov, immediately followed by clanging bullet strikes as the Buick took hits.

Who could miss at that range?

A blind man, perhaps.

Chad Fleming obviously wasn't blind. He put three rounds through Galenka's open door, the last one punching a neat hole inches from her face.

If he fired lower, he could strafe her legs. She suddenly felt naked, terribly exposed and vulnerable to this stranger. They had come to stop him, but it seemed he had the upper hand.

Belasko's pistol popped off two quick rounds, answered at once by another burst from Fleming's Kalashnikov. Galenka couldn't see him, but she reached around the door and triggered a shot from her Gyurza P-9.

Wasted, she thought, but it made noise and told their enemy that she was in the fight, at least.

Fleming sprayed her open door with another burst, some of his bullets scarring asphalt near her feet. The impact of other rounds swung the door back at her, knocking the woman off balance.

Faced with a split-second choice, she lunged back into the Buick's rear seat. The closing door caught her left ankle with force enough to make her grimace, but without inflicting major injury.

She pulled in her leg, felt her shoe coming off in the door's solid grip, and kicked back with her right foot to free it. An AK bullet drilled the window on that door as it swung open, spraying her with shattered glass.

Galenka risked a look between the seats in front of her. Barnum was huddled on the floorboards, counting on the Buick's engine block to stop incoming rounds before they pierced the firewall. Through the bullet-pocked windshield, Galenka saw their target fire a final burst at Belasko, then leap into his car and gun the motor, screeching away from the curb.

Belasko threw himself into the driver's seat and released the Buick's emergency brake.

"All aboard!" he demanded.

"I'm here!" Galenka told him, lurching upright in her seat and reaching for the inside handle of her door.

Acceleration slammed it for her, the big American burning rubber in pursuit of their target. Fleming's car was already two long blocks ahead, widening his lead by the second.

"Hang on!" Bolan said as he floored the accelerator.

They shot through a four-way stop, no other traffic waiting at the intersection, and their car scraped bottom where the street dipped slightly on the other side.

"Oil pan!" Bolan said, driving with both hands on the steering wheel, white-knuckled.

Here and there, pedestrians blurred past them and were gone. Galenka couldn't have described them if her life depended on it. They were gaining on the other car, though, edging closer by degrees.

There was a traffic signal two blocks down, orange flashing lights for caution overhead. Galenka didn't have her map and couldn't name the cross street, but it didn't matter. They had passed outside Atlanta proper now. A few more blocks and Lindbergh Drive would cross Briarcliff.

"He's making for the CDC!" she announced.

"Or Emory. We still don't know. On Briarcliff he can circle back downtown."

"We have to stop him!"

"That occurred to me," Bolan said, and gave the steering wheel an openhanded slap, as if the Buick were a living thing that could be thereby urged to greater speed.

It almost seemed to work, the sedan surging forward as the street sloped gently downhill, gravity doing its best to assist them. One long block ahead, their quarry was driving erratically, swerving back and forth across the solid stripe that marked the center of the street. Oncoming traffic swerved to avoid him, horns blaring in protest, while Fleming shook his fist out the window and gave them the finger.

He's gone mad, Galenka thought.

They'd definitely have to kill him now—as if there had been any doubt.

She'd seen no reason to believe that Seriozha's sleepers could be rehabilitated, rendered harmless in the manner of a kleptomaniac consigned to therapy. They were a team of dedicated soldiers, rising to the challenge of a war already lost.

History had passed them by, but they were still intent on leaving their mark on its pages, perhaps writing the last bloody chapter themselves.

Galenka ducked involuntarily as the point car's back window imploded. She saw a muzzle-flash inside the car and realized that Fleming had to be driving one-handed, using his other to aim and fire his Kalashnikov across the driver's seat.

No sooner did the thought take shape than bullets caromed off the Buick's hood and struck the windshield, spraying the two men with glass.

BURKE BARNUM RAISED both hands to shield his face from flying glass, slipping lower in his seat as he did so to dodge incoming rounds. His seat belt kept him from squirming down under the dash where he wanted to be, Barnum cursing the conformity that had made him secure it in the first place.

Buckle up for safety, he thought, and almost laughed aloud before the ragged sound caught in his throat, choked off by fear.

Coward!

Barnum was used to the label, applied both by others and by himself. It went well with *traitor, turncoat* and a dozen other epithets to which he'd grown accustomed over time.

He could live with it.

Unless, of course, a bullet took his head off in the next few moments.

Up ahead, the mole who called himself Chad Fleming was weaving through traffic like a madman, firing wild bursts of automatic fire through the shattered rear window of his Nissan every half block or so. He couldn't aim and drive at the same time, but he was doing all right. Aside from the hits on their Buick, he had also sprayed a taxi, a bread delivery truck, a biker and several pedestrians.

Barnum wished for a weapon but knew he couldn't have used it effectively. Training be damned—he was too busy trying to duck and cover, wrenching at the buckle of his safety harness now in an effort to release it.

Where's the goddamn button?

There!

The harness whipped away from him as he unbuckled it, Barnum slouching lower in his seat. He caught a sidelong glance from Mark Belasko and responded with a grimace of his own.

"Relax," Barnum said. "I'm not jumping at this speed."

"Or any other."

The voice came from behind him, Galenka's remark punctuated by the kiss of warm metal against his neck. Barnum could smell the Russian agent's pistol, lately fired.

"You got me," Barnum said. "We've done this bit, okay?"

"Remember it," Galenka told him, withdrawing her weapon.

Wind rushed through the broken windshield, stinging Barnum's eyes. He would've closed them or ducked lower, but he was caught up in the chase now, albeit as a piece of excess baggage.

He had brought his escorts to this point in time and space. If they succeeded, neutralizing their target, some small portion of the triumph would be his. If they failed...

We'll probably be dead, he thought, squinting into the wind.

Up ahead, the Nissan veered around slower traffic and gunned through a busy intersection, gunning hard right onto a cross street. Barnum glimpsed the street sign as a family sedan swerved to avoid Fleming, jumping the curb.

Briarcliff Road.

The mole was still on track, making for the Emory campus he knew so well and the nearby Centers for Disease Control.

Which, if either, was his target?

Did he have a plan in mind, even now, or was he simply running for his life along familiar paths?

They'd soon find out.

Belasko fired a short burst from his pistol through a gaping hole in the Buick's windshield. Barnum couldn't tell if he hit the weaving Nissan or not, but the casings spilled into Barnum's lap, making him flinch in surprise.

Relax. It's not the brass that kills you.

More gunfire from the Nissan. Barnum ducked as low as the legroom on his side would let him.

It came down to this, after all his scheming and deception. Jailed for life, he'd been plucked from his cell for a chance to die with strangers who despised him, shot by a stranger he had once protected to the detriment of his country.

And who would mourn his passing if a bullet found him?

He had sacrificed his family to the military, then sold his honor and career for tainted cash. Who was left to feel even a moment of regret if he was killed?

No one.

Barnum wouldn't even mourn himself, but he was still afraid of dying.

"There he goes!"

The warning shout came from Galenka, but their driver was already on it, swerving the Buick in pursuit as Fleming's Nissan left the road, roaring off across a spacious parking lot toward buildings set back from the street.

Where were they? What place was this?

Barnum didn't know and he had no quick way of finding out. Another spray of bullets lashed the Buick, making him duck before he had a chance to look for signs.

FEDORENKA HAD GIVEN UP on his plan to hit the Centers for Disease Control. The dipping needle on his fuel gauge told him that a slug or two had found the gas tank, punching holes that were about to bleed it dry. He wouldn't make it to the CDC, but he could still inflict sufficient damage that his effort wouldn't be entirely wasted.

He could call on his employers and surprise them with a kind of higher education that wouldn't be found on their curriculum.

The main parking lot for Emory University was filling up despite the early hour, students and faculty drifting in for the start of another academic day.

Fedorenka was about to surprise them with a pop quiz the survivors would never forget.

He gunned the Nissan across empty spaces, ignoring the directional arrows painted on blacktop, gaining as much ground as possible before he ran out of gas and was forced to proceed on foot.

Sudden pain ripped through his shoulder, blood spurting from an exit wound to spatter the dashboard. Fedorenka didn't hear the gunshot, its sound swept away somewhere behind him, swallowed by the Nissan's revving engine sounds before he lost the wheel.

It spun free of his grasp as his hand spasmed open, a reflex response to the pain in his shoulder. He felt the car swerving, had time to raise his good arm in front of his face before the Nissan smashed into the left rear side of a green Volkswagen Beetle. Instantly the driver's air bag blossomed, striking him with force enough to sting his face.

Cursing, Fedorenka wrenched his door open and lunged out from beneath the air bag, leaning back inside to grab his heavy gym bag. The AKS assault rifle slapped against his hip as he dragged the leather bag clear, struggling to drape its strap across his wounded shoulder.

The pain was dizzying, but Fedorenka had no choice. The fingers of his left hand wouldn't grip the bag, and he needed his right hand free for his weapons. Staggering around the car, he heard his enemies approaching, tires scorching on asphalt. Startled cries from here and there around the parking lot told him the firefight had an audience.

So much the better.

Anyone within his reach was a potential hostage. If he couldn't capture them to serve as human shields, the next-best thing would be to mow them down.

He gripped the AKS and turned to face his adversaries, squeezing off a burst toward the bullet-scarred

Buick. It used up the last few rounds in his magazine, and he cursed as he tried to reload on the run.

It was nearly impossible to manage one-handed, even worse as he jogged across the parking lot, ducking and weaving around parked cars. At last he had to stop, crouching, to wrestle a fresh magazine from the gym bag, clutching it in his teeth while he pulled the empty one and braced the AKS to receive its replacement. Gripping the weapon's muzzle between his knees, Fedorenka snapped the bolt back to chamber a round.

Finally!

Rising from his crouch, he staggered with the gym bag's unfamiliar weight, colliding with a sports car on his wounded side. Fresh pain flared in his shoulder, wringing a sob from his throat, but Fedorenka pushed off, running on sheer will as he made his way toward the nearest classroom building.

Students and faculty scattered in front of him, some shouting as they ran, others focused strictly on speed. He let them go, brandishing his rifle and snarling at them incoherently, delighted by their terror.

How long before police arrived in force? He didn't even care. A fool could see that he would die this day, perhaps within the next few minutes. All he wanted was a chance to make those final moments count.

Shots rang out behind him, and someone called him by his cover name, demanding that he stop. Laughing through his pain, he spun and fired a burst toward his pursuers, then raked the nearest group of cringing students, dropping several of them on the grass.

It was a start.

The classroom building loomed in front of him, the nearest door opening to frame a pinched, quizzical face. Fedorenka fired into that face from fifteen feet and stumbled past the falling corpse, pausing long enough to kick the door shut behind him.

There were stairs on his left and he took them, stumbling, forced to release his AKS and clutch the handrail as he climbed, to keep from falling backward. Blood pulsed from his shoulder wound with every step he took, draining his strength, but grim determination got him to the second floor.

There were classrooms on either side, students emerging from one on his left, milling about and jabbering questions in response to the sounds of gunfire from below. He herded them like sheep and drove them back inside the classroom, quickly counting heads.

Thirteen.

The sleeper smiled.

It was his lucky number for the day.

BOLAN HEARD GUNSHOTS from the floor above him as he burst into the classroom building, Tasya Galenka on his heels. He hit the stairs running, taking the concrete steps two at a time. Screams mingled with the Kalashnikov's stutter, driving Bolan to a burst of greater speed.

The second-floor hallway was empty when he got there, except for one body lying supine in a spreading pool of blood. The victim had been young, white, male. A textbook lying open, facedown on the floor beside him, had begun to soak up gore as if it were a sponge.

Chaotic voices sounded from a classroom on Bolan's left, silenced by another burst of automatic fire. The top half of the door was frosted glass, obscuring any view of those inside while it admitted filtered light. A second door, positioned at the far end of the room, stood open, held in place by a rubber wedge.

"I need to get in there," he told Galenka, whispering. "I'll take the open door. Can you divert attention on my signal?"

She nodded without hesitation, moving toward the closed door with the inset frosted pane. Bolan took four long strides to reach the farther door, pausing to listen as he thumbed the Beretta 93-R's selector switch to single shots.

They'd left Burke Barnum in the car, with orders to quit the scene and meet them on the far side of the campus if police arrived. It was a gamble, leaving the traitor in charge of their wheels, but Bolan was willing to risk it.

Like the shooter in the classroom, Barnum had nowhere to go.

And the shooter was talking now—make that ranting—to his captive audience of hostages.

"You are privileged," he told them, his voice rasping painfully, "to be part of a great and historic event. You should feel honored to participate. When the story of this moment is recorded, perhaps you will be mentioned in a footnote. If you're lucky, they may even spell your names correctly!"

Cackling laughter interrupted the spiel, high-pitched and hysterical. Beneath it, Bolan heard the sounds of young women sobbing.

Bolan would have paid dearly for a periscope at

that moment. Even a hand mirror would've been welcome—a compact, perhaps—but Galenka had left her purse in the car. He'd be going in blind when he made his move, trusting Galenka's diversion to keep the shooter occupied for a few precious seconds.

And what if he'd found cover? What if Fleming was surrounded by hostages?

Bolan would deal with that problem as necessary, if and when it confronted him. Each wasted moment placed the hostages in greater jeopardy, and placed his team at greater risk of a lethal confrontation with police.

It was coming down to now or never.

He was swiftly running out of time.

Bolan nodded to Galenka, already moving as she swung her pistol hard against the pane of frosted glass, smashing through it, triggering two quick rounds into the classroom's ceiling. He cleared the door as a burst of return fire shivered the door, AK rounds punching through the metal frame as if it were cardboard.

Bolan found his target kneeling on a table with his back to a long bank of windows, firing his Kalashnikov one-handed toward the other door. In front of him, a dozen or more students lay on the floor beside their individual desks. Beside the shooter, on the table, a gym bag stood open within arm's reach.

The shooter turned toward Bolan as he entered, tracking with the AKS. Bolan aimed at the center of mass and triggered a quick double tap, but the guy was already firing as he turned, finger clenched around the trigger of his weapon. Bolan saw him lurch on impact, but the AKS kept spitting bullets, fanning the air overhead.

Bolan ducked behind the flimsy cover of a desk, stung by splinters as an AK round ripped through the laminated desktop. He heard the booming echo of Galenka's Gyurza P-9, unloading in rapid fire, and rolled out of cover to join her as the sleeper began taking hits.

They had him in a cross fire now, students of both sexes screaming as all hell broke loose in the classroom, death hammering away from three sides, bullets snapping through the air above their heads.

The sleeper was reeling, firing as he fell, twisting toward the broad windows behind him. The Kalashnikov sprayed through them, clearing a path as Fleming took more hits to the back and side, propelled from his tenuous perch toward the gray day beyond.

He burst through and was gone, left foot snagging for a moment on the windowsill before gravity took over and dragged him out of sight. It wasn't much of a drop, but it made no difference.

Chad Fleming was dead before he took the dive.

And sirens were closing fast from the direction of Briarcliff Road.

It was time to bail out.

Galenka met him in the hallway, running toward the stairs. Another minute, down and out, turning away from the parking lot and toward the far side of the campus, fronting North Decatur Road.

Barnum was waiting for them in the bullet-scarred Buick, a nervous expression on his face.

"Glad you could make it," he told them. "Can we get the hell out of here, please?"

CHAPTER FIVE

Dothan, Alabama

"Can I change back into a person now?"

Barnum was seated on the end of a motel bed, fingering his beard and eyeing his reflection in a mirror that had cracks at three of its four corners.

"Twenty-one years of bad luck," Bolan said.

"How's that?"

"Nothing. The new face stays."

"I didn't want to go outside," Barnum complained. "I just thought—"

"No."

"What happens when it starts to peel?"

"We've got more spirit gum."

"I hope I can remember what I look like under here."

"I hope nobody else does," Bolan said.

"Okay, I get the point."

They'd ditched the Buick in La Grange and switched plates on a Pontiac Bonneville, driving through a stormy afternoon to reach this place in Alabama's far southeastern corner, equidistant from the Georgia and Florida state lines. There was an airport of sorts ten miles to the north, or they could pick up Interstate 10 in the Florida panhandle, riding it east to Tallahassee or west to Baton Rouge.

It was a decent place to hide, as places went, but they couldn't afford to let the locals glimpse Barnum's true face.

"We still don't know what he was going for," said Barnum.

"Either way, it's done," Bolan replied.

They had another spot on CNN, this time about the campus shootings in Atlanta. Network talking heads had grown accustomed to such stories in the past few years, but this one had a twist. Surviving witnesses had told police an unknown man and woman took down the shooter, then fled before the uniforms arrived. Descriptions varied, and the sketches so far broadcast on the tube were vague enough that Bolan wasn't worried about being spotted on the street.

Not yet.

One of the CNN reports had troubled Bolan, though. It mentioned "startling footage" from a campus security camera that might help identify the missing shooters, and while no tape so far had been broadcast, Bolan cringed at the thought of his visage going international, maybe joining Barnum's on the next airing of *America's Most Wanted.*

He'd already tipped Hal Brognola to the problem, hoping Justice could head off public broadcast of the tape, but he didn't know what the big Fed could accomplish—or if the heads-up had even reached him in time.

Exposure could be fatal. The best-case scenario, if the campus footage aired with Bolan's face, would be a stand-down order and another painful visit to the surgeons who had sculpted him from scratch after he staged his death in Central Park and was reborn into the Phoenix Program based at Stony Man Farm. He'd grown accustomed to this face, but he could get used to yet another new one, if necessary.

As for Galenka, she didn't seem terribly perturbed by the prospect of seeing herself on TV. It helped that she was Russian, working half a world away from home, where it was doubtful anyone she knew would catch her moment on the air.

And if they did, so what?

Galenka was a covert agent, to be sure, but she wasn't a "dead man walking" in the sense of Bolan having staged a funeral and seen his records purged in Washington. Overnight he'd gone from one of the FBI's most wanted to a fading memory, his war on the Mob itemized in a handful of paperback books now long out of print.

A broadcast of his new face wouldn't change that necessarily, but it was a step in the wrong direction—a breach in the wall of security established and defended at great cost.

It was too late to think about that now, though. He could only focus on his mission and proceed as if the goal was still within his reach. If Brognola decided they should scrub the operation, he would have a choice to make.

It might be life or death.

"What's our next stop?" he asked Barnum.

"Scottsdale. I hope you like the desert."

"Name?"

"When we get there."

Bolan leaned closer to the prisoner, holding eye contact. ‘‘We almost missed our man today,’’ he said. ‘‘Five minutes more, we would have. I don’t know what kind of game you think we’re playing here, but I’ll make you a promise—if we drop the ball because you’re being coy, I’ll make you wish you’d never joined the team.’’

Barnum considered it, frowning. ‘‘I’m just supposed to trust you now?’’

‘‘Have you got something better in the works?’’

‘‘I proved myself today. I could’ve left you for the boys in blue. You need to see that I’m on board for this.’’ The one-time soldier blinked, lowering his voice. ‘‘It’s all I have.’’

‘‘Then play it straight,’’ Bolan said. ‘‘Give us something.’’

‘‘If you pick him up beforehand, you’ll have nothing.’’

‘‘We can mount surveillance. If the target moves before we get there, it won’t blow up in our faces. They might even get a fix on Seriozha.’’

‘‘I don’t know.’’

‘‘We’re wasting time,’’ Galenka interjected. ‘‘Jasha won’t be.’’

‘‘Hell, all right.’’ Barnum shifted on the bed, bracing his back against the cheap headboard. ‘‘You’re looking for a man named Byron Cross, age forty-eight. He has a little place outside Scottsdale, on half a dozen acres. Mostly tumbleweeds and cactus.’’

‘‘Occupation?’’

‘‘Last I heard, he drove a cab in Phoenix, with some chauffeur work in limos on the side.’’

‘‘How long ago was that?’’

"Six months before I took the fall."

Call it eight years. How much had changed since then? Was Byron Cross still driving cabs and limousines in Phoenix, living in the Scottsdale desert? Was he even still alive?

The job was unimportant in itself, granting their sleeper no extraordinary access to any sensitive targets in the Phoenix-Scottsdale area. It made no sense for him to move away and leave his stash of gear behind, unless he'd found a better job within a short commute.

Still, anything could happen over eight years' time. People had accidents, got sick and died, had nervous breakdowns, lost their minds—or simply changed their minds, deciding that some goal or concept they'd held sacred simply wasn't worth the trouble anymore.

"I'll make some calls and try to put a watch on Cross, then make arrangements for a flight out west. With any luck we'll catch one heading out tonight."

"Jasha will be ahead of us," Galenka said.

"We'll get him. He's a human being like the rest of us."

"Don't be so sure. His dedication to the cause is all-consuming."

"That's exactly what I'm counting on," Bolan replied.

Fanatics took themselves so seriously that they often made mistakes leading directly to their own downfall. From Rasputin to Hitler, Jim Jones to David Koresh, hard-core zealots had fumbled their way to self-destruction.

The bad news was that they nearly always took innocents with them into oblivion.

Bolan's mission was to minimize the body count and stop Jasha Seriozha before he could light a string of funeral pyres from coast to coast.

So far, they were running behind, but the game wasn't over yet.

Not until he heard the final gun.

BURKE BARNUM SAT and studied his reflection in the motel mirror, wishing the disguise were good enough to hide his real face from himself. It would've been a sweet relief to leave his life behind, wake up tomorrow with a fresh start in a world where no one knew his name or cared what he had done.

Too late.

He caught Tasya Galenka staring at him, after Belasko left the room to make his calls from a pay phone outside the motel's office. Barnum met the Russian agent's gaze and held it with his own.

"I'm surprised the SVR sent you to hunt for Seriozha," he remarked.

"Who better for the job?"

"Don't get me wrong. I'm sure you're capable enough. It's the conflict of interest I'm thinking about."

"There is no conflict," she replied.

"Really? You worked with Seriozha *and* you were his lover. Am I right?"

"You sold him military secrets, Mr. Barnum."

"There's a difference, Major. When I got in bed with Seriozha, it was strictly business."

He saw angry color rising in her cheeks, but she controlled herself, lighting a cigarette to buy some time.

"You think I have some plan to help Jasha escape? Perhaps I'm on his side in this mad scheme to set the world on fire?"

"It wouldn't be the first time," Barnum said. "Are you familiar with the term folie à deux?"

She smiled at that. "You're studying psychology in prison, I suppose? Perhaps you'll have a new career when they parole you, in a hundred years?"

He let that slide. "Some people think the Russian bear's grown old and lost his teeth. I'm not so sure."

"You fed the bear enough. I can't believe it frightens you."

"I'm not afraid of you," he said. "Just curious."

"About my loyalties?" Her lip curled in a sneer. "Unlike yourself, I place my country first."

"Smart money says your boyfriend feels the same."

Galenka frowned at that. "He's living in the past," she said, "unable to adapt. His dedication to the old way blinds him to the new. He doesn't understand that change is sometimes necessary. Russia has to change in order to survive."

"You like what's happened to your country in the past ten years, then?"

She smoked a while and thought about her answer.

"Nations are like families," she said at last. "All have their faults and failings. In America you have the Mafia, street gangs, extremist groups, all with a longer and more violent history than ours. You fight the plague of drugs, as we do. You have politicians who behave like juvenile delinquents in the public eye. You treat minorities with scorn."

"All that," he said, "plus Disney World."

"It is a joke to you?"

"It makes me wonder if you really want to be like us, and why."

"Suspicion. This I understand. My country must seem strange to you. For centuries we had the czar, then we replaced him with the Party. Freedom, as you recognize it in the West, is something new for us. In that respect, Russia is like a child, still learning how to walk and talk."

"While Seriozha wants to start a gang war in the schoolyard?"

"Jasha spent his life in service to the Party," Galenka said. "When that world collapsed, effectively within a few short months, he couldn't change to suit the times. His values, if you will, are absolute. He knows no compromise."

"Unlike the two of us, you mean?"

"We have nothing in common, Mr. Barnum," she replied. "I serve my country and its leaders. You sold yours."

"I'm always fascinated by the double standard," Barnum said. "You purchase documents from me and despise me for selling them. Is that schizophrenic, or what?"

"Police and intelligence agents deal with criminals every day. It's a fact of life. We don't have to admire them."

"And you share no responsibility for their corruption, of course."

Galenka shrugged. "Most people are corrupt in

some way. Preachers, politicians, housewives or lieutenant colonels—it makes no difference. Nearly all have a price. When they finally sell themselves, is it the buyer's fault?"

"You make it black and white. That must be nice for you."

"I never saw the documents you sold to Jasha. I assume they helped our cause somehow and may have damaged the United States. The choice to turn was yours."

"I'm not denying that."

"You seek to mitigate your treason, when you've been caught and punished for it. Like a child, you blame your lapse on bad companions."

"This isn't about me, lady."

"No? You're here today only because you were a traitor to your country. Now, years after you were sent to prison, we discover the extent of your duplicity. You betrayed Jasha, even as you worked for him."

"Call it insurance."

"Which you never used at trial."

She had a point, but Barnum would be damned if he'd concede it.

"I've explained that. By the time they picked me up, the Party was a wreck. I had no way of knowing Seriozha would come back to activate the sleepers."

"You could have named them anyway," she said. "It would've taken you an hour and you've had eight years. Even today, you guard the names like precious coins and dole them out one at a time."

"They're all I've got," he said. And what a godforsaken truth that was.

She laughed in Barnum's face.

"You question my loyalty, when even now you serve yourself alone."

"What else am I supposed to do? I'm serving life without parole. This little road trip is my last breath of free air."

"And yet today you didn't run."

"I've got no money, documents or friends. I'm sitting in a rental car that's shot to hell, wearing a wig and phony beard that make me look like Grizzly Adams. I don't know what constitutes a fair head start in Russia, but where I come from we call that kind of deal jack shit."

"You're not a fool," Galenka said. "I'm not convinced that you're a coward, either, though your countryman may disagree."

"Belasko? I don't give a damn what he thinks."

"On the contrary, I think you do."

"That's your opinion."

"Obviously. He's a soldier, as you were."

"My guess would be he'd take offense at the comparison."

"In any case," she said, "you feel that if you prove yourself to him, it may help you regain a measure of your self-respect."

"Now who's the armchair shrink?"

"Sorry?"

"Forget it. Let's suppose you're right and I have something left to prove. You're still ducking my question about Seriozha."

"It is nearly seven years since I've seen Jasha. We were finished as a couple years before that. I recognize his motives without subscribing to them."

"And you'll kill him if it comes to that?" he challenged.

"Yes, I will."

Bolan chose that moment to return, locking the door behind him.

"Time to go," he said. "We've got a charter waiting on the airstrip."

"Scottsdale?" Barnum asked him.

"All the way."

Dale County, Alabama

THEY CALLED the field Dothan Municipal Airport, although it was closer to Midland City and located in a separate county from the town whose name it bore. They followed Highway 231 northbound, Galenka holding the Gyurza P-9 pistol in her lap and watching for headlights behind them.

"Here it is," Bolan said.

"Already?"

"Eight miles."

It felt to her as if they'd just left the motel, and, in fact, less than fifteen minutes had passed since she'd closed the self-locking door behind her. Traffic was light in this part of the state after sundown, it seemed.

She thought of Alabama in the abstract, as portrayed in *Pravda* through the years, expecting fiery crosses in place of streetlights, lynch-mob victims dangling from every third or fourth tree along the highway.

Maybe the Russian "journalists" had confused it with Albania or Afghanistan. Who could say, when the government censored itself?

The airport wasn't much to look at, but it had the basics: runways, a control tower of sorts, a small terminal. Bolan ignored the latter and veered off toward a pair of hangars squatting on the eastern perimeter of the facility.

The hangar on the left as they approached was home to Bama Charters. A Confederate battle flag drooped from a roof-mounted flagpole. Outside the hangar, under floodlights, a tall man in denim coveralls was inspecting the wings of a vintage Beech Twin Bonanza.

"Are we going up in that?" Barnum asked.

"And loving every minute of it, pal."

"I didn't think Jeff Davis had an air force."

"Live and learn."

They parked the Bonneville beside the north end of the Bama Charters hangar, well back from the tarmac. Galenka holstered her pistol and shouldered her bags, while Bolan pulled his from the car. Burke Barnum had no luggage; he was wearing his disguise and all the clothing he possessed.

They would have to do something about that, Galenka decided. She didn't care if Barnum was stylish, but he'd soon start to smell if he couldn't change clothes. There was bound to be a men's shop in Scottsdale where they could pick up a few things before seeking the next target on their list.

"Y'all must be the Blanton potty."

Galenka frowned before she realized the man meant *party*. Belasko had to have picked the pseudonym.

"That's us," he said, as if in answer to her silent thought. "You'd be Mr. Wilkins."

"Collie. Folks just call me Collie."

Who names their children after dogs? Galenka wondered, but she kept the question to herself.

"Collie it is. You're the pilot?"

"That I am."

"How close are we to taking off?"

"We ready now, except for stowing bags and counting some dead presidents."

Bolan set down his bags and removed a roll of greenbacks from his pocket. "We agreed on fifteen hundred, I believe."

"Ezackly rat," the pilot said. His accent was thick enough to cut with a razor.

Bolan peeled off fifteen hundred-dollar bills and put away the rest. The pilot with the canine name showed no surprise at being paid in cash. He pocketed the money without counting it and graced them with a crooked smile.

"Les gitcher bags abode an' catch a breeze," he said.

Galenka was still translating when Wilkins took her bags and disappeared inside the aircraft. He was back a moment later for Bolan's luggage, pausing for a glance at Barnum's empty hands.

"Y'all travels lat," he said.

"As light as possible," Barnum replied, smiling through store-bought whiskers.

The Twin Bonanza featured seating for six passengers, two rows of three abreast. Galenka boarded first and took the far left seat in the first row. Barnum slipped in behind her, sitting in the middle with a vacant seat on either side of him. Bolan took the right-hand seat in front, leaving an empty in between them for some extra elbow room.

"Y'all buckle ep," Wilkins instructed as he closed the aircraft's door and strapped himself into the pilot's seat. He slipped on a headset and fired the plane's twin engines while engaged in a one-sided conversation with the tower.

"Be a minute," he informed them. "We gat one afore us taken off."

Galenka knew the drill. They had a thousand miles to travel and would stop twice for refueling, at Paris, Texas, and Roswell, New Mexico. Their estimated travel time, with pit stops and inevitable ground delays, fell somewhere between six and seven hours.

Was it fast enough?

She pictured Seriozha waiting at the airport for a scheduled flight, passing for normal in the bustling crowd. If he'd found a nonstop flight between Atlanta and Phoenix, one of the big jets could deliver him within three hours, give or take. That didn't take account of idling at the ticket counter, checking baggage through, more idling at the gate or any of the myriad delays that American travelers found so annoying. Seriozha's ETA in Arizona would be pushed back even further if he was security conscious, bypassing Atlanta's teeming airport to fly out of Macon or Columbus, maybe even land in Tucson as a means of covering his trail.

As they taxied toward takeoff, Galenka wondered—not for the first time—whether Seriozha had ever been in Atlanta, after all. She didn't know what sort of contact was required to activate his sleepers, if a phone call or a simple e-mail might suffice. Was he required to speak with them in person, in the manner of a nightclub hypnotist?

If he could phone the orders in long-distance, Seriozha might be anywhere—and they had little hope of stopping him before he gave the other sleepers on his list their marching orders. He could activate them all within an hour's time and send them on their bloody way.

He wouldn't.

The August death of Jared Hatch in Dallas gave her hope. Barnum confirmed that Hatch was one of Seriozha's people, his execution by point-blank gunshot falling into place between the incidents recorded from Los Angeles and Newport News.

But what about the timing?

Granted, there'd been a month or more between the first five incidents, but Galenka knew they couldn't count on that pace continuing. Seriozha would certainly monitor his pawns, chart their progress in media reports, and he would know by now that Chad Fleming had failed. Coming so close behind Barnum's "escape" and the bungled attempt on his life, the firefight in Atlanta might well drive Seriozha to accelerate his schedule.

It wouldn't slow him.

That much was certain.

The sooner we find him, the better, she thought.

Knowing they'd have to kill the man who'd been her lover once, that she might have to do the job herself, made Galenka feel vaguely ill.

Could she do it, when push came to shove?

Yes, I could.

She had loved Seriozha once, in her way, or lusted

after him, at least. She owed him something for their time together, even if that meant destroying him before he had a chance to set the world on fire.

A gift of death, perhaps.

My gift of death, she thought as the Beech Twin Bonanza lifted off.

Arlington, Virginia

BROGNOLA SIPPED a cup of steaming cocoa spiked with Bushmills Black Label and waited for the double dose of heat to melt the chill inside him. Any minute now the block of ice around his heart should start to thaw.

Too much was happening too fast. Brognola was on top of it so far, but he still worried that the enemy or simple circumstance might slip one past him while his back was turned.

Atlanta had been too damn close for comfort. Bolan's call and CNN reports had tipped him to the presence of closed-circuit cameras in the university classroom building where Bolan and his Russian sidekick had taken out the latest sleeper. Brognola didn't know if Emory had been the shooter's target and he frankly didn't give a damn now that the guy was dead.

His one and only thought, on learning of the cameras, had been to keep his number-one commando's face from beaming into thirty million homes an hour for the next few days.

So far, so good.

He'd called Atlanta PD first, then Emory's chief of police on campus. Both departments had been skeptical concerning Brognola's mention of national security, but they'd come around with some gentle arm-twisting. He used the carrot-stick approach, promising federal favors in return for prompt cooperation, backing it up with not so subtle threats of Washington's extreme displeasure should cooperation be withheld. Campus police relied on state and federal grants when times were lean; municipal departments took the handouts, too, and they were always vulnerable to investigations of corruption and brutality.

His third call, to the FBI field office in Atlanta, had put flying squads of agents on the street, collecting all known videocassette recordings of the campus firefight and dispatching them to Brognola in Washington by overnight express. Atlanta's G-men knew that they'd be held responsible if copies of the tapes eluded them and wound up on the air.

Nobody wanted to spend the winter months in Butte, Montana, watching out for stolen cars.

Brognola reckoned they were covered on the video.

Surveillance of the next suspect was something else.

They had no trouble finding Byron Cross in Scottsdale, but his desert digs made it impossible for a stakeout team to camp on his doorstep without being spotted. Short of spooking him or provoking a siege incident, the watchers had to stay well back and watch the house through field glasses, taking care not to follow too closely when their subject made the five-mile drive to town on Rio Verde Drive and Pima Road.

It would be simpler just to pick him up, but that would never fly unless he made some hostile move. Burke Barnum's word would never be enough to hang a warrant on, especially now that he had been declared a federal fugitive. Same thing for wiretaps that would let them eavesdrop and find out if Cross had any callers with a Russian accent, telling him to head for town and raise a little hell.

The good news was, they'd found their subject safe at home. There'd been no visitors since the surveillance was established, and he'd only left the house to work his shift or feed a swarm of cats that hung around the place. No dogs, which was a bonus if they had to raid the house in an emergency, but Brognola worried about the hardware carried by the sleepers who had tipped their hands so far.

Count on Kalashnikov assault rifles, some kind of handgun, probably frag grenades and enough plastique to put the small house in orbit. His watchers out of Phoenix couldn't tell if Cross's place had been fortified in any way against assault. No modifications were apparent, but he could have damn near anything inside the house, from Kevlar and sandbags to a ferroconcrete bunker.

Public records showed that Cross had owned and occupied the house for nearly eighteen years and seven months. He could've dug escape tunnels from his basement to downtown Phoenix in that time, and no one would know it until he slipped through their fingers like sand.

And what if Barnum was wrong?

What if they were camped out watching the wrong subject while Jasha Seriozha touched base with a sleeper somewhere else, and they had another bloodbath on their hands while Bolan and the FBI were chasing shadows. What then?

Mayhem. And they'd start all over from scratch.

The big Fed sipped his spiked cocoa and thought about failure, what it would mean to miss Seriozha's next sleeper—or to miss the Russian entirely, running around in hopeless circles while he tipped over his lethal dominoes, one after another.

At best, it meant a string of gruesome tragedies.

At worst, global catastrophe.

Brognola told himself it couldn't *really* come to that. The White House and Congress were too level-headed to launch retaliatory strikes on the basis of a rogue madman's crimes, weren't they? Were there enough paranoid war hawks on Capitol Hill to grab the ball and run with it, buying into Seriozha's illusion of a long delayed Russian sneak attack?

Brognola hoped not, but he couldn't be sure.

America had gone to war for less in bygone years. Sometimes her politicians only needed an excuse, and the new regime in Washington had made a point of talking tough to former cold war adversaries, rattling nuclear sabers where a stern word might have been enough to do the job.

How would public Washington react to news that Russian moles, in place for twenty years or more, were surfacing in bloody incidents across the country, directed by a die-hard agent of the former KGB?

Brognola didn't want to know.

He didn't even want to *think* about it, but he had no choice.

Just nail the bastard. Roll him up and finish it, before it's too late.

They'd managed to keep a lid on the story so far, thanks in part to the frequency with which Americans murdered their neighbors and attacked public buildings for no apparent reason. Who said insanity paid no fringe benefits?

Their luck couldn't hold indefinitely, though. Sooner or later, some sharp reporter would start connecting the dots, filling in blanks with imagination that might fall dangerously close to the truth.

Recovery of Russian military hardware at successive, widely separated crime scenes was a clue. If someone in the fourth estate went sniffing after it, they'd soon discover that the lunatic lone gunman in each case was a man without a history, each living an elaborate lie rooted in false documents and fairy tales of childhoods that had never been.

What would he call a team like that?

The Zombie Squad?

Brognola wondered where they'd come from, how they'd slipped into the States and made themselves at home. More to the point, he wondered how many were left and where they could be found.

And whether they'd be found in time.

CHAPTER SIX

Outside Scottsdale, Arizona

The Arizona desert under moonlight may as well have been the surface of the moon itself. It was an alien landscape, bleached of color to a world of shifting grays, alive with scuttling denizens that hissed, bit and stung.

Jasha Seriozha stood within the shadow of a large mesquite and let it cover him. He craved a cigarette but wouldn't give himself away by smoking one. Between its light and smell, it would betray him instantly to any enemy within a hundred yards.

He much preferred to watch and wait, scanning the sprawl of desert that surrounded Byron Cross's modest home.

Seriozha knew about Atlanta. He had wasted half a day trying to catch the broadcast from Emory University's campus security cameras, but the tape never aired and network anchors had stopped referring to the videos in their reports.

Was it an oversight? Acknowledgment of a mistake?

Or something else?

Seriozha had looked forward to the broadcast. He already knew what one of the Atlanta shooters looked like, but he would've paid dearly for a glimpse of the other two, described in breathless media accounts as a man and a woman.

If they were police or FBI, why didn't the reporters say so? No names were required, but law-enforcement agencies always wanted credit for their feats of derring-do. It was a law of nature, as immutable as gravity.

Who were they? How had they discovered Cheslav Fedorenka?

If they were putting the pieces together, Seriozha reasoned, his whole network would be compromised. He'd studied American police procedures prior to his first U.S. visit as a KGB field agent, and while dragnet arrests were technically illegal in most cases, Seriozha knew that lawmen the world over typically ignored rules when it suited them.

If the FBI knew about his sleepers, Washington would find or fabricate a way to take them off the streets before they could go active.

Seriozha had considered calling all of them by telephone, attempting to launch them that way, but the plan had built-in safeguards. There was no hypnotic mumbo jumbo, but his people had been schooled to wait for personal contact, a handler in the flesh whom they could recognize before they went to war.

The Americans had coined a term for it, as they did for everything: fail-safe.

It was supposed to mean that nothing could go wrong, but something obviously had. Now Seriozha was compelled to crisscross the country alone, meeting each of his soldiers in turn and sending them out to do battle with a symbolic pat on the head.

He could've changed the order, though. That much was his fault and nobody else's. Seriozha recognized his own inflexibility where matters of ritualistic detail were concerned, but he refused to deviate from his planned course of action.

Not yet.

Deviation equaled desperation, an admission that the FBI or someone else had beaten him. It hadn't come to that yet, and with any luck it never would.

If worse came to worst, though, and it seemed to him the whole list had been compromised, he might be forced to change his plans.

In fact, Seriozha already had something in mind.

Cross didn't know he was coming tonight, but Seriozha expected a warm welcome. The incident in Dallas had been a troubling aberration, but he didn't let it worry him. None of the others he'd contacted so far were corrupted by their decadent surroundings.

They stood firm and waited for his order to attack.

As it was meant to be.

He would be cautious, though, in case his enemies were more intelligent than he supposed. They wouldn't trap him like a rat who dropped its guard at the first scent of cheese.

The small house was silent, lit from within by low-powered lamps. Cats roamed or lounged beneath a floodlight mounted on a power pole some distance from the building. Seriozha saw one vehicle parked in the yard, another cat sprawled on the roof.

He took the infrared night-vision goggles from his bag and put them on, adjusting the fit before he switched on the unit. A high-pitched whine was audible as the goggles powered up, but anyone who might detect the sound could easily mistake it for a desert insect trilling in the moonlight.

Seriozha's goggles turned the desert landscape green. He made another sweep of the surrounding terrain, stopping abruptly to focus on a small emerald object bouncing along from south to north, some twenty yards out from his cover. The object paused briefly, and he recognized the kangaroo rat before it hopped out of sight behind a clump of cactus.

He kept scanning, taking his time, making sure that he did the job right. There was too much at stake, too much to lose, for half-assed negligence to be permitted. If it took another hour to satisfy himself that he was safe, so be it.

The Russian froze and swung his head back to the left. His goggles moved an inch or two, at most, but out there where it mattered, on the desolate moonscape, his gaze traveled ten or fifteen feet, searching for the image that alarmed him.

Where was it? *What* was it?

There!

Body heat.

He stood immobile, staring through the protruding lenses that made him resemble an alien from a low-budget science-fiction film. Every muscle in Seriozha's body was taut to the point of trembling. He briefly forgot how to breathe.

There were two men, at least. He marked them when one raised his head to look around, the other lying prone and focused on the house where Byron Cross sat waiting with his cats. Their attitude—indeed, their very presence here—told Seriozha they were enemies.

Who'd sent them?

In the end, it made no difference. He didn't care if they were FBI or state police, immigration or military intelligence. They were surveilling Byron Cross, which could only mean they suspected him of something, some criminal behavior.

Seriozha thought it through. He'd had no personal contact with his sleepers for years, since the Soviet Union was officially dismantled and he chose "retirement" over dishonor. One of the sleepers had betrayed him, and it was possible that Cross also had failed him.

How? Had Cross prepared a trap for Seriozha, or was the surveillance a result of some unrelated activity? Had he become a common criminal? Were the police watching his home for some completely different reason?

Seriozha dismissed the notion as unlikely, verging on impossible. To think that after all these years lawmen would come for Cross on the very night he, Seriozha, came calling defied any notion of coincidence. Couple that improbability with the previous day's fiasco in Atlanta and the very thought became preposterous.

No.

Whoever these watchers might be, they were spying on Cross because they knew what he was. That in turn left Seriozha with only two possible answers: either Cross had betrayed him, or the sleeper remained loyal, unaware of the surveillance mounted on his home.

Seriozha had to find out.

One way or another, he couldn't leave the situation as he found it.

Once again he reached into the bag that hung from his left shoulder. This time he withdrew a Polish semiautomatic pistol, the Radom P-83 chambered for 9 mm Shorts. A slim suppressor doubled the weapon's normal 6.5-inch length.

Keeping on the goggles, Seriozha slowly made his way across the wasteland. His shadow trailed behind him like an afterthought of death.

"IT'S GETTING COLD out here," Special Agent Kip Holmes whispered.

"No shit, Sherlock."

His partner, Agent Gary Rexton, grinned by moonlight, enjoying as always the nickname that Holmes had endured since he'd entered the FBI Academy in 1996.

"That's cute, Rex. Soooo original."

Another flash of teeth. "There any coffee left?"

"'Fraid not."

"Dammit!"

They huddled close together on the hard, dry ground and kept their voices down although the subject was inside his house, a hundred yards away. The subject had no watchdog, no security devices visible, but they'd been told to play it straight and watch themselves while they were on the stakeout detail.

SAC Frank Herndon—special agent in charge of the FBI's Phoenix field office—hadn't explained what they were looking for beyond the subject's name, address and vital stats. When Holmes tried to milk a few more details, Herndon had rebuffed him, calling the operation a need-to-know matter of national security.

Holmes and Rexton, the SAC pointedly noted, didn't need to know.

So here they were, wearing desert-camo coveralls, belly down in the dirt watching some guy's house for no apparent reason, making oral observations to a Sony compact tape recorder anytime the subject poked his head outside.

Which wasn't very often.

Subject Byron Cross had driven home from work at 5:05 p.m., rolling surveillance broken off by the day-watch agents Herndon had assigned to follow Cross around his taxi route in Phoenix, burning gasoline at taxpayers' expense. When Cross got home he fed the cats, put out some garbage in the covered cans he kept outside and disappeared back in the house.

Four hours and twenty minutes later, Holmes and Rexton had seen nothing more of him. Even the cats were bored; a few of them looked comatose.

"I'd like to know who this guy is," Holmes said.

"Ours not to reason why," Rexton replied.

"I checked the poster file and warrants. Nothing on him there that I could find."

"That's why they call it need-to-know, old son."

"What does a Phoenix cabbie have to do with national security?"

"You're asking me?"

"I'm asking period."

Rexton lowered his field glasses long enough to glance at Holmes and say, "You've got the cellular. Why don't you give Old Hernia a call and ask?"

Old Hernia was Herndon's nickname, coined by agents under his command because his long face always seemed to bear a vague expression of discomfort, as if he were suffering a sharp pain in his nether regions. No one used it where the boss could hear them, though. Despite a number of reforms in the decades after J. Edgar Hoover's death, internal discipline was still capricious at the FBI, field agents pointedly excluded from the civil-service shield.

Translation—if you crossed the SAC and he got wind of it, your ass was grass.

"Smart money says somebody got their wires crossed on this guy."

"You know the drill," Rexton said. "When Old Hernia says, 'Jump'—"

"We ask, 'How high?' That doesn't bother you?"

"I'm not in charge, Sherlock. We've got chain of command. The shit still rolls downhill."

"I don't mind stakeouts, if they're going somewhere. You remember that militia job last Christmas?"

"I've been trying to forget it."

They'd been staked out in the woods above Flagstaff, six snowy days and nights, watching the members of a self-styled "patriot militia" sit around the nice fire in their camp and shoot the breeze. Six days and nights, before a shipment of illegal weapons was delivered to the rednecks and they dropped the net.

That was a job well done; *this* detail smelled like futile busywork.

"I didn't go to the academy for this," Holmes said.

"Oh, brother. Here we go again."

"I mean it! We're supposed to be crime fighters,

aren't we? How can we make good on this guy if the SAC won't even tell us what we're looking for?"

"You heard the man. He wants surveillance without contact. That tells me we're fishing."

"Fishing I can handle, but for what?"

"You need to turn that broken record over, son. It's getting old."

"Know what your problem is?"

"Enlighten me, Sherlock."

"You lack imagination."

"Wrong. Before you started beating that dead horse, I was imagining myself at Chloe's place, know what I mean?"

Chloe was Rexton's girlfriend of the moment, a caseworker with the IRS. They'd met in April, over mediocre coffee in the Phoenix federal building's cafeteria.

"You need to watch yourself with Chloe, Rex. Piss that one off and you'll be audited back to your summer jobs in high school."

"I'm an open book, Sherlock."

"Derivative and totally predictable?"

"You wound me."

"Yeah, it shows."

"So much, in fact, that now I have to take a leak."

"Again?"

"Damn coffee goes right through me."

Rexton handed Holmes the field glasses, then wriggled backward down the gentle slope they occupied, until the north wall of the gully screened him from the subject's house. The shades were drawn on that side, spilling pallid light from narrow cracks, but it was still procedure, nothing left to chance.

Holmes watched the silent house and listened to his partner's footsteps as they trailed away. Rexton would find a place outside of earshot, maybe take a little extra time to work the kinks out after lying on the cold, hard ground for hours. When he got back, Holmes would take a turn, then settle in for what promised to be a long and boring night.

We should've brought more coffee. Next time—

What was that?

A scuffling sound, from somewhere down the wash. Holmes squinted in the wan moonlight, but shadows cloaked the gully for as far as he could see. He waited, listening intently, but the sound wasn't repeated.

Maybe Rexton was scuffing dirt or kicking sand over the spot where he'd relieved himself. It wasn't as if they were on some great mission behind enemy lines, but Rexton took the job seriously.

Most of the time.

Except where women were concerned.

Holmes had to give him credit. Rexton had a way with ladies and he didn't talk it up the way some fellow might've in his place. Three years he'd been in Phoenix, and Chloe from the IRS was his eighth "steady" girlfriend so far. Holmes made a point of keeping track, lamenting his own painful shyness with women while he watched Rexton score.

It takes all kinds, he thought, turning his full attention back to Byron Cross's house.

A second cat had climbed atop the car, but nothing else had changed. It was a snoozer, any way he tried to slice it.

More noise now, coming back along the gully.

Rexton hadn't stretched his bladder break as long as Holmes had thought he might. Too much excitement for him at the lookout post. He couldn't stay away.

Holmes heard his partner coming up beside him.

"That was fast," he said. "You like this so much, maybe I could take a break."

An unfamiliar voice replied, "I think you should."

Holmes turned to face the voice. He almost recognized the pistol pointed at his face before the moonlight flared to muted orange, then cut to everlasting black.

BORYA KAROLEK, known as Byron Cross to all but one or two people on the face of the planet, sat before his twenty-six-inch Sony television, waiting for a soft knock on the door. The Sony's sound was muted, just in case he missed it and because he hated laugh tracks but adored the situation comedies that featured busty girls in skintight clothes.

He knew the knock would be a soft one when it came, because his caller's business was a secret. There would be no fanfare, nothing to warn his enemies that the day of fire and tribulation was at hand.

Karolek smiled at the lapse into biblical imagery. He was a lifelong Marxist who disdained religion in all forms, but part of the cover he'd devised for his cab-driving cover persona was a devotion to hellfire televangelism and the Good Book. Karolek carried a Bible with him every day in his taxi, enduring the jibes of his jaded, foul-mouthed co-workers.

Who would expect a straitlaced Bible-thumper to destroy them and uproot their cherished way of life?

"Lord, give me strength," he whispered to the TV set, smile widening.

On the aptly named boob tube, a well-endowed blond woman was giving silent hell to her husband, boyfriend—whatever. It amused Karolek to insert his own dialogue, tossing off non sequiturs in the manner of a badly dubbed Asian movie.

"You must appreciate my breasts!" he made her say.

"I would if they were real!" he answered on the man's behalf.

"At least they're paid for," the blonde said, sneering.

"I know, since I—"

The tap-tap-tap silenced Karolek in midsentence. He used the remote control to switch off his TV, then sat and listened, waiting for the knock to be repeated.

His imagination?

No. Not with the phone call to prepare him.

Tap-tap-tap.

He bolted from his chair, dropped the remote and snatched the .38 revolver from the coffee table, stuffing it into his waistband at the back.

It never hurt to be prepared.

Karolek turned off lights as he moved through the house, refusing to provide a backlit target when he opened the door. Assuming he did open it.

If he didn't like what he saw through the peephole, he could simply go back to his chair—or pump a few rounds through the door.

Bending to the eyepiece, Karolek held his breath and found the light switch by touch. A flick of his finger and the yard outside went bright as day. A stocky older man with close-cropped hair stood glaring back at him.

"Too bright, Comrade," said the familiar voice.

Karolek killed the light and unlocked the door, fumbling the security chain in his excitement. Cursing softly, he got it on the second try and threw the door open.

"Come in, please, Comrade!"

"You have a shovel, I presume?"

The question took Karolek by surprise. He fumbled the door's chain again as he replied, "Of course, Comrade."

"We'll use it in a bit."

Karolek's nerves kicked in. "If I may be allowed to ask—"

"I found two spies watching your house," his handler said. "I've dealt with them, but they must be concealed before sunrise."

Two spies?

"Watching *my* house?"

"Must I repeat myself?"

"No, Comrade. No."

A swarm of questions made Karolek dizzy. Who were they? Why were they watching him? How long had the surveillance been in place? What had they seen or heard that might jeopardize his mission?

The sleeper relaxed slightly, realizing there'd been nothing for his enemies to see or hear. His cover had been perfect, airtight.

Except for his handler's recent phone call.

God! Oh, God!

"You didn't know about the watchers, Borya?"

"No, sir! Of course not!"

The older man studied his face, concentrating on the eyes, judging him. It looked bad either way, Karolek recognized. If he had known of the surveillance and done nothing, endangering his handler, then he was a traitor. If he hadn't known, it meant that he was—

"Careless. Very careless."

"Yes, sir. I apologize, sir. I had no idea."

"You have maintained security as ordered?"

"Yes, sir!" Karolek found himself standing at attention and couldn't help it. His shoulders slumped a bit in resignation, though, as he confessed, "I don't check the perimeter each day, sir. That's my failing. It has been so many years..."

"How long since you last checked?" the handler asked.

Karolek cringed. "Six days, sir."

"Six days. I see."

The frown deepened. Karolek prepared for the worst.

"Very well," his handler said at last, surprising him. "I'll show you the bodies before I leave. You'll bury them tonight, without fail."

"Yes, sir! Thank you, sir!"

"Do you have vodka?" the handler asked.

"Certainly, Comrade."

"I'll have some, then."

Karolek ran to fetch it while the other made himself at home on the sofa, studying the small living room as if some particular detail might prove significant, proving or dispelling some preconceived notion. Whatever he learned or felt as he scanned the room, no hint of it was mirrored on his face.

Karolek came back with the bottle and two glasses, pouring his handler's drink first, then a much smaller one for himself. The KGB man sucked down half of his vodka, smiling thinly as it went to work.

"You understand the network has been activated, Borya?"

"As you told me on the telephone, Comrade."

"It is your turn to strike for Mother Russia and the people's revolution."

"Gladly and enthusiastically."

Karolek meant it, too. He had been waiting for this moment nearly half his life. More times than he could count, he'd feared that it would never come. Karolek didn't want to be abandoned and forgotten in America.

"I must warn you, Comrade. There have been some unexpected difficulties."

"Sir?"

"You're not the first I've visited," the handler said. "One had abandoned his commitment to the operation and attempted to betray me."

"Comrade, no!"

"It's true. I dealt with him, of course. Another was exposed and intercepted by a team of capitalist agents on his way to carry out his orders. That concerns me more, in light of what I found outside."

He nodded toward the desert night outside and drained his glass. Karolek poured another hefty shot.

"What does it mean, Comrade?"

"We have been compromised," the handler said. "Perhaps not fatally, since you were merely watched and not arrested. We have time before these two are missed and reinforcements sent. Have you the courage to proceed?''

''Yes, Comrade!''

''Even knowing it may mean your death?''

What did it matter?

''Absolutely, Comrade!''

''Good. I hoped that we can count on you.''

''In every way, Comrade.''

''You've kept in touch with changes at the target site?''

''I visit it three times a year,'' Karolek said. ''I take the guided tours and read the latest government reports.''

''Good man. Is your equipment here?''

''Yes, Comrade.''

Karolek had unearthed it within an hour of receiving the handler's telephone call. The gear was hidden in his bedroom closet, safe from prying eyes outside.

''Go fetch your shovel, then,'' the handler said, rising. ''I'll show you where I left the trash and you can get to work.''

SERIOZHA LEFT Borya Karolek to bury the corpses, content to take their pistols and FBI credentials with him as he walked back through the desert moonlight to his rented car. The Honda Civic waited where he'd left it, parked fifty yards in from the highway on an unpaved access road that showed little sign of use. A moment with a penlight verified that no one had disturbed the car in his absence.

Seriozha had six hours before his flight was scheduled to depart from Phoenix Sky Harbor International Airport. He could've taken more time with the next contact, but he was unsettled by the events in Atlanta. Someone had exposed Cheslav Fedorenka, albeit at the last possible moment, and the FBI surveillance on Karolek's humble home told Seriozha he had problems on a broader scale.

It seemed impossible, but someone was anticipating him.

Who knew about his sleepers? There had only been a few who knew it all, from the beginning. Five or six in Moscow had enough details to damage him, but most of them were dead now, the only known survivor doing hard time on the new, improved gulag. And that one, as it happened, didn't know the names of Seriozha's sleepers in America.

He couldn't betray them individually, even if he wanted to.

Who, then?

He thought at once of Barnum, regretting that his contract killers had failed him in Indiana. Seriozha didn't mind that they'd been killed; he simply rued the fact that they had missed their target.

Executing Burke Barnum was supposed to be a precaution, what the Americans liked to call preventive medicine. A longtime contact at the Department of Justice had noted the plan for Barnum's curious furlough from prison, passing on the news to Seriozha in the belief that he—Seriozha—was a journalist intrigued by real-life cloak-and-dagger stories, willing to pay for hot tips that let him scoop the competition. Seriozha had no reason to believe the move had anything to do with him, and yet...

Why, after less than ten years, would a traitor serving life be granted an experimental work release from

America's toughest federal prison? And why would the move be kept under wraps from the media?

Was it mere coincidence that Barnum's furlough came through in the wake of Seriozha activating sleepers in three states and executing a traitorous fourth?

What did Barnum know about Seriozha that he hadn't already shared with federal prosecutors prior to trial? And how could he know anything about the moles?

Never mind.

The decision had been automatic, pure common sense; Barnum had to die.

But he was still alive, and Fedorenka was dead in Atlanta, while FBI agents shadowed Karolek in Scottsdale.

Coincidence or conspiracy?

That question troubled Seriozha as he drove back toward Phoenix, southbound on Pima Road to McDowell and his right-hand turn toward the airport. He might as well be early, taking time to scan the airport parking lots and terminal for any indicators of surveillance there.

Seriozha hoped he might have nipped his Phoenix problem in the bud, while the federal agents were still on a haphazard fishing expedition. Perhaps it was ego talking, but he felt certain there would've been more than two FBI agents in place if the Bureau had expected him in Scottsdale. Likewise, he believed they would've picked up Karolek for questioning, at least, if there'd been any solid evidence against him.

Were they operating on suspicion, then? And if so, how had they targeted two of his moles in a row?

One solution, Seriozha thought, would be to discard his scheduled order and scramble the list, bypassing Chicago in favor of a mole further down the roster. In that way, he might learn if *all* his agents were betrayed, or if the enemy was somehow tracking him across the map.

It made a fair amount of sense, but Seriozha balked at a last-minute change in his plans. He recognized such stubbornness as a failing, but he didn't believe it was critical.

He'd waited more than a decade to see his plan in action. Why should he allow the enemy to tamper with it now, before he was satisfied that they were truly onto him?

It may be too late when you really know, he thought, but shrugged it off.

He was a covert warrior of the old school, trained to persevere despite adversity. He'd run networks in Western Europe through the last years of the cold war, helped assassinate some of the agents named by Langley's traitor Aldrich Ames, and no one from the CIA or MI-6 had ever laid a finger on him. He was known in certain hostile quarters, but the enemy could never catch him.

As before, so now.

He thought about the Smith & Wesson pistols he had taken from the FBI men and decided he would put them in his check-through luggage, with the Radom automatic. There were penalties for carrying undeclared firearms in checked baggage, but experience had taught Seriozha that bags were rarely X-rayed on domestic flights. He'd traveled widely with the Radom in the past few months and had no trouble, but he always spent some extra time around the baggage carousels just in case, watching out for surveillance before he collected his bags.

For personal protection on the flight itself, Seriozha was limited to a seven-inch fiberglass dagger he'd purchased years ago, at a gun show in Nebraska. It was black, double-edged and sharp enough to cut steak, advertised by its manufacturer as a letter opener, though Seriozha had never used it to slit an envelope.

If push came to shove in an emergency, the blade and his own martial-arts skills should be enough—at least until he could disarm another corpse.

By the time he pulled into the airport parking lot, Seriozha had convinced himself that the discovery of federal agents outside Karolek's home might actually help the sleeper perform his final task. Fear wasn't necessarily a bad thing on the eve of battle; it sharpened wits and gave new focus to a soldier's thoughts.

It wouldn't do, after the business in Atlanta, for Karolek to approach his target in haphazard fashion, too relaxed or too self-confident. His nerves were now on edge, as they should be for any struggle to the death. Karolek would be doubly cautious, and ruthless, in the final hours of his life.

Seriozha congratulated himself, not for the first time, on his selection of the sleepers he'd chosen. Granted, one of them had betrayed him, but the rest were so far loyal, unwavering in their devotion to the cause they served.

As they should be.

Long years of immersion in decadent American society hadn't corroded their ideals or weakened their resolve.

But someone had betrayed him.

Seriozha hoped he'd have a chance to find out who it was and punish the traitor accordingly.

Perhaps the execution of his scheme as planned, against all odds, would stand as punishment enough—both for the traitor and the foul, corrupt society he served.

Next stop, Chicago.

Jasha Seriozha found that he could hardly wait.

CHAPTER SEVEN

Scottsdale, Arizona

It was an hour past dawn when they reached the house off Rio Verde Drive, already sixty-five degrees and climbing with the promise of another scorching day. Bolan drove the Saturn SL2 they'd rented at the airport, checking first for vehicles—none visible on the approach—and then for sudden movements of the drapes in front that would suggest a sniper lining up his shot.

Again, nothing.

"We missed him," Barnum said from the back seat.

"Surveillance says he should be home," Bolan replied.

He'd checked in from the airport to confirm it, calling Stony Man for any updates from the FBI agents in place. There had been nothing since the rolling team handed Byron Cross off to the stationary watchers at six-fifteen last evening.

Not a word.

So, where was he?

Cross drove a four-year-old Chevrolet Cavalier, but

it was nowhere to be seen. Behind the house? Forget it. There was nothing but desert back there, not even a gravel driveway leading around to the rear.

If Cross had left, his watchers should've logged it, and tailed him, too, if there was no backup team available to do the job. Had he bailed out unexpectedly in the half hour since Bolan had made his phone call?

It was damn unlikely.

"What shall we do?" Galenka asked when they had thirty yards to go.

"Drop in for breakfast," Bolan said, and swung the car into their target's unpaved driveway.

"Marvelous." The Russian drew her pistol and flicked off the safety.

"Is this the plan?" Barnum asked. "You call this a plan?"

"We're improvising," Bolan said. "Sit tight."

He killed the Saturn's headlights as they washed across the house, reflected in blind windows. Cats scampered for the shadows as he switched the engine off and set the parking brake.

"You're going in?" Barnum asked, clearly nervous now.

"Feel free to wait out here," Bolan replied.

He drew the Beretta 93-R from its armpit rig as he left the car and closed his door behind him. Stealth was out the window, sudden gunfire still a danger, but the place felt empty. Unless Bolan was very much mistaken, their target had checked out and left the cats in charge.

Galenka was beside him, a hesitant Burke Barnum bringing up the rear, when Bolan reached the front door. He was deciding whether he should try the knob or kick it in when something stopped him—an echo from his briefing with Hal Brognola.

The booby-trapped equipment stash in Kentucky.

"It's no good," he said.

"What's wrong?" Galenka asked.

"I want a window, side or rear."

He moved around the house, cats scurrying before him, until he reached the north side and what seemed to be a bedroom window. He used a penlight on the frame, saw nothing on the sill or edges, but he had a final test to make.

"Stay back," he warned the others, taking a dozen long paces away from the house. Turning in one smooth motion, Bolan raised his selective-fire pistol and put a three-round burst through the window, shattering three-quarters of the upper pane.

Nothing.

He gave it fifteen seconds, and when there was still no blast from a time-delay fuse he walked back to the house, clearing the rest of the jagged glass with a sweep of his weapon. Reaching in, he yanked down the curtains and let them drop. He found the window's latch and pushed it up, brushing more broken glass aside before he scrambled through.

Galenka followed, Barnum grumbling behind her as he joined them in a small and cluttered bedroom. Bolan found the light switch and they made their way along a short hall to the living room.

He found a half-pound block of RDX taped to the inside of the door, connected to a battery and homemade motion detonator that would blow the charge if the door moved more than a few inches.

"*Anarchist's Cookbook,*" Barnum said. "It's classic."

It was a moment's work for Bolan to detach the wires and render the device harmless. Galenka waited until he was done before she said, "He knew we were coming."

"It stands to reason someone would drop by after he makes his splash," Bolan replied. "This is a little 'P.S., Go to hell.'"

"We still don't know his target, though," Barnum said.

"If he left a trail, we need to find it," Bolan replied. "We're on the clock."

"A search?" Galenka asked.

"But carefully. Watch out for trip wires, anything like that."

"I'll help," said Barnum. When they looked at him, the ex-lieutenant colonel added, "Hey, I did some Special Forces time, back in the day. Some things you don't forget."

"All right," said Bolan. "We'll split up and take it room by room."

Barely a minute later, Barnum called them to the spare bedroom he'd been assigned to search. "Is this the mother lode or what?" he asked, as Bolan and Galenka joined him.

Cross had turned the surplus space into a kind of operations room, complete with maps tacked to the walls and a collection of literature on his primary target. The stash included tourist pamphlets, postcards, photographs and books purloined from several libraries. It was apparent that Cross knew his subject intimately.

Hoover Dam.

"How far away is that?" Barnum asked. "Would you say two hundred miles?"

"More like 250," Bolan said.

"He's got a lead. We'll need a time machine."

Already moving toward the telephone, Bolan replied, "I'll settle for some wings."

Kingman, Arizona

SIXTY MILES from his intended target, Borya Karolek stopped to fill the Chevy Cavalier's gas tank. He splurged on premium, paying the extra fifteen cents per gallon without a second thought. What difference did it make when he'd be dead within two hours, anyway?

It felt good to be moving after so much time spent in virtual suspended animation. He had mentally rehearsed these final hours of his life each day for eighteen years, imagining the impact his sacrifice would have on his enemies.

Karolek knew he'd be remembered when the victors wrote their history of earth's final conflict. And those histories would be written in Russian.

His assignment wasn't technically considered a suicide mission. He wasn't required to die in the act, like some misguided Muslim steering a truck bomb into a Middle Eastern embassy. He simply realized that escape was highly improbable, and he had long since come to terms with death.

Nothing mattered but the People's revolution. It had been diverted and delayed, but triumph was inevitable. It was his destiny to strike a killing blow for the cause, and to hell with any consequences for himself.

His life in Scottsdale had been dreary, for the most part. He despised his job but cherished the free time it had allowed for planning, visits to the target, study of materials to help him carry out his mission. When he drove the cab, Karolek marked each fare who treated him with condescension or ignored him altogether, imagining their shock when he carried out his strike against their precious nation.

Would any of the mindless drones remember him? Would his photograph on television stir their sluggish memories? Or would the flood tide of events preclude that recognition, sweeping them away with the corruption of their decadent society?

Karolek hoped a few of them, at least, had time and sense enough to recognize their brush with the Red death. It pleased him no end to imagine their dismay and grief.

His target had been chosen for maximum impact. The Hoover Dam generated much of the electricity for southern California, a region already plagued by power shortages and skyrocketing prices. Within recent memory, the state had imposed rolling blackouts to conserve energy and reduce massive deficit spending. It thrilled him to imagine what would happen when he blew up the dam's huge generators: instant, sweeping loss of power to airports and hospitals, police stations and firehouses, TV and radio stations, shopping malls and theme parks. Auto collisions in Los Angeles alone would claim dozens of lives, as thousands of traffic lights winked out in a heartbeat.

Any flooding on the Colorado River, if his plastique charges breached the dam itself, would be a bonus. There was nothing much between the Arizona line and the Davis Dam, some eighty miles downstream, except the tiny settlement of Willow Beach. Still, that was something. If he had a chance to wipe it off the map, along with sundry campers, rafters and canoers, it would please Karolek all the more.

He only wished that he could be alive the following morning to enjoy the media reports.

There was enough plastic explosive in the Chevy's trunk to shut down the dam's great generators. Of that, he was certain. He had maintained a stringent regimen of exercise—free weights and isometrics, seven days a week—so that he had no trouble carrying 150 pounds of RDX and detonators, plus his AKS and bandolier of extra magazines.

Each time he visited the dam, observing any changes in the layout, he'd kept track of obvious security. The personnel who guided tourists through the dam and answered questions were unarmed, though he assumed there had to be weapons somewhere on the premises. His task would be to take his adversaries by surprise and neutralize as many as he could while they were still off balance, running for their lives, before they could regroup and arm themselves. As for police, the nearest sheriff's substation was seven miles away, in Boulder City; the closest FBI agents and military personnel were in Las Vegas, another twenty miles out.

By the time help was summoned, he would be inside the dam. Before the first reinforcements arrived, he would have at least some of his charges in place. With corpses in view and an armed subject somewhere at large in the bowels of the dam, SWAT officers would take their time seeking him out.

They'd be too late.

Karolek paid the pimply faced teenage clerk for his gasoline, told her to keep the change and walked back whistling to his car.

It was going to be a beautiful day.

Boulder City, Nevada

TASYA GALENKA marveled at the speed with which her American colleague cut through formalities—the proverbial red tape—to get things done. One telephone call from Byron Cross's home, and by the time they drove back to Phoenix a Bell 205 UH-1 Iroquois helicopter from Luke Air Force Base stood waiting for them on the tarmac at Sky Harbor International Airport. The pilots asked no questions, merely helping load their bags for liftoff, while another airman took charge of their rented car. At the helicopter's optimum cruising speed of 161 miles per hour, a grueling five-hour drive was reduced to ninety minutes' flying time.

A nondescript sedan was waiting for them on the deck at Boulder City Municipal Airport, the keys handed over to Mike Belasko by a clean-cut man who could've been a federal agent or a certified public accountant. Again there were no questions, and the stranger paid no evident attention to Burke Barnum in his wig and artificial beard.

At that point, Galenka didn't know if she should be impressed by Belasko's influence or dismayed by the ease with which America's most-wanted fugitive breezed past police and military officers.

She hadn't thought her makeover on Barnum was that convincing, all things considered, but perhaps she'd underestimated her own talent—or Belasko's powers of persuasion.

"How far to the dam?" she asked, when they were in the car and rolling.

"Six or seven miles, once we get out of town," Bolan said. "A straight shot east on Highway 93."

Boulder City resembled any other small town in America. Unlike the other towns and cities of Nevada, though, it boasted no casinos or saloons. Once Nevada's largest city, home to thousands of construction workers, Boulder City was later dwarfed by Reno and Las Vegas, finally incorporated in 1958 after residents were permitted to maintain the former federal ban on gambling, alcohol and prostitution.

Galenka wasn't sure if the attempt to legislate morality had kept Boulder City small, or if time had simply passed the settlement by. In either case, they'd left the city behind within moments, cruising eastward through sparse traffic, Belasko clocking an easy ten miles per hour above the posted speed limit.

She wondered if they were too late, if Jasha's sleeper had already reached the dam and done his bloody work. There had been no alarms, but that could mean Cross was efficient, taking out the guides and guards before they had time to react effectively.

What else did he intend to do?

The other sleepers had been armed with automatic weapons and explosives, antipersonnel grenades and RDX plastique. If Byron Cross maintained the same stockpile, they could assume he meant to sabotage the dam. As far as damages, that would depend on the amount of RDX he carried and how much time they allowed him at his task.

At times like this—thankfully few and far between—Tasya Galenka wished that she knew how to pray. Religion was permitted to the Russian people now, even encouraged, but she'd come of age within a family and a society that recognized no gods. She'd spent her adult life in service to a state that only made its peace with faith inside the past decade, and she suspected she was too old now to find that spark within herself.

It wasn't prayer they needed now, in any case.

It was a little extra time—and firepower.

"How far?" she asked again. The highway seemed to stretch interminably.

"About two miles," Bolan said, not mocking her.

She reached between her feet, unzipped the duffel bag and took out her Uzi submachine gun. It wasn't Russian made, but it would do the job if she could find a target.

Barnum spoke up from the back seat. "Hey, listen, if you want to let me have a gun this time—"

"Dream on," Bolan said.

"Okay. I hope they know we're coming, though," the convict said. "You jump out at the dam with hardware showing and our boy's not there, security may try and take you down."

"I've got a badge, if anybody asks," Bolan told him. "We're FBI today."

Galenka frowned at him. "I don't suppose you have a spare?"

"Sorry."

She pushed the irritation out of mind and concentrated on their goal. She'd memorized a photograph of Byron Cross—a copy of his taxi driver's license, faxed from Arizona's state police before they left Atlanta—and she wouldn't hesitate to kill him on sight.

As for Jasha Seriozha, there was no real hope of finding him with Cross. He still had sleepers to rouse from their long years of torpor, soldiers to send on their way.

But there would be another time.

"Ready?" Belasko's voice cut through her reverie. "We're here. Stay put," he ordered Barnum as he swung into a parking space and switched off the Saturn's engine.

A moment later he was running, with Galenka on his heels.

BURKE BARNUM HAD his orders. They were both specific and concise, no problem with interpretation in the least.

Stay put—as in sit still, go nowhere, put down roots.

He could do that, had no real choice, in fact, since Belasko took the car keys with him, but it was making him nervous as hell. The place would be overrun with suits and uniforms any minute now, and it wasn't where the FBI's most-wanted fugitive cared to spend his day, with or without fake hair.

There was a body lying on the pavement near what Barnum took for an entrance to the dam, perhaps the point where guided tours entered to visit the giant turbines. The body wore a parks department uniform, bloodstained, and two more uniforms knelt beside it, partially obstructing Barnum's view.

He recalled a television documentary about the Hoover Dam, how many of the nimble high-riggers had plunged to their deaths during construction, entombed forever in reinforced concrete. Pink Floyd came out of nowhere, from some recess of his memory, singing about another brick in the wall, and Barnum shook it off.

So many dead to build the dam, but who would've predicted a day like this, when others were killed trying to defend it from a lunatic armed to the teeth?

Barnum wondered if he was far enough back from the dam to be safe if it blew. He should be fine with RDX, all that concrete and steel to contain the blast, and even if the dam went, rushing water from Lake Mead would pour downstream and into Arizona, not back toward the parking lot on higher ground. But if the mole had something more than RDX…

Forget about it.

That was paranoia talking, Barnum knew. A suitcase nuke might've been feasible when Cross went underground, but it still would've been too risky for a low-level sleeper to handle. Radiation leakage alone would be a major problem, both in terms of concealment and security, and none of the moles uncovered so far had been armed with anything more than AKs and plastique.

So far.

First time for everything, Barnum thought, dismissing the small voice in his head as an inveterate troublemaker.

No nukes, then. He'd take that much on faith. It

was bad enough with the standard-issue gear, at least one innocent bystander already murdered, with the dam's great power plant at risk.

It could be termed an act of war, if anyone in Congress connected the dots and traced the ugly pattern back to Mother Russia. It wasn't modern Moscow's fault, of course, but there were still plenty of "ex"-Communists in government who could serve as straw men for a new generation of war hawks on Capitol Hill.

Barnum tried to imagine what course a full-scale reaction would take, then broke it off when he felt himself growing sick to his stomach. They were supposed to be preventing World War III, not bumping it up from a long shot to a virtual sure thing.

Sweating underneath his wig and beard, Barnum resisted an impulse to tear off his spare hair and scratch himself raw. His best bet was to make himself small, remain as inconspicuous as possible until his two escorts returned. Unlike their quarry, Barnum had no ID to explain his presence at the crime scene, traveling with two armed agents who had disappeared inside the dam and therefore couldn't vouch for him. Barnum didn't even know who owned the car he was sitting in, the perfect target for a grand-theft-auto charge.

Emergency, he thought. It was an emergency. With any luck, the uniforms and suits would be distracted by the drama playing out inside the dam and none of them would notice him at all.

But it would take only one look to do him in, and he'd be on his way back to Terre Haute in a flash—or on his way to the morgue, if the arresting officers were trigger-happy with a suspect blamed for murdering two U.S. Marshals.

Barnum wished he had a drink to sedate him, but he couldn't even leave the car to get a drink of water from the public fountain twenty feet away. It would've been too obvious, drawing attention to himself.

"Stay put," he muttered to himself.

IT HAD BEEN relatively easygoing so far for Borya Karolek. He had surprised the parks department rangers, in their uniforms that featured nothing more lethal than the occasional folding knife in a belt sheath. He'd shot one as an example to the rest, scattered the dead man's companions with another short burst from his AKS before he made his way inside the dam.

It felt like coming home. He had taken the guided tour so often that he could recite the spiel from memory. He'd known about the glassed-in office waiting for him just inside the entrance, and he'd made his second kill to stop a female employee from calling for help.

"Not yet," he'd told her as she fell. "I need more time."

But time was running out. His first shot was the starting gun for a desperate race, pitting himself against the men and women who would try to stop him, kill him. Karolek was still ahead of the game, but he knew it couldn't last.

He wouldn't hear the sirens coming in his steel-and-concrete tomb, the massive generators humming like huge wasps' nests. The machinery was loud enough to cause hearing loss from prolonged exposure without proper safeguards, and Karolek had worn shooter's earplugs—not because he worried about long-term deafness in his present situation, but to guard against any and all potential distractions.

He was generous with the RDX, two bricks per turbine, strategically positioned to insure maximum damage. The generators could still be rebuilt, he supposed, but it would be a long and costly process, and by that time, if his fondest hopes were realized, the decadent United States would've ceased to exist in its present form.

His act of war wasn't the last anticipated by his handler, but it could still leave a permanent scar.

That thought—the permanence of it—pleased Karolek more than anything as he fixed his second charge to the fourth generator in line. More than a dozen still remained, and then he'd think about trying to blow the dam itself if there was time.

If not, he would've done enough.

His handler would be justly proud.

The detonators fastened to his plastic charges had no timers. They were radio remote-controlled, keyed to a certain frequency of the transmitter on his belt. He'd spent years tinkering with the transmitter, refining its potential, satisfying himself that the charges wouldn't be blown prematurely by a signal from some passing taxi or policeman's walkie-talkie. They were safe until he armed the detonator and depressed its flat red button, setting off all the charges at once, with one hellacious roar that should be audible for miles.

Karolek was affixing his first charge to the fifth generator in line when a bullet grazed the polished steel before him, striking sparks. He didn't hear a shot but ducked instinctively, firing a short burst from his AKS toward huddled figures at the far end of the catwalk.

There were two of them, at least. The quick glimpse he obtained while scrambling for cover showed a tall man in the lead, a second, smaller form moving along behind him. Karolek couldn't tell if they were pointmen for a SWAT team, but the 7.62 mm rounds from his AKS would drill most lightweight body armor as if it were cardboard.

Assuming he scored a hit, that was.

Karolek was an above-average marksman in optimum conditions, but nearly two decades had passed since he'd had an opportunity to play down-and-dirty war games. He doubted whether his initial burst had wounded either of the gunmen who were closing on him, and he would've bet his life they weren't alone, which meant his time was almost gone.

It was too bad. He'd hoped for time enough to blow the rest of the turbines, at least, but Karolek would make do with what he had. Stealing a moment while his enemies advanced, he took another brick of RDX from his duffel bag and pressed it to the warm steel of the turbine's flank. A flick of his thumb armed the detonator, but he resisted the urge to blow the charges immediately.

Perhaps he could still lead his enemies on a merry chase before they wounded him. It was a gamble, but if it would let Karolek destroy even one more giant turbine, he knew it would be worth the risk.

He burst from cover, staggering slightly as the duffel bag unbalanced him, firing another automatic burst along the catwalk. His bullets rang on steel, whined off concrete, but there were no live targets anywhere in view.

Where had they gone?

A muzzle-flash answered Karolek's silent question, winking at him from near ankle height, behind the second generator. Still no audible sound from the hostile weapon, as he felt a bullet fan the air beside his face.

He was moving, turning to run, when another round struck his left shoulder with explosive force, dropping him to the catwalk. His RDX charges spilled from the open duffel bag, heaped around him like blocks of virgin clay awaiting the artist's touch.

Karolek tried to reach his detonator, but his left arm wouldn't move. His right was tangled up in the Kalashnikov's sling, pinned by the rifle thrust between his elbow and his ribs.

Cursing, he struggled to his hands and knees, mashing a plastic charge beneath his one good hand. Dizzy from pain and loss of blood, he lurched around to face the steadily advancing figures of his enemies.

BOLAN KISSED the catwalk as a storm of AK rounds blitzed overhead. He heard Galenka swearing in Russian behind him as he lined up a two-handed shot with his Beretta and stroked the trigger twice, sending six Parabellum rounds downrange.

His target rocked and staggered, pivoting on one knee and spraying the vaulted ceiling with a long burst from his Kalashnikov as he died. Galenka hit Cross with a quick burst from her Uzi as he fell, and she was on her feet by the time Bolan rose from the catwalk.

"Are you hit?" he asked her.

"Nyet." She caught herself and switched to English. "No, just bruised a bit."

"Okay, let's check him out. Remember that the shooter in Nevada wore Kevlar."

"It won't matter with this," she said, letting her Uzi dangle as she drew the Gyurza P-9 from its shoulder rig.

"Let's watch it, anyway."

"Of course."

They moved along the catwalk, both pistols pointed at the prostrate form of Byron Cross. Bolan went in ahead and kicked the AKS beyond their adversary's reach, then stopped and checked the body for a pulse he couldn't find.

"He's dead."

The bricks of RDX strewed on the catwalk captured Bolan's full attention. He examined one of them, replaced it gently on the deck and unclipped the remote control from Cross's belt.

"No timers," he informed Galenka. "We should still deactivate them, anyway."

"Agreed."

"You've done this kind of work before?"

"Of course."

Bolan was painfully aware of passing time. He didn't know how many charges Cross had planted, or which end of the huge generator room he would've started from. More to the point, police were on the way by now, if not already gathering outside, and there was a risk that their radio transmissions might blow the charges by accident.

Logic told Bolan that his late enemy hadn't had

time to rig the dozen-odd detonators whirring away between the point where Cross died and the far end of the chamber. If he was wrong, a moment's work should be enough to prove it.

"Take this one," he told Galenka, nodding to the nearest generator. "We'll work backward."

"Right."

He left her to it, jogged back to the fourth turbine, and started searching for a brick of RDX. A tiny red light on the detonator helped him out and Bolan plucked it from the plastic charge, leaving the RDX in place for someone else to harvest. Cautiously he scanned the generator for another bomb and found it on the other side, positioned so the two would blow as one and gut the turbine with a single crushing blow.

"Looks like two charges each," he called out to Galenka, plucking out the second detonator and discarding it. Without the small receivers and their blasting caps, the RDX was harmless.

Galenka ran past him on the catwalk, leapfrogging to the third generator in line. Bolan left her to it and took the second, seeking red lights in the shadows as he felt the humming seep into his brain. It would be migraine time if he endured much more of the pervasive background noise, his ears still ringing from the recent blasts of gunfire, but common sense told him they wouldn't be at it much longer.

It was time to think about what would happen outside, in the fresh air and sunlight, when they emerged from the dam.

There would be guns and uniforms, for sure. The FBI credentials in his pocket were the next best thing to real, and Galenka had gone one better, snagging a set of embassy credentials that gave her diplomatic immunity. Between them, he thought they'd be all right—as long as no one recognized Burke Barnum on the sidelines and started asking questions Bolan couldn't answer.

Two more charges down, and they split the last generator, deactivating one bomb each. Galenka seemed edgy, glancing toward the exit door where sunlight spilled inside to glint from polished steel.

"You may want to put that away," he told her, nodding toward the Uzi on its shoulder strap.

She set down the weapon, stripped off her jacket and rehung the SMG, then put the jacket on again. The Uzi's muzzle showed below the jacket's hem, until she wedged it underneath her arm and clamped it tight against her side.

"I can't do any more," she told him, frowning.

"Fair enough. Just don't shake hands."

That sparked a smile and they went out together, with credentials raised, to meet a ring of guns. Barnum was safe outside that circle—for the moment, anyway—while Bolan and Galenka made their explanations to a sheriff's sergeant and a young federal agent who looked more like a college sophomore than a crime-fighting G-man. Telephone numbers were offered, for Hal Brognola's office and the Russian embassy in Washington, before the sergeant helped himself to Cross's radio remote control.

"Take care with that," Bolan suggested as he left them, moving toward the borrowed car and Barnum, "just in case we missed something."

"You finished here, or what?" the young Fed asked, squinting against the sun.

"I've barely gotten started," Bolan said.

They'd cut it fine on this one, and he didn't even know where they were going next. The best Bolan could do was hope they wouldn't be too late.

CHAPTER EIGHT

Washington, D.C.

Brognola had been fielding phone calls since he walked into his office, putting out brush fires. The FBI's special agent in charge of the Las Vegas field office was first, trying to verify credentials he'd been shown by Agent Mike Belasko at the scene of a multiple homicide on federal property. The G-man's usual contacts at Bureau headquarters had bounced his call to Brognola at Justice and it angered him. He wanted explanations "yesterday."

Instead, Brognola gave him bedrock confirmation on the ID Bolan had been issued and made clear in no uncertain terms that details of Agent Belasko's mission were eyes-only, need-to-know, and any other term the Vegas Fed could think of for top secret. He was still angry when Brognola severed the connection, but the big Fed had the agent's solemn promise that there'd be no further inquiries into Belasko's background or assignment. Any lapses in discretion might result in transfer to a post where the Vegas SAC would be neither special nor in charge.

Number two on the hot line was a high-ranking

member of the U.S. Parks Department, venting anger and seeking answers about what had gone down at Hoover Dam a few hours earlier. Brognola played the national-security card on that one, reminding his esteemed caller that the problem had been liquidated and the dam protected once Brognola's team was on the scene. Stretching the truth until he screamed for mercy, he went on to say that details on the shooter would be published when the FBI and Justice had completed their reviews of all the evidence.

The promise was true as far as it went. Police and journalists alike were already going over Byron Cross's background with a battery of microscopes, and most of what was known about the sleeper would be public property by noon that day—minus any allusion to Russia, of course. Brognola was trying to prevent a war, not start one. In the interest of mutual security, Washington and Moscow had agreed to suppress all details of the KGB sleeper campaign and Jasha Seriozha's activation of those moles.

There was never a good time to set the world on fire.

Calls number three and four, respectively, were from commanders of the Las Vegas Metropolitan Police—serving Clark County at large—and the Mohave County, Arizona, sheriff's office. Both agencies had an interest in what happened at Hoover Dam, on their respective sides of the border, but the mayhem had occurred on federal property and both were placated by Brognola's assurance that the case involved no loose ends in either's territory. He didn't tell the metro brass that Agent Belasko and company, including one of America's most-wanted federal fugitives, were currently unwinding at a motel off the Vegas Strip. The locals didn't need to know, and it would only cause more problems if they did.

One can of writhing worms per day was plenty, thank you very much.

The Maricopa County sheriff was harder to shake. His turf included Scottsdale and Phoenix, where the sleeper known as Byron Cross had lived a lie for almost twenty years, driving a cab to make ends meet and looking forward to the grand finale of his life. Brognola put the sheriff off as best he could, explaining that a federal investigation was ongoing and the county's help would be requested if and when it was required. As far as Brognola could tell, the man they knew as Byron Cross hadn't committed any crimes in Maricopa County, except for stockpiling illegal weapons and explosives there. That could go either way, for state or federal time, but there was no one left alive to prosecute.

Scottsdale PD was easy by comparison. The chief wanted "to help," as if his small suburban force could somehow augment efforts put in motion by the FBI. Brognola graciously declined the offer, thanked the chief and promised not to lose his number, just in case.

The media wasn't Brognola's problem. FBI headquarters had a special staff to cope with press inquiries, issue statements and deploy smoke screens. It was a talent cultivated by the Bureau from the early days when Hoover was in charge, finessed and elevated to an art form. There would be no lost or misplaced documents on this one, nothing in the way of scandal or exposure down the line.

The lid was on and it was being welded shut.

Which still left Bolan and his people in the field, at mortal risk. The Executioner did his best work under fire, and his progress had been adequate so far, but the big Fed couldn't help thinking they had grief in store. He didn't know how many sleepers still remained at large, where they were located or which would be the next to blow sky-high.

Brognola's telephone began to ring again. He lifted the receiver, hoping that this time, against all odds, it might turn out to be good news.

Las Vegas, Nevada

THE DESERT ROSE MOTEL had definitely lost its bloom. Counting the plaster cracks and studying the threadbare carpet in his room, Bolan decided it had been a class act once—around the same time Howard Hughes tried to buy out Las Vegas and claim the town as his own personal Monopoly game. Hughes was gone now, dead and buried, but the Desert Rose lingered on, providing Quality Accommodations At A Bargain Rate for visitors who didn't meet high-roller criteria.

The motel was situated two blocks north of the famous Las Vegas Strip, in a zone where day and night lost their traditional meaning. The sun rose and set on Las Vegas, as anywhere else, but Vegas was the original town that never slept. Casinos raked the money in 24/7, and the garish neon of the former carpet joints—now advertised for their contributions to "family fun for all ages"—turned the sky orange at night, as if the city were on fire. You could spend a lifetime in Las Vegas and never see the stars—unless you counted those who turned up periodically in showrooms and cocktail lounges.

Barnum was in a snit of sorts, upset at being left alone at Hoover Dam, surrounded by lawmen, while Bolan and Galenka dealt with Byron Cross. It didn't seem to matter that he'd skated past the challenge without incident. The guy was on a roll, determined to be heard.

"They could've locked me up while you were playing hero in the dam!" he ranted, pacing as an antidote to nervous energy. "They could've recognized me sitting there!"

"They didn't, though," Bolan reminded him.

"But they could have!"

Barnum had been around this track already, working up a head of steam the whole way back from Boulder City to Las Vegas and the Desert Rose Motel. Bolan was sick of it, his patience paper-thin and fading fast.

"All right, enough!" he snapped, with enough command to stop the convict's pacing in midstride. "You've made your daily bitching quota, and unless you want a one-way ticket back to Terre Haute, you'll put a sock in it."

Barnum stood blinking at him, color draining from his face behind the phony beard. Bolan couldn't be sure if it was rage, fear or a combination of the two that blanched his cheeks. The traitor's voice was muted when he said, "You won't do that. You need me."

"Let's get something straight right now," Bolan replied. "I can have people here within the hour to pump you full of Pentothal and pick your brain. Whatever *you* know, *I'll* know by the time they're finished. Once that's taken care of, they can drop you in that garbage bin parked out back for all I care. You get the picture?"

Barnum lost another shade of pigment, swallowed hard and said, "I hear you."

"Good. Now take a seat."

Barnum staked out a corner of the bed and sat with eyes downcast. He had the posture of a sullen child, but he was silent. Bolan took it as a long step in the right direction.

"We nearly dropped the ball today," he told Barnum, "despite surveillance mounted on the target in advance."

"That's not my fault."

"I didn't say it was. My point is that we can't afford to dick around from this point on. You seem to know the order Seriozha's picked for calling up his sleepers, but he isn't giving us a month between events now. If he starts to phone the orders in—"

"He won't," Barnum said.

"You can't know that."

"He's right," Galenka said.

Bolan swung toward the Russian agent, watched her light a cigarette and draw on it before asking, "He's made you a believer now?"

"Not him," she said dismissively. "Jasha."

"How's that?"

"This project is his life, his masterpiece," Galenka said. "He picked the sleepers personally, supervised their training and construction of their covers. They're the children Jasha never had. He'll wake the sleepers personally, one by one, for that reason, if nothing else."

"Give me a break."

She shrugged, exhaling smoke. "It's alien to you, perhaps, but I know Jasha Seriozha. Don't forget, we shared more than assignments when we worked together in the KGB."

"I'm not concerned about his sex life," Bolan said. "You're sitting here describing someone who's insane."

"Is dedication classified as mental illness now?" she asked. "Perhaps. Or maybe he was driven mad by the extinction of a dream."

"It sounds more like a nightmare," Bolan said.

"A matter of perspective, yes? If someone from the CIA had planted saboteurs in Russia, you'd have praised his ingenuity."

"Not if he called them up a dozen years too late and tried to start a World War III. That's lunacy, regardless of the flag you wrap it in."

"You're not a Russian," she replied, as if that said it all.

"I'm glad we cleared that up," Bolan said, "and I'll bow to expertise. We'll play it your way one more time, but hear this, both of you—if anything goes wrong because we backed your hunch—and I mean *anything*—all bets are off. I'll feed you to the U.S. Marshals," he told Barnum, then turned to Galenka, "and I'll see you on the next flight back to Moscow if I have to strap you on the wing myself."

"Agreed," Galenka said.

"I wasn't asking you."

He turned his back on her again and faced Barnum. ‘‘All right, let’s have the name.’’

‘‘THE NAME YOU WANT is Natalie Hyde.’’

‘‘The rest of it,’’ Bolan demanded.

‘‘Last time I checked, she lived in Berwyn, Illinois, and taught fourth grade in the Chicago public school system. She’s forty-eight years old, no children.’’

‘‘Like the rest, so far,’’ Bolan said.

‘‘She married once. It didn’t take. In 1984 she got a plaque for teacher of the year.’’

‘‘The perfect cover.’’

‘‘That’s not half of it,’’ Barnum went on. ‘‘Her husband was an FBI agent, retired in 1993 to work private security. He never had a clue, as far as I could tell.’’

The Russian major smiled at that. ‘‘Jasha must have enjoyed the irony.’’

‘‘I wouldn’t be surprised.’’

‘‘Okay,’’ Bolan said. ‘‘I’ll make some calls and see what’s smoking to the Windy City.’’

‘‘Um, just one thing before we hit the friendly skies again,’’ Barnum said.

‘‘Make it quick.’’

‘‘In case you haven’t noticed, I’m the only one who doesn’t have a change of clothes. Now, I’m all for economy, but in another day or so I’ll have a certain air about me, if you get my drift.’’

The Russian frowned. ‘‘One might say that already.’’

‘‘There. I rest my case.’’

‘‘We don’t have time to shop,’’ Bolan told him.

"We passed a mall on the way in," Barnum replied. "It's maybe half a mile from here."

"Forget it."

"You need time to make arrangements for the flight, yes?" Galenka said.

"Not that long."

"An hour," Barnum offered. "Maybe less."

"You want to stroll around a shopping mall, rub shoulders with the tourists. Is that it?"

"I'm not trying to ditch you," Barnum said. "Where would I go?"

Bolan thought it over, frowning. Finally he said, "All right, here's how it goes. Straight to the mall from here, and then straight back. No stops along the way, coming or going. You get bargain basics, say enough for two or three more days. Go easy on the credit card and keep it simple."

"Maybe I can find an Amish store."

Bolan glowered at him, turning to the Russian major. "You're in charge of him. He talks to nobody but you. He tries to run, you stop him. Don't come back without him, one way or the other."

"I believe we understand each other," the Russian said, pinning Barnum with an icy stare.

"Indeed, we do," he answered, smiling.

They stood and waited while Bolan found a credit card and gave it to the major. Stepping into Barnum's space, he said, "You've got one chance. One hour."

"In case we hit a traffic jam—"

"You're wasting time."

"I hear you, boss."

They made the drive in silence, parked at one end of the shopping mall and made their way inside. The place was fairly crowded, but the shoppers didn't have that tourist look. Most out-of-towners were more interested in slot machines than shirts and slacks.

It had been nearly a decade since Barnum had shopped for clothing or needed to; prison-issue denim had been his standard garb since the arrest that brought his precariously balanced world crashing down around his ears. It felt strange now—even stranger, in a way, than hopping flights and ducking bullets with his two escorts. Shopping was normal, and nothing in Barnum's life had qualified for that label in more years than he cared to recall.

Remembering Belasko's admonition on expenses, they picked a midrange men's store and went in, the Russian hovering and checking her watch incessantly while Barnum scanned the racks. Unsure of sizes after so much time, he had to guess on packaged shirts but took a pair of slacks back to the changing room.

"Five minutes," Galenka said as she took her post outside. "No more."

"The deadline, right," he said.

The changing-room mirror surprised him, as mirrors had done since he first donned the wig and fake beard. A few more days and Barnum thought he might get used to staring at himself from someone else's face, but it hadn't happened yet. He tried the slacks and was surprised to find they fit. It was a lucky guess.

"How many can I get?" he asked Galenka, as he left the dressing room.

She checked the price and frowned. "Two pair, three shirts," she said.

"It feels like Christmas."

"We are finished, then?"

"Not quite," he said. "I'll need some underwear."

If he was looking for a blush, it didn't happen. "Hurry, then," she said. "We're nearly out of time."

Emerging from the mall, Barnum felt almost human for a change. It made a startling contrast from his day-to-day existence in a cell at Terre Haute. The sad part, he decided, was that he'd been unaware of just how much humanity he'd lost.

He thought of running with his new clothes in their crinkly shopping bag, sprinting along the Vegas Strip as fast as he could go until one of the Russian's bullets knocked him down.

Not yet.

He still had work to do.

Bolan was waiting for them when they returned to the Desert Rose Motel. The door was barely shut behind them when he told Barnum, "Get changed, if that's the plan. We've got a flight out of McCarran Airport in an hour and fifteen minutes."

ANOTHER AIRPORT and another charter flight, Tasya Galenka thought. They'd all begun to look the same—air terminals as seen from the outside, the charter planes, the pilots who accepted money without asking any questions.

Back in Russia, as she knew from personal experience, air travel was a luxury reserved for certain government employees and the well-to-do. Most Russians would pass their whole lives with feet planted firmly on the ground, aware of airplanes and airports in the same way they were aware of spacecraft and rockets—as objects designed for others to use, absolutely disconnected from the average Russian's existence. Mobsters and wealthy industrialists had their private jets, of course, but for most simple Russians even traveling on a commercial airliner, in what Americans called coach, was a dream beyond their grasp.

In America, it seemed, everything was so easy—life, death, transportation. Except for dying it all required money, the same as in Russia, but there was so much more to be earned, stolen, spent that Galenka saw no real comparison. And still she was jaded, might've said she was bored except for the ongoing hunt and the possibility that she'd be forced to kill Jasha Seriozha sometime in the next few days.

The gray-haired pilot took Belasko's money and launched into a spiel about his other "clients from Chicago" who had flown into Las Vegas "every weekend in the good old days." She supposed he was speaking of criminals, perhaps spinning tales to make himself seem more important—"connected," in the common American parlance. Just as quickly, Galenka decided he was lying. Surely anyone associated with organized crime in the land of opportunity would have a more impressive hangar and a newer aircraft than the fifteen-year-old Cessna Crusader.

The plane was well maintained, at least, and fairly comfortable. Galenka understood that its top cruising speed was 250 miles per hour, meaning the flight from Las Vegas to Chicago would keep them in the air for seven hours, with stops for refueling in Denver and Springfield, Illinois.

And where was Jasha in the meantime? Was he

perhaps already in Chicago? Had he already activated the next sleeper?

Galenka's last view of Las Vegas was a smear of neon on the vast, dark desert floor below. From high altitude, the city resembled a lava flow or a bed of hot coals, as if the wrath of a vengeful deity had been unleashed upon the gamblers, prostitutes and other sinners who had gathered there. She found it odd to catch herself thinking in such terms, worried for a moment that perhaps prolonged exposure to America and its people had begun to corrupt her thought process.

She had been sent to eliminate her one-time lover and as many of his sleeper agents as she could. That meant killing, since the whole project was destined to remain a secret, removed from intervention by police and prosecutors, and Galenka knew in her heart that she wouldn't flinch from killing Jasha if she got the chance. As for the woman in Chicago, she was no more to Galenka than another target on the firing range.

Belasko had seemed almost surprised at some level to learn that at least two of Jasha's sleepers were women. Galenka didn't think it was a sexist attitude—his reservations against teaming up with her had more to do with nationality than gender, she was certain—but it seemed to gall him somehow that a woman would be used for a virtual suicide mission. There was something vaguely chivalrous about the tall American, though he had been content to let Galenka pull her weight so far.

It was a refreshing change from the old Russian system, where women were perfectly equal in theory but seldom in fact. The asexual label of "comrade" hadn't spared Galenka from her share or gropes and propositions through her years with the KGB. The SVR was different these days, but only, she suspected, because of her rank and reputation for accepting missions that required bloodletting. Galenka had killed and maimed enough enemies of the state that she had become unapproachable on a human level.

Jasha Seriozha hadn't minded that, however. His own reputation preceded him and set him apart from other KGB officers who'd spent their careers in musty offices or embassies. Seriozha was a hard-core covert operative assigned to wet work on a regular basis, directing *konspiratsias* against the West that had cost dozens—perhaps hundreds—of lives on both sides. Jasha won more of the deadly games than he lost, and Galenka believed he could have survived Russia's great transformation if only he'd been willing to bend.

But that had proved impossible. It was a role he could not—*would* not—play at any price. It was better in Jasha's view to lose his rank and pension, even to be hounded from his native land, than to surrender principle. There was a certain irony, Galenka realized, in using such a term to describe Seriozha in action, but he *was* a man of principle, for whom duty took precedence over friendship, family or love.

That was the reason he had to die. There could be no negotiation with Jasha, no reasoning with him. His mind was made up and he wouldn't waver from his task as long as he survived. If captured, he would spend his last years scheming to escape and strike another blow against America. If wounded and disabled, he would find a way to crawl out of the hospital and seek revenge.

Death solved it all—or would, when she got close enough to pull the trigger one more time.

Galenka knew the time would come. She only hoped it wouldn't be too late.

FLYING GAVE Bolan time to think. Galenka and the prisoner both gave him space, preoccupied with private thoughts. Bolan thought he could guess what some of those might be, but he was more concerned with what awaited them on touchdown in Chicago.

Bolan had called Brognola's private line and reported what he knew about their next target, clearing the way for emergency surveillance on Natalie Hyde. The big Fed wasn't sure how many more times he could play that card without explaining himself to the FBI, and it didn't help to learn that two agents from the Phoenix field office were listed as missing in action. Bolan added them to Seriozha's rising body count, convinced they'd never be found alive.

So many dead already, and no end in sight. Bolan was accustomed to violence—he killed instinctively, without hesitation or remorse—but his mission of the moment carried a sense of frustration that was unfamiliar. He lacked a sense of progress, forward movement toward achievement of his goal. Instead, it seemed that he was treading water with no visible signs of accomplishment.

No, that was wrong. They'd stopped two of Seriozha's sleepers so far, saving untold lives in the process. Still, they were no closer to the man responsible for the bloodshed than when they had started.

Bolan resisted an urge to tabulate the dead since Barnum had emerged from prison. There was nothing to be gained from agonizing over strangers lost so far or those who might be killed before he finished it with Seriozha in his sights. He couldn't see beyond the Russian's death and frankly didn't care who pulled the trigger when the time came, but he still questioned Tasya Galenka's ability to drop a former lover in his tracks.

Beyond the culmination of his task in Seriozha's death, Bolan had no idea what would happen to the rest of the sleepers. He could squeeze Barnum for their names and addresses, transmit the intelligence to Hal or Stony Man, but their final disposition would be left to other hands. Whether they were arrested or simply made to vanish overnight, it wouldn't be Bolan's problem or responsibility.

Unless he had to take them one by one, with Seriozha still at large.

That prospect haunted him as they were airborne over Arizona and Utah, flying east toward a rendezvous with Denver and daylight. Fifteen or twenty sleepers, Barnum had said. They had subtracted two from the list, and one more was waiting in Chicago. That left a conservative dozen at large, maybe twice that many if Barnum had been rounding numbers down.

A dozen more lives, minimum, if Seriozha managed to elude them. And then what?

The worst-case scenario, short of Seriozha phoning in his orders to a dozen moles and letting them all run amok simultaneously, was seeing the ex-KGB man escape scot-free. Terminating his sleepers was only half the job, and the less important half, at that. There could be other plans, other contingencies, if Seriozha was frustrated in executing this one. In fact, Bolan was willing to bet on it.

There would be no end to the problem while Seriozha lived. His hatred was boundless, his dedication to a lost cause eternal. Seriozha was one of Russia's last true believers, and that fact made him all the more dangerous.

So Bolan would find him and kill him. The only questions remaining to be answered were where, when and how.

With luck, Chicago might be the end of the trail. It wasn't inconceivable that they would find Seriozha with the next sleeper on his list, or at least in the same neighborhood. The last two had been killed before they could carry out their assignments. Was it enough to tempt Seriozha from hiding to glimpse his pursuers?

Perhaps.

And if not, what then?

Bolan had meant what he told Burke Barnum. If they missed the sleeper in Chicago or otherwise failed to prevent an impending catastrophe, all bets were off. He would give Barnum back to the Feds in a heartbeat, with instructions to extract the list of sleeper names and addresses by any means available. Bolan had zero interest in the traitor's health or happiness as long as he was useful to the mission. If he proved to be an obstacle instead, it would be no problem to dispose of him.

In truth, Bolan felt more in common with his Russian target, Seriozha, than with the turncoat who had spent most of his adult life wearing U.S. Army green. Bolan and Jasha Seriozha were alike in many ways—determined, highly trained, ruthless and dedicated to the sides they'd chosen in a war that many now considered obsolete, passé. They were both of the old guard in that respect, warriors who understood what they were fighting for and balked at compromising basic tenets of their faith.

Barnum, meanwhile, had sworn an oath of loyalty, then violated it for money. His crime was unforgivable in Bolan's eyes; the lives his treachery had sacrificed were irreplaceable. Bolan had no idea what Barnum hoped to gain by helping them stop Seriozha's plan—some greater public sympathy or private absolution, maybe a free pass on Judgment Day, but none of that was Bolan's concern.

He had a mission to complete, and if Barnum wasn't part of the solution, then he was part of the problem. On the one hand, he was useful; on the other, Bolan was inclined to think he might as well be dead.

The ex-lieutenant colonel hadn't proved himself to Bolan's satisfaction yet. What would it take? How much would Barnum have to sacrifice? If pressed, the Executioner couldn't have said. Redemption always had a price, and undeserved redemption was the costliest of all.

Barnum might have to give up everything he still possessed, whatever that might be. If he failed Bolan and Galenka in the next few hours, then the choice wouldn't be his.

So many dead already.

Bolan didn't think one more would hurt.

"We got the Mile-High City coming up," their pilot said. "Get ready for that good old Rocky Mountain high."

CHAPTER NINE

Berwyn, Illinois

Natalie Hyde had been awake all night, but she wasn't fatigued. Adrenaline and coffee kept her up, bright-eyed and mentally alert. She'd always known that it would be this way, from the moment her handler made contact. Nothing mattered any longer but the task for which she'd been selected.

There'd been times within the past ten years, of course, when faith and dedication nearly let her down. The revolution was betrayed at home, and Natalie—born Natalia Helenka in Gorky—had waited in vain for a recall order, determined to swallow her disappointment and obey whatever commands she received. But the order to stand down had never come, and she remained in place, waiting.

Until yesterday.

She'd recognized the handler's voice, although they hadn't spoken in more than a decade. Granted, it could've been a trick—who really knew what could be done with electronics these days?—but even if the voice proved false, her caller knew the proper codes. Helenka listened carefully, absorbing every detail, and agreed to meet him at the rendezvous he'd chosen for their final briefing.

Final? Probably. Helenka had known from the outset that her covert mission behind enemy lines would probably end in her death. She'd accepted that fact as would any good soldier, counting the past twenty years of her life as borrowed time.

And she'd made the most of it, securing her innocuous cover, while keeping track of any changes in the local scene that might affect her mission. Her primary and secondary targets still existed, larger than ever thanks to renovations over time. If one proved inaccessible for some reason, the other was no more than half a mile away, an easy stroll.

The only thing that had disturbed her so far was the handler's mention of FBI surveillance. He'd told her to assume that her cover was blown and federal agents were watching her every move. The thought had startled her at first, no explanation for what had gone wrong or when, but Helenka took the order in stride like the trained freedom fighter she was. If agents were watching her, they did so at their peril.

Helenka had tested her handler's warning, calling in sick for the rest of the week. She missed school so seldom that no one questioned it. A set of backup lesson plans was waiting on her desk, as always—just in case. Step two of her plan had been breaking routine, trusting the deviation from her normal weekday schedule to confuse any watchers and force them to reveal themselves.

It had worked perfectly, two men springing alert in a car parked down the block when she left home at an unaccustomed hour yesterday morning. They'd fallen in behind her Mazda MX-6, trying at first to be inconspicuous, giving in to frustration as she led them through Berwyn's back streets and into Cicero, the suburb where history taught her that Al Capone once ruled like a wicked king from his headquarters at the fortified Hawthorne Hotel. It was a challenge to lose them without seeming to do so on purpose, but she'd managed, ditching them in Oak Park before she passed into Chicago proper.

Another team had been waiting near her condominium when Helenka returned from a leisurely lunch and matinee movie four hours later. She could feel them glaring at her as she passed and pulled into her small garage, but Helenka refused to acknowledge them. She'd left them with suspicion only as she locked herself in and began to prepare for the following day.

The day had been a test. Helenka had to know if she was being watched, and having proved that out, she needed to be sure she could elude the watchers prior to meeting with her handler and retrieving her cache of equipment. They could watch the condo from now until doomsday, but Helenka required mobility and she would kill to achieve it if need be.

To that end, she removed the Glock 19 pistol from beneath her pillow and placed it in her purse. Helenka didn't need to check the weapon's load to know there was a live round in the chamber and fifteen more in the magazine. The Glock wasn't her primary weapon, but it would kill effectively at close range if she had to fight before she could retrieve her cache of gear. Two extra magazines went in the purse and she was ready for the day.

Her working uniform wouldn't attract attention on the street or when she reached her target: black denim jeans, a navy-blue turtleneck sweater and black Nike runners would leave her comfortably anonymous in any urban crowd scene. Her dark brown hair, shot through with flecks of gray, was worn short and rarely needed more than a casual brushing. Helenka wore no makeup, trusting her olive complexion and naturally dark lips to cover for missing cosmetics.

She was just another face, nothing about her that would strike a chord of memory if witnesses were questioned afterward. By then, in any case, it would already be too late.

She took the Mazda out again and waited for the watchers to reveal themselves. They had no choice, but they displayed a bit more cunning this time. Two men parked as yesterday observed her leaving the garage, but one spoke rapidly into a microphone, alerting others down the block. This time the stationary watchers didn't move; instead, a second car was waiting when she passed the first cross street north of her condo, giving her a half-block lead before it fell in behind.

"All right," Helenka said, smiling at her own reflection in the rearview mirror. "You want to play? Let's play."

Downtown Chicago

JASHA SERIOZHA WAITED in a drizzling rain on the corner of South State Street and West Seventeenth. Behind him, the American Police Center and Museum was open for business but drawing few tourists on a gray Chicago morning. The city's trademark wind wasn't in evidence so far, which made the weather tolerable.

At any rate, it was better than Moscow.

Seriozha had chosen the rendezvous in a fit of whimsy, thumbing his nose at the American authorities. Granted, the police museum was staffed by civilian curators, not law-enforcement officers, but he'd stopped short of meeting Helenka outside city hall or Chicago's Federal Building. There was no point tempting fate, after all.

Seriozha stood in the rain, sheltered somewhat by a snap-brim fedora that could have belonged to an earlier age of Chicago's history, when gangsters rode to battle in armor-plated touring cars and carried their weapons in violin cases. His weapon of choice was the Radom pistol, worn in a shoulder rig beneath his sport coat and the lightweight raincoat that kept him more or less secure against the weather.

He didn't plan on shooting anyone this day, but it was always best to be prepared.

Seriozha watched a patrol car glide past, its occupants ignoring him as if he were invisible. He knew the way police minds worked, viewing a moderately well-dressed white man on a city street corner in broad daylight. He wasn't young, black or Hispanic, didn't wear outlandish clothes or act in a peculiar manner, speaking out of turn to passersby or talking to himself. Nothing suspicious there, unless they found him in the same spot when they passed a second time. In that case, they might take a closer look and memorize his face, although they'd still have no just cause to stop and question him.

No problem.

Seriozha checked his watch and saw he only had six minutes left before Helenka was supposed to meet him. The police wouldn't return within that time unless summoned to cope with an emergency. The rain worked in his favor there, reducing foot traffic, along with any likelihood of purse snatching or other minor crimes.

Twelve years had passed since Seriozha's last visit to Chicago. Much had changed in that time, but the gray city still had the same gritty feel he remembered from last time. It was like Moscow—like all great cities—in that way. The hopes and fears and disappointments of its people had seeped into the very stone and concrete of the city itself, making the streets and alleyways a haunted maze. One didn't have to read Chicago's history to know it harbored crime, corruption and despair; it was enough to stand and breathe the morbid air.

Seriozha had an old-line Russian's grasp of U.S. history, as taught in schools whose teachers had been vetted by the KGB. He'd read *The Jungle* at an early age and later learned about Chicago's bootleg wars as an example of capitalism run amok. Chicago meant stockyards where butchers were treated little better than the animals they slaughtered for minimal wages; police more concerned with collecting bribes than arresting criminals; politicians in thrall to swarthy mobsters dressed in gaudy suits and wraparound sunglasses. He understood the Windy City in the same way zealots understand most things, which was to say, not at all.

But Seriozha was a natural survivor, and Chicago

suited him as well as any other city on the planet, from Paris to Pyongyang. Given brief preparation and the proper tools, he could disappear anywhere, eluding those who hunted him, turning the game around and making them his prey. Compared to some of the cities where Seriozha had plied his covert trade, Chicago was what overfed Americans would call a piece of cake.

He saw Helenka coming from a block away. She was afoot, using a black umbrella to obscure her face and keep her dry at the same time. Seriozha watched the scattered pedestrians behind her as Helenka dawdled past the windows of a jewelry store, noting with satisfaction that no one slowed to keep pace with her or even seemed to give Helenka a second glance.

Seriozha allowed himself a thin smile as Helenka crossed the street to join him. They shook hands in the great American tradition, disdaining any more extravagant show of emotion. They were friends, nothing more, perhaps meeting for lunch or a quick shopping spree.

"Were you followed?" he asked her.

"Yes, Comrade. I left my car in Chinatown and lost them at the subway terminal."

"You're certain?"

"Absolutely."

"Good. Walk with me, Comrade."

They walked north on State Street, Seriozha briefing her on the aborted strikes in Atlanta and at the Hoover Dam. Helenka had followed both stories on television without realizing their import. Now, as Seriozha explained her immediate danger, he saw a greater wariness reflected in her eyes.

"I'm obviously compromised," she said when he was finished. There was disappointment in her tone and clearly written on her face. "It's most unfortunate, Comrade. I had hoped to proceed as planned."

"And so you shall," Seriozha replied.

She flashed a hopeful smile. "You haven't come to cancel my assignment, then?"

"By no means, Comrade. Your success in the face of determined opposition is more important than ever."

"I will not fail," she said with perfect confidence.

"It won't be easy, Comrade. You're already hunted through the city like a common criminal."

"That works to my advantage," Helenka said. "They will find I'm not so very common, after all."

"And if they search your home for evidence?"

"I left them a surprise," she said, smiling again.

"You make me proud, Comrade. Refresh an old man's memory about your primary and secondary targets."

There was nothing wrong with Jasha Seriozha's memory, nor did his sleeper buy it for a moment. Even so, she did as she was told, reciting from her memory the layout and security provisions currently in place at both of her prospective targets. If one was inaccessible today, the other would do just as well.

"I may be watching you today," Seriozha advised her as they reached the corner of West Fifteenth Street. "A bit of extra security, perhaps. I hope that will not inconvenience you?"

"By no means, Comrade. It's a compliment."

"Until this afternoon, then."

"For the revolution, Comrade."

"For the revolution. Serve it well."

Washington, D.C.

THE NEWS HAD GONE from bad to worse within the past two hours, leaving Hal Brognola with a feeling that the case was slipping through his fingers in a deadly rush. He worried that it might already be too late to save the situation, that he had committed Bolan to a no-win situation where a loss could cost him everything.

The first bad news had come from Arizona, where a retired police officer and would-be prospector had turned up two corpses in the desert north of Scottsdale. The guy had been working a section of arid landscape with his metal detector when the bells and whistles started going off big-time. Ten minutes digging in loose soil revealed no treasure chest, but rather the first of two bodies planted side by side, betrayed by belt buckles and coins in the pockets.

Missing FBI agents Kipland Thomas Holmes and Gary Arthur Rexton were accounted for, minus their badges, ID cards and pistols. Both had been dispatched by close-range gunshots to the head. Rexton's single killing shot had entered behind the left ear, fired at something close to skin-touch range as revealed by the powder tattooing. Holmes had died facing his killer, shot twice—in the forehead and right cheek—from a distance greater than three feet. Superficial abrasions and scuff marks on the dead men's shoes revealed that they'd been dragged some distance after they were shot. A search was under way to find the place where they'd been shot, but Brognola was betting on a lookout point near Byron Cross's house.

Two G-men dead, and now the FBI was up in arms. Headquarters was demanding full disclosure on the mission that had led to Holmes and Rexton being killed. Brognola had referred the angry messages to Justice, where a bureaucratic firewall was in place and holding—for the moment, anyway. In Hoover's day the Bureau might've pulled out on its own, refusing to participate further, but times had changed and FBI directors worked on a considerably shorter leash these days.

Brognola hoped so, anyway, because the news from Illinois had sparked another case of nerves at what the FBI still liked to call the seat of government.

No government employees had gone missing in Chicago yet, but they were mad as hell after the woman they'd been watching on Brognola's orders—a mild-mannered schoolteacher named Natalie Hyde—had shaken off surveillance twice in as many days. The first time, yesterday, her trackers had passed it off as coincidence, one of those glitches that happened now and then to even the best shadow teams. That verdict had been reevaluated when Ms. Hyde gave another team the slip that very morning. Two slips in two days defied the laws of coincidence and happenstance.

It was enemy action.

Where had she gone? The question left Brognola numb with dread, eclipsing any irritation suffered by the FBI field office in Chicago. He knew what the Bureau brass couldn't—specifically, that Ms. Hyde's first disappearance had been practice, while her second might be a signal of critical danger.

The evasive maneuvers told him that their subject knew she was under surveillance and, more to the point, that she knew how to beat it. The first fade would've confirmed watchers in place, her reappearance hours later denoting a dry run. How had she known the Bureau had her covered? In Brognola's mind there were only two possible answers: either Chicago's G-men were sloppy to the point of incompetence, or else the sleeper was forewarned.

By whom?

There was only one name on the list, and while Brognola hated to think that Jasha Seriozha was aware of a concerted move against his moles, the revelation was inevitable. How else to explain the violent interception of his last two sleepers within moments of blitzing their appointed targets? Only a fool would think it was coincidence, and whatever else he might be, the ex-KGB man was nobody's fool.

Call it bad news squared, then, if the Russian was aware of efforts to corral him and prevent his moles from carrying out their assignments. The only good news so far was that Seriozha seemed intent, for whatever reason, on launching his human projectiles one at a time, rather than unleashing them en masse.

That could change in a heartbeat, though, if Seriozha deemed it too risky to continue on his present course. Brognola didn't know if their adversary could activate the sleepers via long-distance, and Burke Barnum had thus far declined to part with the full list of names.

Chicago would decide that problem, at least. If Bolan and Major Galenka missed their target in the

Windy City, all hell would break loose from the strike zone to the Oval Office. Barnum would find himself suddenly devoid of wiggle room, compelled to give up the names by one means or another.

And what would happen then? Brognola was embarrassed to admit he didn't have a clue. Would any federal judge in his right mind accept the unsubstantiated word of a fugitive from justice as probable cause for the issuance of twenty-odd arrest warrants? And if so, would any of the charges stick without corroborating evidence in the form of confessions or captured Soviet weapons?

Brognola felt a headache building in the space behind his eyes. He rummaged in his top desk drawer until he found a tin of aspirin, washing four tablets down with tepid coffee. The bitter taste stayed on his tongue, matching his sour mood.

It was going to be a long, brutal day.

Brognola wondered who would come through it alive.

Chicago

NATALIA HELENKA DROVE her rented Hyundai Sonata north on Narragansett Avenue toward Jefferson Park, until she reached a private storage facility. The place had been repainted six or seven times and renamed twice since she had rented unit 42, but her belongings hadn't been disturbed. Twenty dollars per month bought anonymity and a measure of security, the latter enhanced by her own heavy-duty padlock.

A guard on the gate checked her through without

incident and wished her a good morning. Helenka gave him her best smile, then switched it off the moment his back was turned. Another foolish American, smug in his complacency. She would've enjoyed killing him, but it wasn't part of her mission. As a professional, Helenka knew better than to indulge her personal whims.

She drove the rented car between two rows of storage sheds and parked outside unit 42. Stepping from the Sonata, she glanced both ways along the alley, satisfying herself that she had the place to herself. Helenka had left her Mazda parked in Chinatown and watched her rearview mirror closely all the way from the car-rental agency on East Cermak Road, insuring that she wasn't followed.

Success!

She rummaged in her purse, pushing the Glock 19 aside to reach the extra key ring that held only three keys. One unlocked a safe-deposit box at her bank in Riverside, containing her escape kit—documents supporting a second false identity and ten thousand dollars in cash. One of the smaller keys, which she selected now, fit the padlock on storage unit 42.

When she'd unlocked the metal shed, Helenka raised the square garage-type door, went in and lowered the door behind her for privacy. It wouldn't lock from the inside, but she was confident no one had followed her—and if they had, against all odds, she had the Glock.

A large, old-fashioned steamer trunk sat in the middle of the shed, raised off the concrete floor by two chunks of four-by-four lumber. The trunk was covered with a fine layer of dust, its hasp secured by another sturdy padlock, which Helenka now unlocked using the third key on her ring. Inside the trunk were several military-surplus duffel bags.

She lifted out the bags and opened each in turn, checking the contents for the first time in nearly two years. The items required no maintenance, but Helenka visited the cache sporadically, to make sure it hadn't been disturbed. After nearly two decades of waiting, the objects would be put to use.

One duffel bag contained an AKS assault rifle, carefully wrapped in oily rags to prevent rust. Likewise wrapped in a second bag were Helenka's magazines and ammunition for the rifle, four hundred armor-piercing rounds in all. A third bag contained a dozen RGD antipersonnel grenades. The fourth held bricks of RDX plastic explosive, detonators separated in a plastic sandwich bag. The last item, a field radio, she left in the trunk as superfluous.

The original plan, as conceived at the outset, had called for sleeper agents in America to coordinate their strikes with an invasion force or in support of air and missile strikes, requiring secure means of communication. Perestroika and the collapse of the Soviet Union had closed out those options, and Helenka's communications gear was thus unnecessary, deadweight she could ill afford to carry with her into battle.

The weapons were all she required this morning, en route to her primary target.

Her targets—all the sleepers' targets—had been preselected with maximum shock value in mind. No agent was restricted to a single target, though, their handler anticipating that some would be demolished or relocated over time, requiring a measure of flexibility on D day. As long as sleepers maintained periodic surveillance on their targets and kept abreast of local changes, there should be no problem.

There had been none for Natalia Helenka. Her targets remained unchanged beyond superficial remodeling over time. She'd spent protracted time in both and knew her way around inside both buildings well enough to draw their floor plans from memory. Security was tighter on the secondary target, including metal detectors and visible armed guards, which, in fact, explained its relegation to backup status if she couldn't score on number one. But it should be no problem, she decided, while loading her gear into the Sonata's back seat.

After all, everyone was welcome at the Sears Tower.

The targets were Helenka's choice. Upon arrival in what the Americans were pleased to call Chicagoland, the first assignment from her handler had been compilation of six proposed targets, ranked in order of desirability and maximum impact. She'd originally ranked Chicago's Federal Building first on the list, in those distant days before domestic terrorism and suicide truck bombings transformed government facilities into fortresses. The other four targets on her list—all enthusiastically approved as fallback options in the event of war between Russia and America—had been the Midwest Stock Exchange, Chicago's city hall, the Mercantile Exchange and Tribune Tower, home of what had once been America's foremost reactionary newspaper.

Any one of those targets, her handler agreed, would

make a fitting funeral pyre for decadent Chicago on the day of reckoning. If she could strike at more than one, so much the better.

But one would be enough.

When all her gear was safely settled in the car, Helenka locked the rental unit one last time and drove away to keep her rendezvous with destiny.

Berwyn, Illinois

TWO FEDERAL AGENTS WERE waiting when Bolan's team touched down at Chicago Midway Airport. The older of the pair gave Bolan's FBI credentials a cursory once-over, pointedly ignoring Galenka and Barnum. He passed Bolan a set of keys in lieu of shaking hands.

"You've got the Buick Century," he said, nodding toward the nearer of two late-model sedans. His partner sat behind the other car's steering wheel, pointedly avoiding eye contact with the new arrivals.

"Thanks, Agent...?"

"Drop the wheels back here when you're done, if you can. Otherwise, call the field office and give us an address for pickup."

"Will do," Bolan said.

"Anything else?"

"I'll let you know."

The G-man blinked at him and turned away, retreating toward the second vehicle. His partner had the engine running when he got there, and the agents wasted no time pulling out, neither affording Bolan or his team a backward glance.

"Some friends you've got," Barnum remarked.

"They've heard about Scottsdale. Get in the car."

Brognola had broken the news when Bolan checked in from their Springfield pit stop. Two more bodies had been added to Seriozha's rising tally, and this time the victims were FBI agents executed in cold blood. Bolan didn't know if they'd been shot by Seriozha personally, or by the sleeper known as Byron Cross. It made no difference to the dead or to their fellow agents nationwide, who would be itching for a chance to settle the score.

Tasya Galenka understood the problem at a glance. "Will they attempt to interfere?" she asked.

"I hope not," Bolan said as he settled into the Buick's driver's seat.

In fact, he had no way of knowing whether the men and women assigned to the Bureau's Chicago field office were disciplined enough to keep their cool, under the circumstances. Bolan hoped they were, but experience had taught him that a world of hurt often lay between hope and reality.

The Buick had a police scanner mounted underneath the dashboard. Bolan turned it on and drove north from the airport on Central Avenue, passing through Stickney before he turned left on Pershing, then right on Narragansett into Berwyn. Midway Airport lay barely four miles from their destination on a quiet residential street where nothing newsworthy had ever taken place.

Until that morning.

Bolan saw the smoke from two blocks out and felt a worm of apprehension make its wriggling way along his spine. By the time he pulled into Natalie Hyde's cul-de-sac, he knew they were too late.

The sleeper's condominium was gone, for all intents and purposes. A smoking crater occupied the place where it once stood, bristling with jagged beams and bits of shattered masonry, including rubble from the condos flanking it on either side. Firefighters played twin streams of water on the smoking wreckage, while grim-faced neighbors, uniformed police and clean-cut types wearing FBI jackets surveyed the damage from a safe distance.

"We're too late," Barnum said from the rear.

"Maybe not."

Bolan left Galenka in charge of their prisoner, leaving the Buick parked behind a blue-and-white squad car. The Buick's police scanner was crackling with emergency traffic as he palmed his federal ID and moved toward a huddle of agents, scoping out the gray-haired man who seemed to be in charge.

"I want deep background on the Realtor, while you're at it," the agent told his crew. "No stone unturned on this, people. Get cracking!"

Bolan approached with his ID on display, introducing himself by the name on the card. "Supervisory Special Agent Michael Blanski, from D.C.," he said. "Can I get a sitrep, Agent…?"

"Sundberg," the gray-haired agent replied. "That's special agent in charge for Chicago, and I don't recall asking for any supervisory assistance."

"We're never invited, Agent Sundberg. You know that as well as I do."

Wariness crept in around the older man's eyes. Any G-man with gray in his hair would be familiar with the FBI's Byzantine bureaucracy and methods of spot-checking agents in place. Bolan's putative appearance from Washington could only mean trouble for local agents caught in his path.

"All right," Sundberg replied, "so what's the problem? You can see we've got a situation here."

"Your situation is the reason for my visit," Bolan said. "I was sent out to coordinate investigation of one Natalie Hyde, residing at this address."

"What address, son? You're looking at a crater here."

"What happened, Agent Sundberg?"

The SAC released a weary sigh, leading Bolan a few more paces away from the rubble. "We had orders to mount surveillance on this subject," he said. "You must know that, right?"

"That's affirmative."

"Then you should know she slipped us twice in two days. The first time she was only gone a short while. This time, I figured maybe she was running."

Bolan saw it now. "You authorized a penetration."

"Well..."

"Against direct orders, you went beyond your brief. And what happened here?"

Sundberg shrugged, looking defeated now. "I guess she had some kind of booby trap in place."

"You guess?"

"It's the best I can do right now, okay? I've got two agents dead—vaporized is more like it—and we won't have forensic results on the cause of the blast for a while. The fire department has some notion about saving lives before they let us bag the evidence. Go figure."

Bolan didn't have to fake the anger when he told Sundberg, "You're on notice. This is a major breach and it comes down to you. The buck stops right here."

"I know that. Do you think I don't know that? Jesus!"

"Indulge the self-pity on your own time. Was there any indication Hyde might be at home when it went up?"

"No way. The two I lost were sitting on the place from when she left this morning till I sent them through the door."

"Tell me you had a warrant, at least."

Sundberg averted his eyes. "They were just supposed to have a look around," he said. "That's all."

"How many years do you have in?"

"I've got my twenty-five," Sundberg replied.

"Consider starting the retirement paperwork before the press gets hold of this and runs with it. You could do worse."

Bolan left the gray man standing by himself and walked back to the rental car. Before he'd fairly settled in the driver's seat, Galenka asked, "Is she inside there?"

"No such luck," Bolan replied. "She lost her second tail this morning and the Feds got jumpy. They were working on a black-bag job, but she surprised them with a little house-warming present."

"Bad news for somebody," Barnum said.

"That would be us. Our target's running, and we don't know where she'll go."

"We're screwed," Barnum said. He was staring at the back of Bolan's head but likely seeing prison gates slam shut. "There's too many potential targets in Chicago. If she spotted the surveillance—"

"She won't care," Bolan interrupted him. "She's already ditched her watchers. My guess is she'll try to go ahead as planned from the beginning."

"Great. We're back to square one."

"She'll keep it simple," Galenka suggested.

"Say what?" Barnum craned forward, frowning in confusion.

"If she believes herself superior to those set against her, she won't be afraid of the direct approach."

"Direct approach to what?" Barnum demanded.

"Start with something close to home or to her job," Bolan suggested. "Something she could keep an eye on year-round, maybe five or six days a week."

"Like what?" Barnum challenged.

"There's a map in the glove compartment. Let's see it."

Galenka unfolded the standard auto club street map of greater Chicago, arranging it as best she could between them, Barnum peering over the back seat.

"She teaches school," Bolan observed, "but where?"

"An elementary school on West Quincy Street," Barnum said, adding a street number.

Bolan consulted the map's index and let his fingers do the walking. His eyes narrowed as he found the block containing Natalie Hyde's workplace. "She's got two targets within walking distance," he announced. "Sears Tower and the Federal Building."

"It's a start," Galenka said, already folding the map as Bolan turned the ignition key.

"I have a bad feeling on this," Barnum said.

"Join the club," Bolan told him.

They were halfway to their destination, rolling north on Clark Street, when the dash-mounted police scanner came to life. "All units in vicinity of Sears Tower," the dispatcher said, "respond Code Three. We have shots fired and two officers down. I repeat—shots fired and two officers down!"

CHAPTER TEN

Downtown Chicago

Natalia Helenka wasn't sure who had called the police, but she accepted their arrival as inevitable. It would've been nice to complete her mission unseen and escape, but her backup plans felt like hubris now, a fantasy she never should've trusted in the first place.

Fair enough.

She'd come this far, and there could be no turning back. Before her first AKS magazine was exhausted, she had taken down two uniformed patrolmen, a private security guard and three screaming civilians who'd fled too slowly for her liking. The policemen were dead—she'd made certain of that and taken their pistols for good measure—but she didn't care about the rest.

If the rest of her plan was successful, they'd all be dead soon enough.

Helenka had primed her explosive charges in the car, then repacked them in the largest duffel bag before she left the Hyundai Sonata and made her way into the Sears Tower lobby. She hadn't expected police to be there, but once she'd seen the two officers huddled in conversation with a private security guard she was forced to proceed aggressively.

The patrolmen had their backs turned to Helenka when she'd drawn her AKS assault rifle, already cocked, from underneath her knee-length coat. The rent-a-cop saw her coming with the weapon, but he had no chance to warn the others before she opened fire and dropped all three. A single head shot for each policeman, ignoring the shrill screams while she bent to retrieve their side arms, then Helenka turned toward the bank of waiting elevators.

She hadn't expected to fire on civilians so quickly, but when she turned away from her first three victims, Helenka found a trio of high-powered types—a man and two women—obstructing her path to the elevators, all gaping at the carnage she'd wrought. One of the women bleated a warning to her friends and turned to flee, but they were too late. Already irritated at the way her plans had been thrown off, she swept them with a burst of automatic fire and sent them sprawling over blood-slick marble.

Were they dead? Dying? Helenka didn't know and didn't care. She had important work to do and she was on borrowed time once the first shots were fired.

Two elevator cars were waiting for her, doors standing open, as Helenka stepped around the spreading pond of blood her last three targets had released. She was halfway to the nearest open door when a third elevator arrived and a tall black security guard emerged. His first glimpse of the lobby battlefield was startling, but the man recovered quickly, drawing a pistol as he leaped back into the elevator car.

Helenka tried to catch him with an AK burst, but

her bullets merely ricocheted off steel and marble. She was advancing toward the elevators when the guard thrust his hand around the corner and triggered two blind shots in rapid fire. To her surprise, one of the wild shots passed within a hand's width of her face, the other missing by at least a yard.

Helenka returned fire, cursing as she retreated toward a circular island in the middle of the lobby, where a uniformed guard normally sat, observing foot traffic and answering simple questions from visitors. That guard was dead or dying now, and there was no one to object as Helenka threw herself across the counter, dropping out of sight within the small enclosure.

Enraged by the potentially fatal delay, Helenka popped up long enough to fire another short burst at the elevators, driving the security guard back under cover. It might've been a stalemate, but she knew each elevator contained an emergency telephone, and the guard was undoubtedly calling for reinforcements if he hadn't already done so. Even if the elevator's phone malfunctioned, Helenka knew someone had to be dialing the police, either from somewhere in the building or along the street outside.

As if on cue, she heard a distant wail of sirens drawing closer by the heartbeat, clearing traffic as more men and guns were rushed to cut off her retreat. Escape was now the last thing on Helenka's mind, however. Even though she might have slipped away before the first squad cars arrived, she was determined to proceed at any cost.

She reached inside the heavy duffel bag and lifted out two fragmentation grenades. Letting her rifle dangle from its shoulder strap, she held a grenade in each hand, yanking the safety pins from both with hooked index fingers. She was smiling as she rose from cover and hurled the first grenade toward the nearby bank of elevators.

THREE BLUE-AND-WHITE squad cars were double-parked outside the main entrance to the Sears Tower, roof-mounted lights flashing, when Bolan pulled up in his federal sedan. Another five or six cruisers were inbound, making it a hellish sound-and-light show on South Franklin Street. The SWAT team hadn't rolled in yet, but uniforms were busy chasing pedestrians along the sidewalk, herding them away from the bullet-pocked windows and glass revolving doors.

"Badge time," he told Galenka, removing from his pocket the FBI credentials he hoped would get him past the first cops on the scene. He turned toward Barnum and found the prisoner sitting back with his open palms extended.

"I know the drill," Barnum said. "You go play while I sit here and hope nobody sees me, right?"

It wasn't Bolan's first choice for an optimal arrangement, but events had overtaken him and he was out of time. "It might help if you mingled with the crowd," he said, "but don't get lost."

The traitor flashed a smile. "No sweat. I'll be around when you get back."

If we get back, Bolan thought, but he didn't share the gloomy thought. A moment later he was showing his ID to a beleaguered sergeant, Galenka flashing her own too quickly for the cop to take it in.

"I've kinda got my hands full," the sergeant told

them. "If you wanna take a number, we can shoot the shit when I get some relief out here."

"We're not here to observe," Bolan replied. "You've got a federal fugitive inside who's probably equipped with high explosives, in addition to whatever guns she's carrying."

"Say what?"

A detonation from the lobby brought windows crashing down before Bolan could repeat himself. A second blast came close behind, flames pulsing in the shady cavern of the lobby.

"Those are frag grenades," Bolan said. "We have reason to believe she's also carrying plastic explosives."

"She?" The sergeant gaped at him. "Did you say *she?*"

"I don't have time to lay it out for you," the Executioner replied. "We need to get inside there, and I'd rather that your people didn't shoot us while we're working."

"I've got SWAT inbound," the sergeant said.

"And you've got squat for an excuse if she brings down the house before they get her and deploy. We need another way inside, and I mean *now.*"

"Well, shit!" The sergeant turned and shouted at a nearby uniform, "Rankin! Run these two over to the side entrance on Jackson. They go in, nobody leaves. If anybody shoots the Feds, I'm holding you responsible!"

"Yes, sir!"

They ran behind their guide to Jackson Boulevard, an east-west artery that ran along the Sears Tower's southern flank. They found another entrance there, undamaged by the gunfire and explosions from within.

"Good luck!" the young cop said as Bolan pushed his way inside.

They'd need it, Bolan thought, drawing his pistol as he crossed the threshold with Galenka on his heels. They found themselves inside a smaller version of the tower's main lobby, with access to the front of the building along a short corridor lined with understated works of art. The air was redolent with cordite here, and Bolan picked up his pace as their target cut loose with a Kalashnikov, somewhere beyond his line of sight. A pistol answered, barking twice, before the AK smothered it with automatic fire.

Bolan had his Beretta 93-R set for 3-round bursts, and he held it ready as he moved along the corridor. Galenka paced him, her Gyurza P-9 braced in a two-handed grip. Ten more paces brought them to a corner with a slice of open lobby visible beyond, but no view of their shooter yet.

Somebody had to make a move, and it was Bolan's turn. Galenka had him covered as he launched himself into the lobby, running in a crouch, and heard the AK's rapid fire veering to meet him on the run.

JASHA SERIOZHA WAS an expert at mingling with crowds. He had practiced the art in a dozen world capitals and countless smaller cities, priding himself on the very lack of distinction most people considered a personal fault. It was more difficult in Africa and Asia, though he'd enjoyed some success in the Third World, as well. Downtown Chicago, by contrast, was simplicity itself.

Seriozha had staked out the southeast corner of Jackson Boulevard and Franklin Street, well back from the police line and surrounded by scores of those vultures in human form whom Americans call rubberneckers. The ex-KGB man had no fear of being spotted in the crowd. If his nameless companions were vultures, Seriozha himself was a chameleon, adept at changing hues to match his background.

Still, he knew, there might be certain risks involved. His sleepers—some of them, at least—were under FBI surveillance, and while it hadn't helped the Bureau yet, that very fact suggested someone might be conscious of his presence in the country. That knowledge, and the tantalizing mystery behind it, had made Seriozha decide to follow Natalia Helenka and see what became of her raid in the heart of Chicago's thriving financial district.

He expected her to die, of course. That was a given, in the circumstances. Helenka was prepared to give her life for the revolution, had volunteered to do so, and Seriozha wouldn't mourn her passing. She deserved a hero's praise if she succeeded, but the time for celebration hadn't yet arrived. Seriozha still had far to go before his mission could be rated a success.

And if he failed, there was a chance that he would be erased without so much as footnote status in the history of these tumultuous times. Traitors at home wished him to disappear, along with all his efforts to defend the revolution they'd betrayed. But he wouldn't go quietly. The old war dog wouldn't lie down and die without a fight.

He listened to muffled echoes of gunfire from inside the Sears Tower lobby, watching patrol cars converge on the scene. How long until the officers worked up their nerve to charge inside? Would Helenka have time to plant her charges before a lucky shot brought her down?

Seriozha frowned as an obvious unmarked police car pulled up and its driver got out, advancing toward the officer who seemed to be in charge of the crime scene thus far. There was nothing remarkable about the driver, but his female passenger was something else. Seriozha recognized her at once.

Tasya Galenka.

She'd been blond the last time he saw her, but there was no mistaking that face, the athletic body. Long strides caught her up with the brown sedan's driver, and they huddled with the uniformed policeman, speaking urgently. Seriozha couldn't hear their words and the angle was wrong for lipreading, but he already knew what Galenka wanted.

She was stalking him.

No other explanation fit the fact of her appearance at a crime scene in Chicago. Why else would a major in the SVR and Seriozha's one-time lover show up in the company of an apparent U.S. federal agent, at the very moment when one of Seriozha's sleepers went into action? And who was the unmarked sedan's back-seat passenger?

Seriozha watched as the bearded man emerged on the passenger side of the car, reaching up distractedly to scratch at his whiskers. Instead of following the driver and Galenka, though, this one immediately moved in the opposite direction, toward the east side of Franklin, where he mingled with the growing crowd of onlookers. His behavior was curious enough to draw Seriozha's full focus away from Galenka and her companion, his eyes narrowing as he studied the man's hairy face in profile.

What was it about this stranger that made him uneasy? The way he touched his hair and beard for one thing—not so much scratching, Seriozha decided, but *patting* them, as if to reassure himself that they were still in place. A disguise? And if so, for what purpose?

Seriozha examined the profile more closely, concentrating on the brow and nose, the cheek above the beard. Why did he feel as if he ought to know that face, against all odds and logic? Could it be…?

The fugitive.

Burke Barnum, in the flesh.

His teeth clenched in fury, Seriozha began to make his way through the crowd, excusing himself as he shouldered the vultures aside.

If Barnum didn't see him coming, they would soon have something else to watch.

GALENKA FLINCHED as a burst of Kalashnikov rounds rattled off the wall above her head. They seemed to miss Belasko as he charged across the lobby toward a kind of circular desk or counter fifty feet away. She couldn't see the shooter, but when Belasko returned fire he angled his gun to the left, blasting two short bursts toward a target beyond Galenka's line of sight.

He had to have missed, since the Kalashnikov responded instantly, another stream of 7.62 mm rounds hammering across the lobby, this time chewing up the circular island Belasko had chosen for cover. Galenka risked a glance around the corner and saw a woman running backward toward a bank of elevators, firing from the hip as she retreated.

It was a long shot but she tried it, squeezing off a double tap from the Gyurza P-9. Galenka missed the woman, but her second round slapped hard against the heavy-looking duffel bag her target carried slung across one shoulder. The impact startled Natalie Hyde but she recovered like a true professional, swinging around her AKS without a heartbeat's hesitation to bring Galenka under fire.

It was a losing game unless she reached the elevators, since Hyde couldn't cover both of them at once. She'd have to reload soon, and if she tried it standing in the open she was dead.

Crouched in hiding, Galenka tried to remember what she'd just seen of the lobby in detail—how many elevators were open and waiting, what other concealment Hyde might have available. She thought two open elevator cars were visible behind the shooter, with at least three others in the line, but Galenka couldn't swear that she'd seen everything there was to see. And that could be a problem, since an error at this point, when she made her move, could easily prove fatal.

Belasko fired another 3-round burst from his Beretta, and she seized the opportunity to break from cover, slipping gracefully around the corner before she broke into a run. It wasn't really far—no more than thirty yards, if that—but it was open ground all the way, with a firefight in progress. Galenka charged toward the bank of elevators, squeezing off two more rounds from her pistol without a clear target, the figure of Natalie Hyde a blur of motion and hammering sound.

The woman was poised between two elevator cars, both doors open. She could go either way, but now she'd stopped dead-center, pivoting to face Galenka with the automatic rifle braced against her hip. She fired for effect, a determined effort to kill, but Galenka saw it coming and threw herself aside with force enough to bruise her ribs on touchdown. Chips of marble stung her face and scalp, one slicing through her right eyebrow, but Galenka was still in the fight, firing again and again at Seriozha's sleeper.

Hyde leaped backward into one of the open elevators, slapping at the control panel with one hand. Galenka picked a spot on the wall where she hoped the circuits might be and triggered four quick shots, hoping the Gyurza P-9 would live up to its awesome reputation this time. She needed damage to either stop or slow the elevator, prevent Hyde from slipping away. If she escaped into the upper reaches of the tower, she could hide for hours, maybe days.

It wouldn't take that long to plant the RDX and set its fuses. Minutes, maybe, but not days.

Galenka heard a string of bitter Russian curses emanating from the open elevator car. She felt a surge of triumph but it quickly died as her opponent reached out through the open door and flicked a metal egg in her direction, wobbling and bouncing across the polished floor.

Galenka recoiled from the grenade, had time to turn her back and throw one arm across her eyes before it blew and sent her spinning through a smoky thunderclap.

NATALIA HELENKA RELOADED her AKS while the echoes of her latest grenade blast still echoed through the cavernous lobby. Taking advantage of the momentary smoke, she lunged from the decommissioned elevator, fired a short burst toward the central desk where another enemy lay waiting and slipped inside the nearest waiting elevator with an open door.

Again she punched the control panel indiscriminately. Floors meant nothing to her now. She had no specific targets in the building. She only needed time to plant her charges and prepare for their sequential detonation. For Helenka's purposes, a blowout on the third or fourth floor would be as good as any other choice, rocking the massive monument to capitalist greed, bringing it down in an avalanche of stone and steel.

Helenka wished that she could be alive to see it, but at least her handler would be justly proud. And the ruins of the Sears Tower would make an appropriate marker for her grave.

The elevator stopped on four and she exited uncaring, conscious only of the weapon in her hands and the milling crowd of lackeys who were now aware of danger in the building. Whether they'd heard sounds or been alerted by phone calls, she neither knew nor cared. Some started screaming at sight of her rifle, prompting Helenka to fire short bursts in either direction and set them running pell-mell for their lives.

As if it would help.

Where to start? She'd been on almost every floor of the Sears Tower at one time or another, dressing up and feigning business there or simply roaming at will, pretending she was lost if anyone stopped to question her. Security was farcical, she'd found, and trespassers who seemed to know where they were going seldom faced a challenge. This day, on the fourth floor, there were no guards in sight.

She had also studied works on architecture, some of them including diagrams of this very building, until she knew the locations for optimum placement of demolition charges. It was a mix of art and science, application of strategic force to drop a building cleanly in upon itself, but cleanliness wasn't Helenka's top priority. She frankly didn't care if shrapnel flew across the street to damage other buildings, claim more lives. If anything, she sought more collateral damage, rather than less.

She was an angel of death, anxious to share.

A stocky gray-haired man emerged from an office to her left, brandishing a fire extinguisher as if he meant to spray her with it, or perhaps toss the whole thing at her head. Helenka shot him in the chest before he could decide and sent him reeling back through the doorway with a strangled cry of pain.

How many had she killed so far that morning? Helenka wasn't counting, and she wasn't finished yet. She smiled, thinking about the booby trap she'd left at her town house, wishing she could watch police or federal agents trigger it.

So many wishes now, so little time.

She counted doors and found an office that, if she had calculated properly, should grant her access to one of the tower's massive support beams. A block of RDX plastique secured in the northwest corner of the room would snap that pillar, even as other charges strategically placed around the fourth floor severed others, permitting the tower to collapse of its own ponderous weight.

Helenka was reaching into her bag for the first plastic charge when she heard a distant chime and realized another elevator had arrived on four.

She had company.

BOLAN LUNGED through the door in a crouch, Tasya Galenka close behind him. The Russian was still bleeding from a ragged shrapnel cut along her hairline, but she didn't let it slow her. If the close-range grenade blast had damaged her in any other way, it didn't show.

The counter on Natalie Hyde's elevator had shown them where to go, and the familiar smell of cordite told Bolan they had the right floor. If his nose had failed him, there was fresh brass scattered in the hallway, bullet damage to the walls in both directions and a pair of feet from an open doorway on his right, three doors down.

The sleeper was running up her score, but where was she now?

Bolan paused, listening, but there was too much extraneous noise on the floor for him to chart a cautious shooter's movements. Telephones were ringing off the hook, a fax machine was whirring, at least two different women were sobbing in offices nearby, and water was noisily dribbling from a bullet-punctured watercooler at the intersection of two corridors. Scraping sounds from another office down the hall suggested that someone was barricading the door with furniture. It wouldn't help if plastic charges brought the building down, and Bolan took for granted that his target wasn't looking for a place to hide right now, as much as seeking places for her bricks of RDX.

Without knowing exactly what she had, Bolan could make some educated guesses. The Kalashnikov and frag grenades he knew about from personal experience. The blast at Hyde's condo had required something heavier than antipersonnel grenades, and since all the other sleepers so far had come equipped with plastique, he was willing to assume Hyde had to have a stash of her own. The trick now was to find and neutralize her before she could set them off and start a chain reaction that would leave them all buried under several thousand tons of smoking rubble.

That meant a search, rapid but reasonably thorough, and for Bolan's money the dead man lying thirty feet in front of him was a fair indicator of which direction Hyde had been moving when she left the elevator. As to whether she'd maintained that track or changed her mind and turned around, maybe veered off down another hallway, only precious time would tell. They could split up and cover twice as many offices, but Bolan was prepared to play a hunch this time.

He moved out toward the pair of jutting feet that looked like something from *The Wizard of Oz,* except that these were obviously men's feet and they weren't protruding from beneath a misplaced farmhouse. Bolan leaned across the corpse to check the office out, letting Galenka take the room across the hall. They worked that way until they'd covered eight more offices. He was about to enter number nine when gunshots and a muttered Russian curse behind him said they'd found their target.

High-rise architecture is a mixture of utility and art. Skyscrapers have to stand against the elements, earthquakes and time itself, but contractors cut corners when they can. Few interior walls are meant to withstand direct fire from automatic weapons cycling armor-piercing rounds, and the fourth-floor Sears Tower offices were no exception. Bolan snaked across the slick floor on his belly, joining Galenka where she lay against the wall, a zigzag line of bullet holes marking the office door and wall above her at waist level.

Bolan crawled toward the door, which had swung nearly shut but failed to latch. There was an inch or two of daylight showing down the frame, which meant it should swing open at his touch. He would be under fire as soon as it began to move, but he was betting on the sleeper not to have a clear shot through the door at ankle height. If she was crouched behind a desk or something similar, he just might have a chance.

Galenka crept up on his left, stretched out beside him, angling her P-9 toward the door. He didn't argue, since her weapon was reputed to have better penetration than his own. If Hyde had cover, he could use the help. If she didn't, two guns were still twice as deadly as one.

"Ready?" he whispered.

"*Da,*" she answered, forgetting her English for a moment.

Bolan shoved the door back, braced and ready for the storm of automatic fire that broke above his head an instant later. Natalie Hyde was firing across a modernistic desk, some kind of sheet-metal construction painted chocolate-brown. She fired off half a magazine before she recognized her mistake, and by that time Bolan and Galenka were returning fire.

He milked 3-round bursts from the Beretta, Galenka firing her P-9 as rapidly as her finger could flex and release the trigger. Together, they turned the desk into a sieve, Natalie Hyde jerking and tumbling over backward behind it, firing her last, wasted rounds at the ceiling above.

Bolan reloaded as he scrambled to his feet, Galenka once again beside him as he approached the desk. Behind it, their adversary lay sprawled in blood, past caring whether her mission was a success or failure.

It took another moment to locate and disarm the charge she'd planted. Bolan shouldered Hyde's duffel bag and took the AKS with him as they moved back toward the elevator. It was a long ride down in silence to the lobby, where a ring of guns and men in black lay waiting for them.

"Take it easy, will you, guys?" Bolan said. "It's all over but the mopping up."

BURKE BARNUM LISTENED to the muffled sounds of gunfire, grimacing each time another burst of shots rang out. He watched policemen milling in the street and felt frustration radiating from them as they paced behind their cars or duckwalked between vehicles, staying below the line of fire.

In fact, no one had fired a shot at them, so far. Ironically, that seemed to increase the frustration level among the assembled officers, as they were left out of the action, consigned to a spectator's role while assembled television cameras broadcast their inactivity live across the width and breadth of greater Chicago.

Barnum, for his part, was glad to be excluded from the battle. His combat experience had been limited to a brief rear-echelon tour of the Persian Gulf during Operation Desert Storm, and while he'd worn the campaign ribbon proudly before his arrest, he'd never truly shared the zeal of his brother officers for logging combat time. It had always been easier to coast and avoid the grim duties, while others took the risks and banked the hazard pay. Barnum didn't know if that made him a coward, but that was the least of his problems right now.

If he *had* been a combat soldier, perhaps he would've sensed the movement on his flank before it was too late. A shifting in the crowd at first, nothing to be concerned about, and then a strong arm snaked around his neck from behind. Barnum dropped his chin in time to keep the unseen stranger from crushing his larynx or cranking his head back and snapping his neck, aware of a woman crying out somewhere beside him in the press of bodies as he was dragged backward, struggling to stay on his feet.

At first he thought one of the officers or G-men milling at the scene had spotted him and crept around behind him to score a major-league arrest, but the voice rasping in his ear was instantly familiar, its message chilling.

"Goodbye, Comrade Barnum."

Seriozha!

Barnum brought his hands up, clawing at the arm

that threatened to strangle him, trying desperately to recall the self-defense tricks he'd been taught in boot camp, so many years before. Kick backward and down at the shins or instep. Failing that, slump forward and try to flip an adversary over one shoulder, using his weight and momentum against him.

One thing at a time.

Barnum struggled, kicking feebly backward with one foot, then the other, terrified of losing his balance and giving Seriozha the leverage he needed to finish the job. It only took a second to crush the hyoid bone, and Barnum would choke to death from there, even if Seriozha released him and vanished into the crowd.

The world was going dark in front of him, a sure sign of oxygen deprivation, but he could still see well enough to watch the crowd fall back around him. They were typical Americans, dreading involvement in someone else's trouble, especially if danger was apparent.

Now his ears were popping, a sharp sound Barnum had never heard inside his head before. It took a long, disoriented moment to realize he was hearing gunfire, and then Seriozha released him, landing a vicious blow to the side of Barnum's head before he turned and ran. Tasya Galenka shoved her way through the gaping ring of spectators, a pistol smoking in her hand, and knelt beside Barnum long enough to check his pulse before she ran on past and disappeared.

Barnum tried to catch his breath, but the world was spinning. He saw Mike Belasko standing over him, bending down to offer him a hand, before a curtain of darkness descended.

Shit! he thought, as consciousness deserted him. I've done it now.

CHAPTER ELEVEN

Danville, Illinois

"So tell me once again," Bolan said, "how you lost him."

Galenka glared at him and cocked her head in Barnum's direction. "I stopped for a moment to see if *he* was all right," she replied. "If I'd left him for dead, I might've gained a few seconds."

"Or if you'd used your gun," Bolan suggested.

"As I've told you, it wasn't possible. The crowd sheltered him and blocked me. It's how he managed to outrun me. Also, the P-9 has too much penetration for use in crowds."

"Meaning you could have shot him *through* bystanders," Barnum quipped from his position on the motel bed.

Galenka stared daggers at him. "You could have captured him yourself," she said, "if you weren't such a weakling and coward."

Barnum didn't seem to take offense, as if he'd heard the epithets so often they no longer stung him. "The bastard came up behind," he said. "It's lucky for me he wasn't armed."

"Jasha is *always* armed."

That took some color out of Barnum's face and prompted another question from Bolan. "Why not use a weapon, then, and finish it?" he asked.

"I can only speculate. Seeing our *friend*—" she stressed the word as if it were obscene "—he may have understood he'd been betrayed. To Jasha's mind, revenge for such an insult should be personal."

"What 'insult'?" Barnum challenged her. "If he saw me, smart money says he sure as hell saw *you*—his former lover—working with the enemy. You want to talk about betrayal, there it is."

Galenka took it in stride, seeming relaxed in a cheap captain's chair near the window. "I'm sure he saw me, but he couldn't reach me without exposing himself. You were more convenient, predictably careless."

"Oh, yeah? If you'd—"

"Enough!" Bolan snapped. "We're getting nowhere with this."

In fact, they'd gotten as far as a budget hotel on Highway 136, ninety miles south of Chicago. It seemed to Bolan that they'd come full circle. Terre Haute's federal prison lay not more than forty miles to the southeast.

"Who knew Seriozha was watching these people?" Barnum asked. "Did either one of you think so? I never heard it mentioned."

"It wasn't expected," Bolan admitted. "That was our mistake. We won't make it again."

"It's too much," Galenka said.

"How's that?"

"For Jasha, it's too much. I don't believe he

watched the others, or he would have taken steps against us earlier. After Nevada, though, he recognized that we were catching up to him. He'd want to know his adversaries, see their faces. He would take a risk for that, I think."

"And seeing them?"

"He had a chance to finish this one," Galenka said, nodding once again toward Barnum, "but we chased him off. Now that he's seen us, I cannot predict what he'll do."

"He'll go ahead and try to finish it," Barnum stated.

"You can't be sure of that," Bolan replied.

"It's what I'd do if I were in his place and had his personality."

"But you aren't and you don't," Bolan said, "so you're guessing."

"I agree with him. Jasha has a certain..."

"Arrogance?" Barnum suggested.

She nearly smiled at that. "Perhaps. Or call it determination, self-assurance."

"I don't care what you call it," Bolan said. "We need to think ahead of him and get a jump while there's still time. I want the list," he told Barnum.

"We had a deal."

"It's off. We cut it too damn close this time. If he jumps out of order or starts making phone calls, we've had it."

"He won't," Barnum insisted.

"You're guessing, by your own admission. It's not good enough."

"Two of us in this room know Seriozha," Barnum

said, "and you're not one of them. Ask her, if you don't believe me."

Bolan faced Galenka. "Well?"

"I still agree with him," she said. "Jasha's determination verges on fanaticism. He won't quit unless we stop him."

Bolan frowned. "I'm not concerned about him quitting. Now he knows we've spotted him and both of you are on his case, what is there to prevent him skipping names to throw us off or activating all the sleepers overnight?"

"I can't give you a guarantee," Galenka said, "but—"

"He can." Bolan jabbed a finger at Barnum for emphasis. "He can give us the whole list of names, right here and now. We can put them all under surveillance tonight."

"And then what?" Barnum asked. "Drop a net on him when he shows up for a meeting?"

"I've heard worse ideas," Bolan told him.

"It won't work," Barnum said. "He's too smart."

"Smart enough to jump you in a crowd of witnesses and nearly get himself busted?"

"It's the 'nearly' that gets you," Barnum replied. "Nobody laid a finger on him. No one ever does."

"By that logic, we may as well give up and drop you back at Terre Haute. We're close enough. Call it an hour, if the traffic's not too heavy."

Barnum paled at that, beneath his phony whiskers. "I know where we are," he said. "I haven't been inside so long that I've forgotten how to read a highway sign. Unloading me won't help you do your job."

"What could it hurt? We've played the game your way so far, and all we've got to show for it is rising body counts."

"Without me, you'd have missed the last three sleepers altogether," Barnum said.

"We won't miss any more, when you give us the list."

"You had surveillance on the last two. It didn't do much good."

"The agents didn't know what they were dealing with. We can fix that," Bolan replied.

"And what about the press?" Galenka interjected. "You cast a net so wide, they're bound to know about it soon."

"They're breathing down our necks already," Bolan said. "You saw them on the street today. For all we know, they may have us on tape—again."

"Your people are supposed to deal with that."

"I made the call," he said, remembering Brognola's weary voice. "They're working on it, but we operate without the benefit of Russian censorship."

"Too bad," she said, lighting a cigarette.

"I'll take my chances with the First Amendment," Bolan answered, silently adding, And hope someone loses the tapes. "Right now I'm more concerned with what blows up tomorrow than I am about what's running on the TV news tonight."

"You must understand Jasha's mind, how he thinks," she replied through a pale haze of smoke. "For him, the crusade has now become a contest. He believes he can defeat you, the American, because he always has."

"And you?" Bolan prodded.

"He won't discount me as a woman or because I've shared his bed," Galenka answered, "but because he's always been the best. Jasha is in his element. He lives for the clandestine game."

"If I buy that, I'm gambling countless lives on your say-so," he told them both.

"And if you don't believe us, then what?" Barnum asked. "Suppose you put a tail on all the other sleepers. Will it stop them? They're already batting two for two on ditching the surveillance and you've got dead agents now, along with the civilians."

"Forget the tails for now," Bolan said. "There's another reason why I want the names."

"What's that?"

"Your old friend blew his shot at you today. He may be luckier next time. We need the names and addresses in case you're not around to finish it."

The explanation put a scowl on Barnum's face. "Thanks for the vote of confidence," he said, then added, "Okay. Has anybody got a pen?"

TASYA GALENKA SMOKED and watched the prisoner as he began to write. He took his time, printing the names and addresses on motel stationery, making two neat columns. It was quiet in the room, now that they'd finished arguing, and she was grateful for the silence that allowed her time to think.

Belasko was suspicious of her failure to apprehend Seriozha, and she couldn't really blame him. Knowing that the two of them had once been lovers and devotees of a hostile government, he had to question everything she said or did. Galenka had her doubts about the tall American, as well, but he had never shared their target's bed and so remained uncompromised on that score.

She replayed the morning's action in her head, while Barnum concentrated on his list. Emerging from the elevator, they had been surrounded by a SWAT team, the commander carefully examining Belasko's FBI credentials and her own diplomatic ID before he'd accepted the bag of explosives and had them escorted outside. Galenka had barely cleared the lobby's revolving door when she looked across the street and saw Barnum grappling with a man who held him from behind.

At first, she'd thought some policeman or FBI agent had seen through Barnum's disguise and was trying to arrest him, but in his struggle Barnum lurched about until she had a glimpse of Seriozha's face. She would've known him anywhere, and in a heartbeat she was racing toward the crowd across the street, telling Belasko, "There he is!"

She hadn't known if he would follow her or whether the police would try to cut her off. She'd run full speed, the P-9 pistol naked in her hand as an inducement for the innocent to scatter from her path. Some of them did, but many members of the crowd were watching Seriozha and Barnum as she cleared the curb and plunged across the street.

Seriozha had seen her first; she wasn't sure that Barnum ever did, until she stopped beside him, feeling for his pulse. Jasha had given him a mighty shake, as if he meant to tear the traitor's head off, then shoved him into the nearest rank of gawkers. Several had fallen with Barnum, men cursing and women crying out in alarm, Galenka leaping over them to waste a precious moment with the prisoner.

She knew he'd live when Barnum blinked at her and gasped out, "Nail his ass!" By then, Seriozha was halfway down the next long block, southbound and running like an athlete half his age. He ducked and dodged among startled pedestrians, deliberately clipping some so that they sprawled across her path as thrashing, cursing obstacles. He hadn't drawn a weapon, hadn't even glanced back to confirm that she was chasing him. He'd known she would and ran as if his life depended on it.

Which it did.

Galenka's stated reason for not firing in the crowd was true enough. She would've had to stop and aim, thereby giving Seriozha a greater lead, and there were too many civilians in her line of fire. Even a clean shot would've been too risky, since the P-9's armor-piercing bullets might have drilled Seriozha and traveled on another hundred feet or more with lethal force.

Galenka was supposed to stop a bloodbath, not create one, and she'd already killed once that morning. If they'd had the sidewalk to themselves—or, better still, a nice blind alley—she'd have risked the shot. But as it was, no way.

Seriozha hadn't outrun her. She was younger and believed herself more fit than he, able to run him down on any manner of terrain. And she'd have done it, too—Galenka was convinced of that—except for the young woman with the baby in a stroller.

Seriozha hadn't hesitated when he saw the golden opportunity. Almost without breaking stride, he plucked the baby from its nest of blankets and swung around as he ran, his right arm going back, clutching the surprised infant by its fuzzy jumpsuit. He moved so swiftly that the baby's mother couldn't stop him, barely had time to unleash a breathless scream before he hurled the infant back downrange, for all the world like a quarterback passing a football.

And the bastard was smiling!

In that split second, Galenka realized Seriozha had to have known she was behind him—but she also realized he didn't care. If she had broken off the chase, his cruel diversion would've been a wasted effort, but he would've done it anyway. It meant the baby's life, and Jasha Seriozha had been smiling like a happy psychopath.

Galenka hadn't dropped her pistol. It was cocked and might discharge on impact, but she also didn't care to leave herself unarmed, perhaps have someone in the crowd scoop up the gun. She blurted out a curse in Russian as the baby wobbled toward her in midair, its mother shrieking now, Galenka's arms outstretched to catch the pass. She almost shut her eyes, but forced them open for the baby's sake, willing to live with what she'd see if it fell short or if she fumbled.

But she didn't.

What she did was stumble, losing balance as the baby landed in her outstretched arms. Falling, she clutched the wailing bundle to her breast and twisted like a leaping skater in the air, so that she fell backward and took the brunt of the impact on ribs and buttocks, while the baby gave a startled cry and gaped at her with bright blue eyes.

The bawling mother was beside her in an instant, sobbing, "Thank you! Jesus, thank you!" as she wrenched the infant from Galenka's arms. Galenka, bruised and breathless, struggled to her feet knowing she'd lost the race. Seriozha was nowhere to be seen when she went after him, and she'd given it up at the next intersection, turning back toward the Sears Tower in a blue funk of disgust.

The baby toss had throttled any latent feelings that she might've harbored for her one-time paramour. It didn't help to tell herself the move had been a textbook ploy, an inspiration to be proud of. She couldn't have done as much herself, and if that made her weak—somehow deficient as an agent in the field—she'd simply have to live with it.

And now she knew that if their roles had been reversed, Seriozha would certainly have gunned her down without a second thought. He wouldn't have concerned himself with bystanders, ballistics or trajectories. He would've fired until the pistol was empty, killing everyone between them if he had to, but he would've done the job.

Next time, she thought. Next time, my love, you are mine.

BURKE BARNUM FINISHED with the list and read it over once before he set down the pen, making sure he'd left no one out. His memory was crystal-clear as always, thanks in equal parts to some innate ability and concerted mental exercise he practiced in his prison cell. They'd caged his body, but his mind was free—up to a point, at least.

"That's it," he said, and pushed the sheet of motel stationery back. "All done."

Bolan took the list and scanned its fourteen names. "You said fifteen or twenty when we talked, before."

"You've taken care of three," Barnum replied. "That's it, the whole enchilada."

"No accidental omissions?"

Barnum shook his head. "What would I gain? You take me back, I'm looking at the needle now, unless you put in some kind of good word with the U.S. attorney's office. My life isn't much, but I don't want to wind up like McVeigh."

Bolan seemed to think about that for a moment, then nodded. "Upstate New York's next, then?"

"If he doesn't change the rules."

"Gregory Millward, in Albany."

"Unless he's moved. None of the others have, so far."

"What is he?"

"Last I heard he was a cop."

Bolan hesitated over that, not liking it. "Okay," he said at last. "I'll make a call and get some people out to these addresses. Be ready for the first flight I can line up, headed east."

"Maybe someone should warn the tails this time," Barnum suggested.

"It's a thought."

He knew what that meant. Law enforcement was a mirror image of the military, only broken down across the country into several thousand smaller, independent agencies. In each, the grunts took orders from the brass; the brass, in turn, was jealous of its power—even if a ranking officer commanded no more than a single deputy—and all it took to start a blood feud was the hint of a suggestion from some outside agency that tried-and-true procedures ought to change. The FBI, for all its reputation, was worse on that score than any small-town police department in America, perhaps in the world.

Barnum was apprehensive about sending out more federal agents to shadow the remaining sleepers. He had enough collateral deaths on his conscience already, without adding more. Two moles in a row hadn't only shaken their watchers, but had also killed them. If the other fourteen were as deadly as those two, the FBI body count would hit double digits in no time.

Their problem, he thought. They insisted.

So why didn't he feel better about it?

Bolan left to make his call from a more secure line, leaving Barnum alone with Galenka. He watched her light another cigarette and said, "You'll kill yourself with those."

She blew smoke at him and replied, "How would you have me die?"

"That isn't what I meant." He hesitated for a moment. It was hard to say. "You saved my life."

"Coincidentally," she said. "I wanted Jasha."

"You let him go to save a child."

"I had no choice."

"Thanks, anyway."

"You're welcome. Next time, be more careful, yes?"

"Ten-four on that."

"Excuse me?"

"Never mind."

Barnum thought about the moment when he'd been convinced Seriozha would kill him. His defensive tactics had accomplished nothing, which told Barnum that he'd either done the moves wrong or the Russian was immune to pain. Neither idea was calculated to improve his confidence.

Seriozha knew them now—or two of them, at least. He probably wouldn't have Belasko in his memory banks, but Barnum and Galenka were fully exposed. Seriozha would be thinking about them, and there was a decent chance, better than fifty-fifty, that he'd try to take them out for old times' sake. Hell, he'd already tried it once and very nearly did the job.

Choking to death was a strange sensation, and the more he thought about it now, the more Barnum agreed with Galenka that the attack had been intensely personal. Seriozha had chosen to make the kill bare-handed, his hot breath whistling in Barnum's ear.

Did it go beyond simple payback for Barnum working against him? Would Seriozha risk so much next time, knowing Galenka was also on the job? It never once occurred to Barnum that there might not be a next time. He was simply thinking tactics, wondering *how* Seriozha would try to snuff out his life.

His name was on a list now, along with Galenka's. Seriozha had marked them both, and he wouldn't rest until he'd killed them both. Call it a backup crusade to the main event. The ex-KGB man knew they were after him now, and his innate arrogance would demand retribution. Seriozha might not jeopardize his primary mission to kill Barnum and Galenka. Then again…

"I guess we're bait," he said.

"Sorry?"

"From here on out, we've got two problems for the price of one. Stopping the sleepers only covers half of it."

"You mean Jasha."

"Bingo. He wants us dead, and now Belasko's counting on it, too."

"He's a professional."

"Which one?"

She smiled through smoke and answered, "Both. They do what's necessary."

"And you're cool with that? You don't mind playing rubber ducky in the shooting gallery?"

"I'm not confined to Jasha's plans. Knowing he hunts me is enough to let me be prepared."

"Speaking of that, I'd like a fair chance to defend myself next time he comes around. Think you could help me out?"

"You want a weapon." There was mockery behind Galenka's smile.

"It crossed my mind."

"Would it have helped you on the street today?"

"Bringing a pistol to a fistfight? I'll take those odds every time," Barnum replied.

"Jasha won't try to strangle you again."

"That's comforting. Since you can read his mind, what *will* he do?"

Galenka shrugged, lighting another cigarette. "Who knows? I doubt if he's decided yet, himself. It will depend upon the circumstances."

"So, a gun could help."

"No gun," she said.

"Belasko wouldn't have to know."

"I'd know. Do not mistake me for a friend."

"Okay. You don't mind if I ask the big guy, though?"

She smiled at that. "Belasko? Be my guest. It should be entertaining."

Right. Barnum already knew what Belasko would say. His keepers didn't trust him with a weapon, and why should they? For all he knew, they were gambling their careers just letting him remain at large. It was a squeaker in Chicago after Seriozha tried to strangle him, dumb luck that Barnum hadn't lost his wig or beard in the attack. Belasko had convinced the local dicks that he was no one worth their time, but they'd been fuming when the borrowed FBI sedan pulled out and left them to the cameras.

That kind of magic couldn't be repeated often without someone seeing through the trick and spoiling it. Burke Barnum had a sense that he was running out of time. The only question now was whether it meant going back to prison or a cold hole in the ground.

Washington, D.C.

SOME MORNINGS, Hal Brognola wondered why he didn't have an ulcer. There were days when he heard nothing but bad news, when problems came at him from all directions simultaneously, each demanding his immediate attention. How he handled all of them and kept his sanity intact was anybody's guess. Perhaps it was a gift, honed with decades of experience.

Or maybe it was just dumb luck.

The news was worse than usual. Instead of one more sleeper, Bolan had delivered fourteen names and addresses, ranging from Portland, Oregon, to Albany, New York—the next one up, in fact—and from Detroit to New Orleans. The only pattern visible in Jasha Seriozha's choice of which sleepers to activate was that he was moving down the list in order, one by one.

So far, at least.

Bolan was worried that the pattern might evaporate after Chicago, and Brognola shared his concern. Seriozha knew they were after him now; he'd seen the team in action and identified two of them. Why in hell would he stick to the schedule and thereby place himself at greater risk?

Because he could, the big Fed thought, frowning.

The Russian was an arrogant bastard, on top of everything else. He'd failed in an attempt to kill Burke Barnum, but abandoning his private schedule was the same thing as admitting he'd been beaten. If he had to change his plans, it meant his enemies were smarter, stronger than he was.

Or maybe he'd change everything and fool them, leave them shadowing a cop in Albany while one of the other moles blazed into action.

Surveillance should limit that risk, at least in theory, but Brognola was having problems with the FBI. Four agents dead in half as many days, and headquarters was screaming for blood. It didn't matter whose, as long as someone paid the tab. Reluctance to participate in any more surveillance on the case went all the way up to the director's office, but unlike Hoover in the bad old days, the new guy couldn't ignore direct orders from the White House and attorney general. The problem now would be controlling trigger-happy G-men who were looking for some payback for their comrades.

Correction: that was one problem.

Another was waiting for Bolan's team at Albany, in the person of Detective Sergeant Gregory Millward, assigned to Albany PD's robbery-homicide division. Millward had sixteen years on the job, two commendations for valor and three righteous line-of-duty shootings behind him. According to Burke Barnum's list, he was also a lifelong deep-cover Soviet mole.

That, in itself, wasn't the problem.

The problem was Millward's gold shield.

They hadn't discussed it in years, but Brognola was well aware of Bolan's private rule against killing lawmen. From day one of his lonely war against the Mafia, Bolan had steadfastly refused to drop the hammer on a cop, and nothing in his recent history suggested that he had abandoned the rule. Police were sacrosanct in Bolan's eyes. Regardless of their nationality, gender, race or state of personal corruption—even if they were found guilty of multiple murders—Bolan simply couldn't bring himself to kill a cop. They were soldiers of the same side in his view, and while some disgraced themselves by trampling on the very laws they'd sworn to enforce, they were exempt from final judgment by the Executioner.

Granted, Bolan had put his share of dirty cops away, setting the stage, doling out rope for them to hang themselves, but he stopped short of deadly force. Cops had done time or lost their jobs because of Bolan, but he'd never been responsible for a blue funeral. There'd been times when Brognola believed his friend might die because he wouldn't go the extra yard against a uniform.

This day was one such time.

Brognola hadn't asked how Bolan meant to handle Millward when he got to Albany. He didn't like to second-guess a soldier in the field if he could help it, and the odds were good that Bolan hadn't worked the problem out himself. It would've put the big Fed's mind at ease if Bolan simply made a one-time-only personal exception to his rule, but he guessed that would happen the day Hell froze over.

Would it make a difference to Bolan that Millward had joined the force under false pretenses? That he wasn't even really an American, much less an honest cop? Did intent count for anything with Bolan, once his target put on a badge and uniform? Brognola was afraid it wouldn't matter, that the warrior's scruples might just get him killed this time.

The Russian could probably help, if Bolan let her. Somehow he suspected she wouldn't mind ventilating a New York detective, any more than she'd minded taking out a Chicago schoolteacher. Russian operatives were more practical than many Yanks when it came to wet work. Ice a kiddie TV star? Why not? Need a radical nun taken care of? No sweat.

Brognola hoped the faux cop didn't get the drop on Bolan first, before Galenka had a chance to deal with him. More to the point, what would the Russian think when Bolan balked at taking out the next sleeper, before Millward could run amok? Unless Brognola missed his guess, there was ample tension brewing on the team already, without introducing fresh doubts.

Bad news, and nothing but. Some days it felt like a lifestyle Brognola couldn't shake. He won more than he lost, but none of them were exempt from the great law of averages. Disaster lay waiting for all of them somewhere. It was only a question of when it would strike.

But not this time, he silently pleaded with someone or something he couldn't have named if he'd tried. Not just now.

A pair of FBI agents would be waiting for Bolan and company at the Albany County Airport, handing off another set of wheels and a report on Millward's movements in the past few hours—if they hadn't lost him yet. Brognola, meanwhile, set about to rack his brain for targets in the area.

Albany was New York's state capital, but it still offered fewer choice targets than any given square mile of midtown Manhattan. There was the governor's mansion and state legislature, of course, with three or four colleges and an equal number of large hospitals. Beyond that, the landmarks ran toward museums and historical sites from colonial times. Even the shopping malls had names like Mohawk and Colonie Center.

There was something he'd missed, Brognola decided. But what?

Which particular targets would appeal to a Russian sleeper who believed a third world war was imminent? More to the point, which targets would've been considered choice when Seriozha put his moles in place, two decades earlier?

"Hell if I know," Brognola muttered to himself.

He went back to the map of Albany spread on his desk and started from the top.

If at first you don't succeed, he thought, try, try again.

Until the answer clicked.

Until he found a way to help his friend survive.

CHAPTER TWELVE

Albany, New York

Detective Sergeant Gregory Millward hadn't worn the blue serge uniform of his police department for the past nine years, except at job-related funerals, and he wouldn't be wearing it today. His clothes were casual but sporty—a navy blazer over light gray slacks, an open-collared shirt in powder blue that almost hid the Kevlar vest he wore beneath and no necktie. The one exception was his footwear—black Dr. Martens boots, spit shined—but since the flared cuffs of his slacks concealed most of the boots, they'd pass for clunky shoes if anyone looked closely.

He wore the boots habitually for their extra support, in case he was involved in foot pursuits, fence climbing, kicking doors—the usual. Most of his average day was cut-and-dried routine, whether he was processing another murder scene or filing paperwork, but there were moments when it went to hell without much warning. That was life behind a badge—but it was winding down.

Millward had worn old jeans and a faded sweatshirt while removing his covert gear from the crawl space underneath his house near Lincoln Park. He'd double-checked the equipment and cleaned the AKS assault rifle before he showered and changed into his street clothes, getting ready for his day. The bags were hidden in his bedroom closet now, behind a double lock. The door itself was steel, a special item no one else had ever seen.

He wasn't sure what would happen tomorrow, when all hell broke loose, but one thing, at least, was sure in Millward's mind: this was the last day he'd be forced to use the name borrowed from someone who had died within a month of birth. *That* Gregory Millward was buried at Taunton, outside Syracuse, forgotten by everyone except the parents who'd mourned his passing back in 1954. Were they even still alive?

Misha Mishenkovich had no idea and didn't care. His life had never intersected theirs, to the best of his knowledge, beyond expropriation of their dead child's name and birth certificate. Everything else he'd achieved, Mishenkovich owed to himself or the Soviet state—more specifically his handlers from the KGB.

They were gone now, those handlers, the KGB itself, even the state he'd served—except for one man who stood fast against a rising tide of treason. Mishenkovich trusted his handler as he trusted no one else on Earth, except himself. Who else was there to care for him and see his mission carried out?

Mishenkovich would go to work as usual that morning and receive his assignments, then proceed to take an hour of personal time his lieutenant had already approved. It was supposed to be a doctor's visit, but in fact he would be going nowhere near his doctor's office. He had a very different kind of meeting scheduled for that morning, one his public employers knew nothing about.

He was meeting his handler, for the first and last time in more than a dozen years. There'd been dark days between 1989 and '91, when he'd believed the people's revolution was collapsing, unraveling before his startled eyes, but a long-distance telephone call had saved him from despair.

"Nothing has changed, Mishenkovich. Be strong."

And so he had been, waiting for the next call that would send him into action. Waiting through the years when he suspected that his handler might've been arrested, even executed by the traitors who now commanded Mother Russia. Waiting when simple logic told him he'd waited too long, that even former colonels of the KGB were mortal men, subject to cancer and car wrecks, senility or simple disillusionment.

Now his patience and fidelity had been rewarded. His handler was coming to meet him, and it could only mean one thing. Mishenkovich would be allowed to shed his sham identity and show the world his true face in a blaze of glory, even if it meant his death. Before he left the house, Mishenkovich attached a clip-on holster to his belt and filled it with his standard-issue Beretta Model 96 Centurion, a 10-shot semiautomatic pistol chambered for the powerful .40-caliber Smith & Wesson round. At thirty-two ounces, it dragged his belt down on the right, but he balanced it with two spare magazines and handcuffs on the left.

Ready.

He'd go through the motions at roll call and the morning briefing, just like always. There were bad guys to watch for and warrants to serve, victims and witnesses to interview and evidence to scrutinize before he finished his shift—but none of it really mattered. In every way that counted, Gregory Millward was already gone.

The next day, when his so-called friends and brother officers gave him another thought, they'd be amazed, astounded, horrified. Some of them might be sent to bring him in, believing they were up to it, that they possessed an edge from knowing him since they were all cadets at the police academy. In fact, they'd never known Mishenkovich at all, and he would prove it to them if they tried to interfere with his mission.

Reporters yammered endlessly about the thin blue line of law enforcement, corruption and a code of silence in the ranks that protected wrongdoers in uniform. They were in for a shock when Mishenkovich exploded from the closet with a vengeance. Reporters could be martyrs, too, as they would learn if any of them crossed his path.

Misha Mishenkovich believed this night would be the best night of his life. And if it also proved to be the last, he didn't mind at all.

JASHA SERIOZHA ARRIVED at the rendezvous early, anticipating trouble. He'd deliberately chosen a public place—a strip mall on Fuller Avenue, in suburban McKownville—so that he'd be able to observe pedestrians and motorists from any one of several vantage points. So far, he hadn't spotted any spies, but that proved nothing.

The watchers would be following Mishenkovich, not Seriozha. They would trail his sleeper to the meeting, if they came at all. The best that he could hope for was that Mishenkovich would recall his training and observe security precautions. If he did so, then their brief but crucial meeting should be safe.

If he didn't…

Seriozha wore the Radom P-83 pistol in a holster at the small of his back. Beside him on the front seat of his rented Geo Prizm, the two Smith & Wesson autoloaders he had taken from the dead federal agents near Scottsdale were concealed beneath a folded copy of the *New York Times.* In an emergency, Seriozha could fire thirty-one rounds without pausing to reload, assuming he survived that long in an ambush situation and he wasn't busy fleeing for his life.

Seriozha had purchased a cheap police scanner, using his knowledge of such things to discover both the local police department's chosen frequency and the "secure" channel used by agents of Albany's FBI office. The police were busy as expected, with sundry crimes against property and persons—the sort that made American newspapers such dreary reading on days when some national leader or clergyman wasn't facing trial on morals charges. The FBI channel had produced some cryptic chatter but revealed far less activity than the police band. Seriozha had been interested, however, in a terse exchange he'd overheard some fifteen minutes earlier.

A male voice had intruded on the air, saying, "HQ, this is Shadow. Priority, HQ. Come in!"

To which a female voice replied, "HQ to Shadow, roger. What's the problem, guys?"

"We seem to have misplaced the package," Shadow told his supervisor. "Over."

Terse and clipped, the woman's voice came back, "Is there a chance you'll reestablish contact, Shadow? Over!"

"That appears to be a negative, HQ. It's gone. Over."

The woman dubbed HQ—for headquarters, no doubt—spit back at Shadow in a sharp, disgusted voice. "All right, get off the air. HQ to Ranger! Do you copy me, Ranger?"

"Um, Ranger reading five by five, HQ," another male voice said.

"Please tell me you have contact with the package, Ranger. Over?"

"That's negative, HQ. No contact here. Over."

"Dammit!"

The air went dead and Seriozha smiled. There might be two surveillance operations under way in Albany at any given time, he realized, but the exchange gave him hope for Mishenkovich and their mission. He waited, scanner hissing softly on the seat beside him, right hand resting lightly on the folded newspaper and weapons underneath.

Misha Mishenkovich drove a Mercury Grand Marquis, a carbon copy of the Ford Crown Victoria that had become a law-enforcement cliché across the United States. There was no difference between the two vehicles except for their name and the sticker price, with the Mercury averaging one thousand dollars higher than the Crown Vic with identical equipment. In deference to the car's "unmarked" status, Seriozha knew its department-issue shotgun would be racked beneath the driver's seat, or maybe in the trunk.

He watched Mishenkovich select a parking space and lock the car as he got out. Seriozha's sleeper had him spotted, moving easily across the strip mall's lot to join him in the Geo.

"You were followed," Seriozha said while they were shaking hands, not making it a question.

"As you said I might be, Comrade Colonel. They were stubborn but predictable. I lost them."

"Excellent. Is everything prepared?"

"As planned and ordered. There'll be surveillance on my home tonight, but I anticipate no problem losing them again."

The colonel had debated whether he should warn Mishenkovich about specific dangers, finally deciding that he owed it to the man and to their mission. "Misha, I must tell you that our operation has been compromised."

"You mentioned the surveillance, Comrade, but—"

"There's something else," Seriozha said, interrupting him. "You've heard about the former Army officer—the traitor—who escaped from prison earlier this week?"

Mishenkovich nodded. "He's on the FBI's most-wanted list. We have a poster on him at the station house, for what it's worth."

"You'd know his face, then, if you saw him on the street?"

The sleeper frowned. "I think so. Why, Comrade?"

"The details aren't important, but he's joined a team that means to stop us from achieving what we've worked and planned for all these years."

"A fugitive?" Mishenkovich was frowning. "What the hell—?"

"There's more, Misha. A former comrade who worked closely with me years ago has joined the traitor in his effort. She serves the greedy pigs in Moscow now. I don't have photos, but she has dark hair of shoulder length, a slender woman in her early forties. Be prepared to see the traitor in a wig and beard, also."

"And if I see them, Comrade?"

"Kill them both, along with any others who accompany them. Make it your first priority, Misha. They jeopardize not only your assignment, but the whole network."

"I'll watch for them," the sleeper said.

"And if I see them first, they'll never have a chance to bother you." They shook hands once again, and Seriozha said, "Good luck, Comrade."

"I don't need luck," Mishenkovich replied. "I've been preparing for this moment all my life."

Over Lake Erie

CRUISING AT fifteen thousand feet and 270 miles per hour, the Piper Mojave had covered half the distance from Chicago to Albany in just over ninety minutes. Its twin turbocharged engines were loud enough inside the cabin to required raised voices, but conversation had been minimal since takeoff, each member of Bolan's team consumed with private thoughts. Lake Erie, far below, glimmered with the reflected sunlight of what could be someone else's perfect day.

It was another charter flight, for reasons of security and speed, their bags and weapons evenly distributed between the Piper's long nose and its engine nacelles. Their pilot was a thirty-something African-American who'd started out all smiles, then took his key from Bolan and reverted to the silent type. He seemed content to fly the plane and pocket the remainder of his bonus on arrival at the Albany County Airport, north of town.

Bolan wondered how Jasha Seriozha was traveling, and whether he'd reach Albany ahead of them—or whether he was bound for New York State's capital at all. The FBI was checking takeoffs from Chicago, Hal Brognola had assured him, but that didn't mean they'd started soon enough or covered all the airstrips in Cook County and environs. There were only so many G-men in Illinois, and they'd been fumbling every step along the way, so far.

He couldn't blame the FBI for everything, of course. Brognola would've held back crucial information from the agents sent to shadow Seriozha's sleepers in Scottsdale and Chicago, perhaps encouraging them to treat the surveillance as a lightweight assignment. That illusion had vanished with the deaths of four agents and twice that many civilians, but the damage was already done. Brognola had his hands full with the Bureau brass in Washington, and Bolan was expecting something less than wholehearted cooperation when he hit the ground in Albany.

The FBI worried Bolan less, however, than the enemy who waited for them on arrival. Whether Seriozha was in Albany or not, their target—Gregory Millward—was a cop, and that raised special problems for the Executioner if they came face-to-face with weapons drawn.

Brognola, though a lifelong member of the blue fraternity himself, had always puzzled over Bolan's private vow that he would never kill a cop, regardless of the provocation or the officer's abandonment of anything that passed for human decency. Perhaps *because* Brognola was a lawman, he was doubly hard on those who overstepped the bounds of his profession and disgraced it in the name of greed, racism, politics—whatever. More than once he'd counseled Bolan to abandon his peculiar scruples on this subject and drop the rotten bastards in their tracks, but Bolan still stood firm in his resolve.

Bolan couldn't explain his private decision to anyone who didn't understand, and for those who did, no explanation was needed. He wasn't some starry-eyed idealist, much less one of those dreaded bleeding-heart liberals. Bolan understood that dirty cops were criminals, and he wouldn't have argued with folks who believed corrupt lawmen were the worst, deserving of harsher punishment than civilians who committed identical crimes. A cop who crossed the line not only broke the law, but he also broke his sacred oath to stand between the savages and those who paid his salary. In effect, he became one of the savages. Aside from child-raping preachers and teachers, Bolan was hard-pressed to imagine a greater breach of trust.

And still he wouldn't drop the hammer on a lawman.

Never.

It wasn't a matter of ethics, per se. Rather, it was a matter of personal loyalty to the vast majority of men and women who put on their uniforms each day and did what they were paid to do, risking their lives for people they'd never met—if not always without complaint, at least with dedication to the job they'd chosen for themselves. They faced mortal danger every day, year-round, but they would never be at risk in any confrontation with the Executioner.

Brognola had tried to rationalize the specific case of Gregory Millward, noting that the sleeper wasn't even really an American, much less a dedicated cop. If his charade had been exposed, he would've been arrested or deported, but they had no way of doing that before the next attack was triggered.

Brognola's advice was simple: take him out. The fact that Bolan couldn't bring himself to do it was an argument they'd have to have some other time, assuming they were both alive. Right now, less than two hours from touchdown at Albany, Bolan needed to focus on the practical side of his problem.

Millward was dangerous, whether Seriozha chose to activate him next or not. Either way, he had to be neutralized, and they had no evidence sufficient for anything resembling a legal arrest or indictment. They could always try to snatch him, but they had no holding pen for prisoners and he was bound to resist violently, which brought them back to square one.

It came down to killing, and Bolan knew he couldn't bring himself to do the job this time. The self-imposed restriction made him virtually useless to Tasya Galenka; worse, it made him downright dangerous. She counted on Bolan to pull his own weight and watch her back. If he couldn't do either, he ought to step off.

But he couldn't do that, either.

It was too late to send in a Stony Man substitute, when the delay itself could prove fatal. Bolan had a job to do, and he would simply have to find a way to get it done. He was forbidden on his own account to kill a cop, but that still left a range of rough options.

Bolan simply had to find one he could live with.

And hope his companions could live with it, too.

TOUCHDOWN WAS smooth enough, as small-plane landings went. The pilot taxied toward a hangar where three suits and two brown Ford sedans stood waiting for them. Barnum was the last one off the plane, joining the others to retrieve his sparse baggage from one of the storage compartments.

Belasko paid the pilot and they walked the final thirty yards or so to meet the waiting G-men. Once you'd seen your share of FBI agents up close and personal, they were unmistakable. Barnum hoped they were better undercover, when it came to masking their identity, but he suspected most of them gave off a smell like pheromones, which hardened felons could pick up from miles away.

The agents didn't say much to Belasko, and their few comments were terse. The news was bad: they'd lost Millward that morning but were sitting on his house, assuming he'd come home before the day was out.

Barnum stood with his escorts, watching as the G-men drove away. "You think they're right?" he asked of no one in particular.

"Let's go to work," Belasko said, "and keep our fingers crossed."

CHAPTER THIRTEEN

Albany, New York

Bolan had barely left the airport, driving south on Albany-Shaker Road toward the state capital, when the police scanner mounted on the dashboard of their borrowed car crackled to life.

"Shadow to HQ, over."

"HQ, Shadow. What's the sitrep?"

"We have contact," said the agent code-named Shadow. "Make that home delivery on the package."

"Roger, Shadow. Maintenance of discreet contact is your top priority."

"You don't want us to take delivery, HQ?"

"That's negative. I say again, discreet contact."

"Affirmative, HQ. We're sticking. Out."

"I need a fix on Millward's home address," Bolan said, bearing down on the accelerator while Galenka took a street map from the bag between her feet and opened it, running a finger down the list of indexed names.

"Two miles ahead, turn left—that's east—on Osborne Road. It takes you into Loudonville. Drive on through town until Osborne meets Highway 377, then turn right—that's south. Millward's house should be within a quarter-mile of Littles Lake."

He knew the street address already, and now the route was fixed in Bolan's mind. He could picture the house, a team of G-men parked nearby and trying to be inconspicuous.

Bolan drove in silence, concentrating on the highway and the evening traffic. Most of the flow was outward bound, escaping Albany for the suburbs, and he made good time to Loudonville. As they were rolling out of town toward Highway 377, the radio came alive once more.

"Shadow to HQ, urgent! We have movement here, bags and all. It's looking like a road trip. Over!"

"Maintain visual, Shadow. Avoid contact as far as possible."

"Roger, HQ. We just thought— Hey, what's that? Oh, shit!"

The speaker crackled with another sound, not static. Bolan recognized it as an automatic weapon firing at some distance from the transmitter, the first shots followed swiftly by a nearer crash of breaking glass.

"Shots fired! My partner's down! Send backup *now!*"

The female voice of headquarters was no longer composed. "Ranger!" it snapped. "Shadow is under fire! We have an agent down! Move in! Repeat, move in!"

"Moving!" another voice—presumably Ranger—came back at her, as Bolan stood on the accelerator. "We have a visual, HQ. He's running. Shall we stay with Shadow?"

"Negative, Ranger. An ambulance has been dispatched. Secure the subject."

"Roger that, HQ. We're in pursuit."

And so was Bolan, although starting from a distance that discouraged him. The Bureau car was closer and they'd have a swarm of reinforcements on the way by now, to intercept Millward. He should've been relieved, but instead he felt left out. The contradiction troubled him, but there was no time for soul-searching at the moment.

"North on Highway 377, turning east now on 378," the agent known as Ranger broadcast. "Where's that backup, HQ?"

"They're en route, Ranger, tracking your progress."

"Roger. Heading north on Highway 32, now. Damn! I think he's heading for— We're under fire, HQ!"

There was no sound of gunfire this time, but the crack of bullets striking windshield glass was unmistakable.

"Jesus! Goddammit!"

"Language, Ranger," HQ said.

"Screw that! We're taking hits! I think he's headed for the arsenal. We'll try to—"

The voice was suddenly cut off, replaced by hissing for a moment while HQ took stock of the situation. "Ranger? Ranger, please respond. Ranger!"

"No Ranger," Barnum said from the back seat.

"What arsenal?" Bolan demanded of Galenka.

She was studying the map, holding it close to her face. "I've got it!" she said, index finger jabbing crinkled paper. "It's the Watervliet Arsenal, no further description. Take Highway 378 eastbound when we reach it, then north on 32 a mile farther on. It's less than two miles from the turnoff."

"Got it."

Bolan had it, but he didn't like it. Millward was within striking distance of his apparent target, armed with whatever weapons and gear he'd retrieved from his house. The arsenal made it that much worse, a potential bloodbath as FBI agents and SWAT teams closed in.

Crowded, hectic, violent. It had all the makings of a classic Executioner strike, except that the target was a cop.

Zeroing his thoughts down to the solitary goal of getting there, he jammed the pedal down and let the federal Ford cut loose with everything it had under the hood.

MISHA MISHENKOVICH HAD taken out the second team of agents with his AKS, while speeding north on Highway 32. The Hudson River was a dark slash on his right, ignored as he decided on the risk he had to take to buy himself some time. It was a dangerous maneuver, driving blind while he turned back to fire the AKS one-handed through his rear window. Aiming was difficult, if not impossible, but he had steady hands and nailed them on the second try, watching the dark sedan swerve wide across both lanes of traffic, raising clouds of dust before it stalled out on the shoulder.

He was clear, at least until the next team found him, and by that time he should be on target. Getting past security would be another challenge, but Mishenkovich had worked it out to his own satisfaction as a mental exercise. Ironically, if there were sirens on his tail the racket might work to his ultimate advantage.

It was worth a try, at least. He was committed now, with nothing left to lose except his life.

The basic plan was simple and it hadn't changed. Mishenkovich would show his badge to the arsenal's security officers, spinning a tale of some terrorist threat. If he couldn't charm or bluff his way inside, he'd kill them where they stood and enter over their dead bodies. It was all the same to him. He hoped for an impressive body count, aside from physical destruction of the arsenal. It would be disappointing if his final hours didn't count for something more than twisted steel and shattered stone.

The pursuit would help Mishenkovich, as long as he didn't let the agents get too close, too soon. A certain note of panic, even chaos, would be perfect window dressing for his story, pressing those on duty at the arsenal to make a snap decision with their own security in mind. They only had to drop their guard a little, move anxious hands ever so slightly away from their weapons, and they were his.

He swung into the parking lot, past large Restricted Access warning signs, the red light on his dashboard flashing. Mishenkovich parked nose in toward the arsenal's main entrance, as close as he could, trusting darkness and confusion to disguise the Mercury's shattered rear window. As he stepped out of the car, his mind ran down the checklist he had memorized years ago, revising and rehearsing it as changes occurred over time.

Three men were normally assigned to guard the Watervliet Arsenal at night. They were uniformed guards, each man armed with a Ruger Security-Six .357 Magnum revolver, four inch barrels standard, with at least two speed loaders apiece. They had other hardware inside—shotguns and automatic rifles, racked and ready—but Mishenkovich didn't believe they'd bring their big guns to the door, first thing.

And if they did, he had the AKS.

He didn't hide it, stepping from the car. He had the rifle slung across his shoulder, pressed against his right side with the muzzle pointed toward the ground, so his intended victims would have only a vague glimpse of it, hidden by his arm. The piece, while startling at a glance, would fit his story of a threat against the arsenal and make them take it seriously.

The front door opened when he was halfway there, two guards emerging, the one in front raising a hand to shield his eyes against the Mercury's headlights. Mishenkovich had left them on deliberately, for just that reason—another small distraction when the guards needed to focus for all they were worth.

"I'm Sergeant Millward, New York State Police," he said, flashing the badge they couldn't make out with the light behind him. "We're responding to a threat against the arsenal."

"What kind of threat?" the squinting leader asked.

Mishenkovich put on his most determined frown and said, "It's better if we talk inside."

THERE WERE THREE CARS in the parking lot when Bolan swung in from the highway. All three had flashing red lights on their roofs or dashboards, the detachable kind often carried in unmarked police cars. FBI agents with drawn pistols crouched beside two of the cars, while the farthest from the street—and nearest to the arsenal—looked empty, its rear window missing.

Galenka got out on the passenger side of the Ford and trailed Bolan toward the nearest pair of agents. They were half turned with their weapons ready, visibly suspicious even when Bolan showed them his credentials.

"That was quick," one of the G-men said. "The bodies aren't cold yet, and here you are from Washington."

Bolan ignored the gibe and asked, "Who have we got in there, besides Millward?"

"Should be some security," the agent said. "We don't have numbers yet."

"I heard what sounded like gunfire as we pulled in," his partner said. Catching a sidelong glance, he added, "But I can't be sure."

"You have a layout for the place?" Bolan asked.

"I've been here once," the second agent said, almost reluctantly. "Outside, is all. They have a loading bay for trucks around in back."

"That's us," Bolan told Galenka as he edged back from the federal men.

"Hold on," the first one said. "We already reached out for hostage rescue."

"We're just looking. If the ninjas want it, they can be my guest."

Facing Galenka as he passed, Bolan said, "Come on."

She followed him, still crouching, but she hesitated long enough to scan the street as far as she could see in both directions. There was no sign of Jasha Seriozha anywhere, but that wasn't as reassuring as it should've been, under the circumstances. Leaving Barnum in the car with warnings to sit tight, they jogged around the east side of the arsenal, no windows to expose them as they left the street and parking lot behind.

"We're going in?" she asked as they approached the loading dock.

"Affirmative," Belasko said. His mind was back in military mode, preparing for the action that would come. Galenka didn't like the pinched look on his face, but she dismissed it as a by-product of concentration.

The loading dock was a concrete slab elevated chest high from another parking area, this one clearly designed for large trucks to back in to remove or deliver cargo. A flight of concrete steps led upward to the platform and a metal door some fifteen feet across, seven feet tall. Beside it, set into the gray stone wall, a smaller door was locked and labeled with a sign instructing them to Ring And Wait. A small closed-circuit camera watched them from the southeast corner of the loading dock, above their heads.

Bolan made no move to punch the doorbell mounted on the wall. Instead, he drew his sound-suppressed Beretta and squeezed off a single shot that left the camera a dangling wreck. That done, he took a set of lock picks from his pocket, knelt before the metal door and went to work. Galenka covered him, facing the darkened lot behind since there was no way to surprise them from the front. She half expected to see Jasha gliding through the shadows, closing in to take them from behind.

"We're in," Bolan said a moment later, rising as he put the picks away and drew his gun once more. "You ready?"

Nodding, she gripped her weapon in both hands, standing aside as he opened the door and stepped across the threshold. When he wasn't met with gunfire from within, she followed him. A dimly lighted corridor received them like a monster's open throat.

MISHA MISHENKOVICH WAS careful not to step in either of the spreading blood pools that already covered nearly half the lobby floor. Two of the men he'd shot lay slumped together near the center of the smallish room. Their backup had been standing in a corner near the rack of long guns when Mishenkovich raised his AKS and swept all three with automatic fire. The two pale faces he could see both registered surprise.

Mishenkovich wasn't concerned about staining his shoes, but blood-slick soles were hazardous on concrete floors. It was embarrassing to fall, even without an audience, and a disabling injury had to be avoided at all cost. He still had work to do, before the troops gathered outside and stormed the arsenal.

It would've been amusing to unpack some of the weapons and defend the place until they took him down, as if he were the last soldier at Rorke's Drift or the Alamo, but that would leave most of the arsenal intact. Mishenkovich had an assignment to complete, specifically destruction of the Watervliet arms cache, thereby depriving New York State militia units of equipment valued in the high seven figures. He might've hoped for a more flamboyant target, but arms were always critical. Destruction of the arsenal would sap morale and pave the way for—what?

Mishenkovich shrugged off an urge to think beyond the moment. He was here; he had a job to do. He was about to leave the lobby, moving toward the main room of the arsenal, when he glanced over at a bank of four small television monitors mounted above a military-surplus desk.

One screen showed him patrol cars pulling up in front, to join the units already in place. Two others showed the long sides of the arsenal, no movement there. The fourth was blank.

Mishenkovich didn't believe the camera covering the rear approach had failed at just that moment by coincidence. Pulling the nearly empty magazine from his Kalashnikov, he shoved it in a pocket and replaced it with a fresh 30-round clip. A round already in the chamber left him ready to fire at the first sign of trouble, moving briskly past the stacks of crates containing arms and ammunition, toward the loading dock in back.

Mishenkovich knew the arsenal's layout. He had studied it at every given opportunity for years on end, from drive-bys in his squad car and ride-along overflights in a police helicopter to night-crawling expeditions carried out by the dark of the moon. He'd photographed the place from every angle, mostly using high-speed infrared film on nocturnal forays, and he knew exactly where the surveillance cameras were mounted on each of the building's four sides. The camera that had failed had been installed to protect the facility from a flanking attack. Now it was broken at a crucial moment, and Mishenkovich had to know why.

He had a firm grip on his AKS, barely felt the weight of the gear-laden duffel bag slung across his shoulder, as he neared the arsenal's loading bay. He couldn't see the personnel door yet, with a partition in the way, but his ears picked up scuffling sounds of movement dead ahead.

Intruders!

Mishenkovich was duly impressed. He hadn't expected them to move that quickly, especially when no more than three or four cars had responded so far. Where had the SWAT team come from? Or was it a SWAT team?

He thought about the conversation with his handler and frowned. Some counterforce had been at work for days, striving to block the grand design. If he, Misha Mishenkovich, could face and stop the enemy right here, right now, his sacrifice would doubly benefit the team at large. The thought pleased him and turned his frown into a smile.

Edging closer to the source of that single furtive sound, Mishenkovich called softly, "Come out, come out, wherever you are!"

BOLAN HEARD the taunting voice and froze in his tracks. He felt rather than heard Galenka stop behind him, poised and ready to respond if Millward sprang at them from hiding. From his tone of voice, though—Bolan took for granted that the lilting challenge hadn't come from any of the arsenal's assigned watchmen—it sounded as if Millward wanted to play games.

That could be good or bad, depending on what he'd accomplished in the short time since he'd penetrated the facility. Bolan was guessing that he hadn't planted many of his charges, and that should mean that he'd resent any distractions from his duty. On the other hand, there'd been no opportunity to run a psych evaluation on the sleepers they'd identified so far, and it was possible that not all of them were dealing with the proverbial full deck.

Isolation, stress at leading double lives, feelings of abandonment, ambiguity over their assignments a dozen years after the collapse of the system they served—all that could be combined with a long laundry list of personal foibles to create unstable personalities in deep-cover agents. In police work, they were widely recognized as the first to crack under pressure. And when had any lawman been left under cover for twenty-odd years?

Call it never, and hope for the best.

Bolan was edging forward, risking it to circumnavigate a stack of crated M-60 machine guns, when a burst of automatic fire ripped through the air-conditioned room, slugs gouging divots from the crates above and behind him. He hit the deck, almost returning fire before he caught himself. It was Galenka's pistol that answered the burst of Kalashnikov fire, banging out two quick rounds, then two more in rapid succession. Her brass hit the smooth floor near Bolan, jingling and dancing.

Bolan rolled between two piles of crates, and waited for Galenka to join him. When she didn't show, he took for granted that she'd found another shelter, farther back or possibly across the aisle.

There'd been no fire from Millward after she'd cranked off her rounds, meaning she couldn't have been hit.

The mocking voice came back, a bit more respectful this time. "Not bad," the sleeper said. "You can't win, though. It isn't in the cards."

Bolan retreated silently along the narrow strip of floor between crated mortars and machine guns. At the other end he found a wider aisle and started edging closer to the sound of Millward's voice.

What would he do when he caught up to Millward? Bolan wasn't sure. He couldn't kill the man, but that still left a wide range of disabling injuries, assuming he could pull it off without sacrificing himself or Galenka.

In other combat situations, Bolan's private scruples had endangered no one but himself. This time he had a comrade to consider—no pun intended, he thought, nearly smiling—plus all the lawmen gathering outside, preparing to storm the armory. If Millward murdered anyone because Bolan had passed on a clear killing shot, the blood would be on his hands, as much as on the mole's.

And still he knew he couldn't bring himself to do it. There would simply have to be another way.

Another burst of AK fire shattered the brooding silence in that room of death, echoing among the boxed piles of weapons and ammo. There was enough hardware within arm's reach to supply a small army, but Millward didn't want to steal it for his one-time Russian masters. He'd be going for a blow-out, scorched-earth destruction, and the blast could easily be great enough to kill or wound the suits and uniforms gathered outside the arsenal.

Bolan still had to stop him without using deadly force, but that didn't necessarily mean the sleeper would be going off to jail alive. There was more than one way to skin a mole, in fact. All Bolan had to do was find the means and get it done, without killing himself or anyone else in the process.

BOLAN HAD LOST TRACK of Galenka after they were separated, but he hoped she'd be advancing on a course that roughly paralleled his own, to flank their enemy. Millward conserved his ammunition like a pro, but he still made little shuffling, scraping sounds from time to time.

Or were those noises generated by Galenka?

If that turned out to be the case, he would've wasted precious time stalking the wrong target, while Millward either fell back to plant his explosive charges or waited in ambush to kill them both the moment they came together. Neither image appealed to Bolan, so he put the prospect out of mind for now and concentrated on stalking the only target available.

Unless his ears were playing tricks on him, Millward was roughly twenty feet ahead of him and nearly equidistant to his left. That made it something close to point-blank range, but he was hunting in a maze constructed out of heavy-duty crates with military hardware packed inside. The arsenal's acoustics weren't designed for easy tracking, and the only time he had a clear view of the big room from end to end was when he stepped into one of the wider aisles and made himself a target.

The confrontation, when it came, would be up close and personal, a split-second thing with no time for hesitation, second-guessing or trick shots. Kill or be killed was the name of the game—except that Bolan wouldn't, couldn't kill. And that would be a fatal handicap.

He had a plan in mind, but it depended on a clear view of his prey, however brief, before the sleeper opened fire. If he was right, Bolan could take his shot and see what came of it, without breaking his private code. If he was wrong, he'd either be a corpse or a cop-killer when the gun smoke cleared.

And of the two, as strong as his survival instincts were, he'd rather be the corpse.

Not yet, Bolan chided himself. You're not done yet.

But maybe soon.

Passing a stack of crated M-203 grenade launchers and their 40 mm high-explosive rounds, he hoped Millward wouldn't choose that moment to unleash a probing burst. Most of the hardware in the arsenal could take hits all night without posing any threat to bystanders, but the HE rounds could detonate on impact, one grenade setting off the remainder in its case or in the larger pile.

Bolan was thinking past that problem when he heard another of the scuffling noises that had lured him this far from the loading dock. He recognized the sound of leather soles on concrete as different from rubber's squeaky sound or the noise of dragging boxes. Galenka wore rubber-soled athletic shoes, and Bolan knew he'd found his man.

Getting an audio fix was one thing, though; making visual target acquisition was something else entirely.

Bolan crept forward, doubly cautious now as he edged past long crates of M-16 assault rifles, stacked six feet high. They offered good, solid cover, but he knew he'd have to give that up for his shot at Millward.

Make that his nonlethal shot.

Bolan had the 93-R's selector switch set for single shot, eliminating any chance that he'd lose control on a 3-round automatic burst. There was still a flinch factor involved, but Bolan was an old hand at face-to-face combat. He trusted himself to put the bullets where he meant for them to go, assuming he felt free to fire at all.

One more stack of crates, by the sound of it, and he should have a glimpse of Millward before the cop-turned-killer spotted him. Not much of one, perhaps, but Bolan was gambling everything on this one-and-only chance. He waited, listened for another sound of leather on concrete, and when it came he made his move.

Millward was suddenly in front of him, crouching beside an OD duffel bag, gripping an AKS assault rifle. They were no more than twenty feet apart, and Bolan had his pistol braced in a two-handed grip for accuracy's sake as he zeroed the target. In a heartbeat he made out the bulky shape of a Kevlar vest beneath Millward's dress shirt, and Bolan knew he had a chance.

His first shot hit dead center, lifting the cop and propelling him backward. Number two was a gamble, with Millward lurching from the impact, but he fired and scored again, an inch or two left of the first shot's striking point. Millward went down, stunned by the double tap that had to have bruised his chest and winded him, but he recovered swiftly. Bolan had closed barely half the gap between them when Millward rolled over on his side, bracing the AKS against his hip, prepared to fire.

Galenka made her move then, coming from behind him, her Gyurza P-9 blasting three quick rounds into the fallen sleeper's back from ten or twelve feet out. The armor-piercing rounds drilled through Kevlar as if it weren't there, and Millward died facing Bolan, a startled expression on his face.

Standing above the man she'd killed, Galenka turned him over and examined Bolan's handiwork. She probed torn fabric with her fingertips, frowning when they came away dry.

"You need a bigger gun," she said, "or maybe better ammunition for the one you have."

"I'll make a note," Bolan replied.

CHAPTER FOURTEEN

Washington, D.C.

The phone calls had been coming in all morning, and the news was bad across the board. Brognola had relayed the worst of it to Stony Man, though for the life of him he didn't have a clue what any of his people at the Farm could do to help. Bolan and his companions were in trouble, but they didn't know it yet. All the big Fed could do was wait for Bolan to make contact in his own good time and pass the word along.

Sleepers were on the move. So far, of the thirteen still alive from Barnum's list and under around-the-clock surveillance, six had left their homes within the past four hours, packing baggage in their vehicles and taking to the road. Brognola didn't think it was coincidence that all of them were based in Southern states, all driving south or southeast toward the next target city on Bolan's hit parade.

It spelled trouble, and Brognola could only guess how bad the fallout might be if Bolan couldn't head them off before Seriozha put his new plan into action.

The moles in motion were a mixed bag, as Brognola had come to expect from Barnum's list. Abel Decker was a forty-five-year-old newspaper advertising salesman from Biloxi, Mississippi. George Jamison, also forty-five, was the night-shift foreman at a steel plant in Birmingham, Alabama. Thomas Atkins was a forty-six-year-old certified public accountant employed by a midsized firm in Baton Rouge, Louisiana. Franklin Watts, age forty-one on paper, was a clinical psychologist in private practice at Pine Bluff, Arkansas. Edward Cowan was a forty-eight-year-old long-haul trucker based at Myrtle Beach, South Carolina. It troubled Brognola that he'd left home in his rig with a long semitrailer attached. The only woman on the list so far was forty-two-year-old Millicent Bullard, a Baptist church secretary from Nashville, Tennessee.

All six fit Seriozha's mold. They were Caucasian, middle-aged and singularly unattached in terms of family, lovers or long-term friends. They were respectable and law-abiding, got along with folks at work and socialized enough that no one would've thought to call them hermits, but they shied away from the entanglements that made life "normal." None had ever married; none had children; none claimed any living siblings; all listed their parents as deceased.

It was remarkable, but only if a hunter knew what he was looking for. Without Burke Barnum's pointers from the list he'd memorized, they could've passed unnoticed for the rest of their dreary, predictable lives.

The FBI had done its best to find out what the moles were up to. Phone calls to employers told the

Feds that five had called in sick to work, claimed family emergencies or suddenly decided it would be a good idea use up some vacation days before they went to waste. Cowan was self-employed but left a message on his answering machine advising callers that he'd booked a run to Richmond for the weekend, thereby sending any casual inquirers north while he drove south.

At a glance, from the routes they had followed so far, a casual observer might not have known the six runners were heading for Florida. Brognola wouldn't have seen it this soon in the hunt, but he knew where Bolan's team was headed next, seeking the next sleeper on Barnum's list, and once he knew that all the rest of it made sense.

It made sense and it scared him.

Seriozha had broken his pattern. There was no other way to explain it. The mass movement of sleepers told Brognola their opponent had put out a call to his troops on a regional level, rallying them to the next flash point. Even so, the Russian was working his way down the old list in order, as provided by Barnum—and that worried Brognola more than anything else.

By this time, Seriozha obviously knew his moves had been anticipated, but he wasn't following the logical course of diversion to a different sleeper. Instead, he was rallying the troops, and that could only mean he planned to have his people fight it out, inflicting as much damage as they could. With the Florida sleeper already in place and Seriozha waiting in the wings, Burke Barnum no more than deadweight on the home team, Bolan and his Russian ally could find themselves outnumbered four to one.

And they didn't know it yet.

His telephone chose that moment to ring. It was the private line, no secretary or switchboard between Brognola and the ten or twelve people on earth who knew the unlisted number. One of those sat in the Oval Office; two others spent their days at Stony Man. As for the rest—

He picked it up and growled, "Hello?"

"It's me," Bolan said. There was static on the line, long-distance from the neighborhood of Albany. "We're out of here in thirty minutes, headed south."

"You're not alone," Brognola said.

"How's that?"

Brognola hit the highlights, filling Bolan in. The Executioner was silent while he spoke, asking no questions until the big Fed had finished. Even then, the line hissed at him, voiceless, for another ten or fifteen seconds, until he began to worry the connection had been lost.

"You there?" he asked at last.

"I'm here. There's no mistake about the destination on these other six?"

Brognola caught himself shrugging, as if his friend were there to see. "We won't be absolutely sure until they show up in Orlando," he replied. "But if they're going somewhere else, it's one far-fetched coincidence."

"Okay, then," Bolan said. "Surveillance updates couldn't hurt, until we know what's going down."

"You got it. I could try scaring up some reinforcements, if you think—"

"I don't," Bolan said, interrupting him. "Let's play the cards we've got for now, and see what happens."

"Right, your call."

"And my responsibility, if anything goes wrong."

"Don't sweat it, pal," Brognola said. "If it goes wrong, there'll be enough to go around."

TASYA GALENKA HAD to have seen it on his face as Bolan let himself into the motel room. She stubbed her cigarette in a plastic ashtray, frowning at him through a veil of smoke and asked, "What's wrong?"

"We have a complication in Orlando," Bolan said.

"He's skipping Reynolds?" Barnum asked.

The sleeper in Orlando, Florida, was a construction worker named Otis Reynolds. He was forty-six years old and, like the others on the list, had passed his double life without any noteworthy incidents, hiding in plain sight.

"Not skipping," Bolan answered. "Reinforcing."

"Say again?" The convict managed to look worried and confused at the same time.

"Surveillance says we've got six other sleepers on the road right now. They're all from Southern states, within a day's drive to Orlando. They've been rolling out at intervals since 6:00 a.m., all headed south or east."

"Toward Florida," Galenka said, not asking him.

"Smart money leans that way," Bolan replied. "If there's another answer that makes sense, I'm missing it."

"That still leaves six unaccounted for," Barnum said.

"The Bureau has them covered, safe at home. My

guess would be they're too far north or west to make the drive in time."

"And they can't fly with their equipment," Barnum said.

"Not safely," Galenka stated. "Jasha wouldn't want them booking six charter flights at once and risking intervention by the FBI."

"We ought to count on seven, then," Bolan said. "Maybe eight, if Seriozha feels like jumping in."

"Eight against two," Galenka said.

"Hey, folks!" their prisoner chimed in. "I'm sitting here, you know?"

"That's all you're doing," Bolan said.

"Guy tries to help," Barnum muttered, "this is the thanks he gets."

"Don't even ask about a gun."

"Not me," Barnum replied, sulking.

"A question," Galenka said. "If Jasha's bringing six more sleepers to Orlando, will they all attack one target, or divide their forces?"

Bolan had been pondering the same question, without result. Raw logic told him there'd be no point bringing reinforcements to Florida for random strikes, when they could raise hell in their own backyards as planned from the beginning, without risk of being tagged by Bolan's team while he was tied up in the Sunshine State. It would've been the way to go if chaos was the only goal, but he sensed something else at work in Seriozha's mind. They'd blocked the Russian's play four times and taken out his hitters before they could wreak major havoc. That had to sting an ego like the whopper Seriozha carried with him, and it might well be enough to make him risk another beating for the possibility of sweet revenge.

Viewed in that light, the rush to Florida only made sense if Seriozha was fielding all his troops against the same target—or, more accurately, against the hunters he expected to come looking for Otis Reynolds. He'd know the others were under surveillance, but Seriozha would trust them to shake their pursuers at some point between their doorsteps and their destination. It shouldn't be that tough, each sleeper driving anywhere from 250 to 500 miles across Dixie, with back roads and bayous all the way. If they could reach Orlando unobserved, maybe link up with Reynolds at the target while the FBI was scrambling to find their tracks, they had potential to inflict some major damage in the final hours of their lives.

But where? What was the target that demanded seven guns instead of one?

Bolan decided he could think about it on the way. He had a charter flight lined up from Albany to Orlando, twelve hundred miles as the crow flies, with a pit stop for refueling at Raleigh, North Carolina. Say six hours in the air, another hour to ninety minutes on the ground, and they should still reach Florida by early evening. Seriozha's troops were widely scattered, dodging federal tails and local speed traps. Bolan's team still had an edge.

The trouble was, they'd have to wait and let the sleepers gather if they wanted to be done with it. They could get rid of Otis Reynolds on arrival—if his watchers hadn't lost him—but that wouldn't stop the others from collecting and proceeding with their hit.

Bolan was anxious to be on his way. "Is everybody packed?" he asked.

"You mean all two of us?" Barnum replied.

"The answer's yes or no."

"Make mine a yes," the convict said.

"I'm ready," Galenka added.

"Good. We're wasting time."

It was a short drive to the county airport, where their pilot waited with a Cessna Golden Eagle gassed up and ready to fly. He was another silent type, which suited Bolan fine. The flyboy checked out Galenka briefly, while helping Barnum stow their bags, then saw them buckled in and took his seat at the controls. Liftoff was smooth and uneventful, Bolan watching from his window as the earth dropped out from under them, houses and cars dwindling to the size of objects portrayed in an aerial surveillance photograph.

Soaring, the soldier closed his eyes and concentrated on the desperate fight that lay ahead.

BURKE BARNUM DIDN'T like the way this trip was going. He was troubled by the thought of Seriozha's sleepers massing in Orlando, even if the Russian had been forced to leave the other half of them at home. He'd seen how close Belasko and Galenka came to losing it their past two times at bat, civilian casualties and all. Those narrow victories had each involved one shooter. Barnum didn't want to think about the carnage that might follow if they had to cope with eight.

He didn't *want* to think about it, but he had no choice.

There was good news and bad news, just like always. Good news first: they'd be in Florida before most of the sleepers had a chance to get there, with the possible exceptions of Abel Decker from Biloxi and Edward Cowan driving down from Myrtle Beach. The rest had longer trips to make while trying to avoid surveillance. That would take some time and put the good guys on the ground ahead of them, with any luck.

It felt strange to Barnum after all this time, ranking himself among the good guys. He wasn't "born again," by any means, but he couldn't deny it felt good for a change, being on the right side. There was a chance he wouldn't make it through the day to come, and while he was the last person on earth to claim immunity from fear, the years in prison had made Barnum philosophical about his own mortality.

Belasko and Galenka were opposed to his participating in their plans as anything beyond a finger-pointing font of information. Barnum had expected them to dump him on the Feds after he'd given them the list of sleepers, and he was pleasantly surprised when neither of them moved to cut him from the team. That didn't mean they trusted him, of course—much less that they regarded him with anything akin to friendship. Barnum wasn't looking for a group hug from his keepers, but as long as he was going to the party in Orlando, he'd have liked to play an active part.

Maybe there was still a way, he thought. But how? What would it take to swing the votes his way?

If he could spot the target in advance, Barnum thought that might do the trick. That stumped him going in, since he'd spent little time in Florida and most of that around Miami, on vacation. What was there in Orlando that would make Seriozha pull half of his remaining sleepers in from other states?

A football fan in his former life, Barnum thought first of Tinker Field and the yearly Citrus Bowl. No good. Sea World? The Universal Studios theme park? Not much better. When he pictured central Florida, Barnum saw citrus groves and migrant workers sweating underneath the tropic sun. There was some swampland, snakes and alligators for the tourists to admire before mosquitoes sent them running back to their motel rooms. Boating on the lakes.

What else?

It hit him like a slap across the face.

"Oh, shit!"

Galenka swiveled in her seat to stare at him, frowning. Barnum grimaced, resting one hand on his stomach. "Sorry. I'm just a little airsick. Don't mind me."

Barnum was sick, all right, but not from altitude or turbulence. The vision that had shocked him was the mental picture of the only target near Orlando that made sense—and what a nightmare it would be if seven dedicated shooters ran amok with automatic weapons, frag grenades and RDX plastique. The label "massacre" would barely cover it.

Barnum was sweating, hands trembling where he clenched the armrests of his narrow seat. Scenes of carnage played out in his head like trailers for a low-budget horror movie—bodies torn and broken, leaking crimson, maimed survivors crawling for cover where none could be found.

The target was so obvious, Barnum couldn't believe one of them hadn't thought of it sooner. It had everything Seriozha could hope for: an unsuspecting crowd of victims numbering in the thousands; worldwide name recognition, with the guarantee of global publicity; enough combat stretch that the sleepers could work independently, widely scattered for maximum damage and evasion of police, or join forces for a concentrated bloodbath where the targets were most numerous.

Jesus!

He fumbled with his seat belt, rising halfway from his seat before he caught himself. What if I'm wrong? thought Barnum, hesitating. Surely there were other likely targets in Orlando and environs. If he sold his notion to Belasko and Galenka, would he be diverting them from the real target, thereby jeopardizing countless other lives?

It wouldn't hurt to wait and tell them his idea when they were on the ground. They couldn't move against the enemy before then, anyway, and the sleepers were under surveillance—supposedly, at least. Barnum decided to relax as best he could, wait out the flight and float his supposition to the others after they'd picked up their wheels. They had a lead on Seriozha's sleepers. It would still be soon enough.

Please, God. Let it be soon enough.

CHAPTER FIFTEEN

Orlando, Florida

The day had been a long time coming, but Otis Reynolds had never given up hope or lost sight of his goal. He'd been shaken like everyone else when the Soviet system collapsed, but he'd maintained sufficient self-control that he could laugh and joke about it with his so-called friends on the construction crew, going out for beers after work and sneering at the stupid Russians like a true American, gnawing Buffalo wings and repeating the mindless shit that passed for political insight among his sweaty peers.

Cuba next! Fuck Fidel! Better dead than Red!

Before another day was done, many of those who held that view would get their wish. Oleg Romochka—born in the Ukraine, reborn in Florida at age twenty-two—made that vow to his own mirror image and smiled.

It wouldn't be long now, before he could discard the sham of his existence as a real American and give the self-satisfied bastards around him what they'd been craving for decades. Central Florida was a hotbed of right-wing sentiment, worse in some ways than

Miami's own Little Havana, and it had galled Romochka to play along with such ignorant nonsense, but that was the sum and substance of undercover work. He had become a chameleon, adopting the protective coloration of his surroundings—and he'd done a fine job, false modesty notwithstanding.

Now he was ready for payback. Past ready, in fact.

He had retrieved his gear despite the puny efforts of the FBI to shadow him. It was amazing to Romochka, after all the years he'd lived in dread of being found out and arrested by the Feds, that they were only human after all. They did their best, but he'd had twenty years to plan evasive movements, cutouts and escape hatches. He had a dozen ways to shake pursuers in the city, and they all appeared to work without a hitch.

The best part of it, to Romochka's mind, was that he could discard his mask within the next few hours, stop pretending to be someone he wasn't. He thought his twenty-year performance should have qualified him for an Oscar, but the committee would've been forced to create a new category just for him. Best performance by a socialist warrior posing as an American redneck, perhaps? Something a bit more subtle?

The thought made Romochka smile again, not the usual shit-eating grin he'd rehearsed for his peers on the job, but an expression of true satisfaction. This night he would amaze them all, and there was nothing the police or FBI or CIA could do to stop him.

Romochka was honored by his handler's personal attention and the fact that reinforcements had been summoned to assist him in destruction of his targets. Some warriors might've taken offense at the gesture, but Romochka saw the move for what it was—an acknowledgment that his target was greater and more important than those selected for the others. By extension, his selection as the primary agent of that target's destruction set him apart from the rest, made him special.

Romochka's handler would have dismissed that logic, had they discussed it, but he didn't need to know everything that went on inside his sleeper's mind. Romochka understood that the people's revolution was a vast collaborative effort, but it also needed heroes in these times of trial, as Mother Russia had needed heroes in the Great Patriotic War of 1941-45.

Oleg Romochka was one such hero, whether his handler knew it or not. In a few short hours he would prove himself and win a place in history.

He checked his watch against the bedside clock and found them synchronized, as always. He had three hours to kill before he left the house and put his watchers through their paces, shaking them at one turn or another. They were so predictable, they almost took the sport out of it, but he still enjoyed humiliating them. The gear was in his Ford Contour, parked outside. When he had lost the Feds, he would be ready to proceed.

Three hours.

He had time to watch a video before he left. Smiling, Romochka grabbed his favorite cassette and put it in the VCR, reclining on the unmade bed as credits rolled.

He loved *Red Dawn.*

Glynn County, Georgia

THE COP WAS DEAD before he hit the ground. It was his own damned fault for setting up a speed trap in the first place, hiding on his Harley-Davidson behind a billboard for the New Life Christian Church and waiting for the chance to ruin someone's day. Bad luck had sent Ed Cowan down that stretch of Highway 99, skirting the county seat at Brunswick, and the cop had seen his chance.

Now he was history.

It would've done no harm for Cowan to accept the ticket, but he wasn't in the mood. He'd made a long drive down from Myrtle Beach already, and he wasn't even halfway to his destination yet. The FBI had dogged him for a while, until he dealt with them, and by the time he got to Georgia he was in no mood for pissant traffic cops who chewed tobacco and wore mirrored sunglasses.

The cop—he'd been called Myerson, according to the brass nameplate he wore above one of the leaking bullet holes—had tagged Cowan when he was doing sixty-seven miles per hour in his Peterbilt with the refrigerated semitrailer. He was speeding, true enough. The posted speed limit on Highway 99 was fifty-five, and Cowan normally would've been willing to accept the citation without complaint.

But not this day.

This day was special, and the cop would never know how close he'd come to altering a piece of history. If he'd been smarter, even quicker on the draw, he might've been alive and standing over Cowan's corpse. Their close encounter might've ended differently and saved some lives in Florida before the day was out.

Too late.

The cop was young and cocky—meaning stupid—and he hadn't banked on Cowan stepping from the Peterbilt's cab with a 9 mm Makarov pistol in his hand. He wasn't even wearing Kevlar, as the spout of blood from Cowan's first shot proved. Two more, and he was down. Threat neutralized.

Almost.

There was the matter of disposal to be dealt with, and Ed Cowan—born Evgenii Khoklov—wasted no time cleaning up. No cars had passed since he was stopped, but that could change at any moment. Every second counted now, before more killing was required.

He opened the back of his freezer rig and dragged out the loading ramp. Khoklov was strong. It took only a moment for him to grip the dead cop by the shoulders of his leather jacket, hauling him up the ramp and into the long semitrailer. The trailer was empty except for two bodies stashed way in the back. Khoklov left the cop beside them, telling the dead FBI men, "You've got company. Play nice."

He smiled at his own witty joke and went back for the bike. It was bound to draw attention if he left it parked beside the road. Better to take it with him, then, since he'd be out of Georgia by the time dispatchers started looking for the cop he'd shot.

The Harley started on his first attempt. It was a bigger bike than he was used to, but he'd driven one before and was familiar with the various controls. At that, a novice could've handled it, since Khoklov only had to drive it twenty feet or so, then up the metal ramp into his rig. Inside the trailer, he switched off the engine and dismounted, gave the bike a shove and dropped it on the body of its late rider. It wouldn't slide around that way and pester him with grinding, scraping noises on the long drive still ahead.

Khoklov was fastening the big doors on his trailer when a station wagon passed, its driver waving at him through the windshield as if they were long-lost friends. Khoklov waved back at him and smiled, thinking, You hopeless idiot.

Back in the cab, he switched his police scanner on to keep track of any premature alarms. A highway map lay open on the vacant seat beside him, with his route traced out in red.

"Don't start without me, people," Khoklov said, and put his truck in gear.

Diamondhead, Mississippi

THE FBI AGENTS HAD trailed him as far as St. Tammany Parish, but Thomas Atkins lost them outside Bogalusa, before he crossed the Pearl River on Highway 26 to enter Mississippi. He'd risked a stop in Poplarville to make sure they were gone, dawdling the best part of an hour at a drive-in restaurant on the small town's main drag, but there'd been no sign of the clean-cut federal men in their obvious car and their off-the-rack suits.

He was clear.

Atkins—born Tolya Aksenov, in Novgorod—worried that he might be forced to kill the agents, but it hadn't come to that. He lost them, finally, by putting on an unexpected burst of speed and swerving his Volvo 850 onto a narrow side road at the last moment, when his pursuers were nowhere in sight. They passed his hideout, racing to catch up, and Aksenov doubled back to skirt Bogalusa on the south, following Highway 16 and the Bogue Chitto River until he picked up Highway 21 at Sun and started north again.

He wouldn't have minded killing the agents, in fact, but disposing of their vehicle and bodies would've cost him precious time while increasing his risk of discovery and arrest. There was too much at stake now for Aksenov to be careless or impetuous. He had his orders and would carry them out to the letter—or at least to the very best of his ability.

It was what Tolya Aksenov did best, following orders. That proclivity made him a perfect sleeper agent, just as it had made him a reliable—if undistinguished—member of the Tower, Forbes & Dane accounting firm in Baton Rouge. He was the kind of man who went unnoticed for the most part, taken for granted by his employer and co-workers, ignored by his neighbors, dismissed without a second glance by women in search of a mate or a simple good time.

He was perfect.

None of those who knew him as Tom Atkins would've guessed that he'd been trained to fight beside Spetsnaz commandos and defend himself with a variety of weapons—or with none—in a variety of lethal situations. They would never have suspected that he'd killed two men in East Berlin when he was just eighteen and that he'd been chosen ten days later for a special task in the United States. His Boston accent was impeccable, as were his transcripts from a list of schools he'd never seen, much less attended. When his colleagues called him Yankee, gently poking fun, he smiled and played along, wishing them dead behind his smile.

It was unfortunate that he'd have no chance to destroy them now, but Aksenov's handler knew best. He was needed in Florida for a special assignment, no advance training required, and he obeyed the way he always followed orders, instantly and without question. If his handler said it was essential, Aksenov had no complaints.

He wondered if the FBI would circulate an all-points bulletin, now that he'd given them the slip. Would they involve local police departments or attempt to limit their embarrassment by leaving other agencies out of the loop? He didn't know, and there was nothing he could do but stay alert and watch for anyone who paid too much attention to him on the road.

It was a benefit of being unremarkable that individuals who noticed him stood out, thereby drawing attention to themselves. If it happened again before he reached Orlando, Aksenov wouldn't be so forgiving of his enemies.

He had a rendezvous to keep, and he didn't intend to miss it, even if he had to wade through blood along the way.

Washington, D.C.

"YOU'VE LOST *how many?*" Hal Brognola blurted out. His grip tightened until it felt as if he'd crush the telephone receiver.

"Three, so far," the soft, embarrassed voice replied.

"Three out of six."

"Unfortunately, yes."

"Fifty percent," Brognola said.

"I've done the math, sir."

"That's just freaking great!" Brognola's FBI contact made no reply, leaving dead air between them until the big Fed spoke again. "What about the other three?"

"Still tracking, as of ten o'clock. The teams are checking in at thirty-minute intervals."

"You've lost which three, again?" Brognola knew the names but needed time to think.

"Atkins, Cowan and Decker," the G-man replied. "There's something else," he added.

"Go ahead."

"The agents who were watching Cowan don't respond by radio. They've missed their last four check-ins."

Shit! "No sign of them?" Brognola asked.

"We've found their car. Just turned it up at Kensington, before I called."

"Where's that?"

"Along the coast, southbound. I make it twenty miles or so from Myrtle Beach."

"What are the circumstances?"

"A patrolman with the Kensington PD surprised some local juvies stripping it, behind a fast-food dive that's been closed down for years. The kids all got away, but we've got latent prints up the wazoo—our guys, some unidentified, but nothing yet on Cowan."

"Signs of foul play?" Brognola inquired.

"None obvious, but we assume the agents didn't leave their vehicle and take off voluntarily."

"At least we know where Cowan's going," Brognola said.

"Do we, sir?"

"He's headed for Orlando."

"Maybe he was headed for Orlando when he left this morning, but he's taken out two agents now. That changes everything. We don't know where he's going now or what he'll do."

"It changes nothing," Brognola replied, putting more confidence into his tone than he felt in his heart.

"We're leaning toward a five-state APB," the G-man said.

"Forget it. Heat like that would ruin everything right now."

"The director—"

"Takes his orders from the same attorney general who's been breathing down my neck all morning," Brognola said, interrupting. "Does he need another call to spell out terms of his cooperation on this deal?"

The G-man hesitated for a moment, tempted to come back with some sarcastic answer, but he managed to resist the urge. "No, sir," he said at last. "That won't be necessary."

"Excellent. I'm glad to hear it. And I won't be hearing APBs on any of these subjects, right?"

"No, sir."

"All right, then. Try to find these people, but discreetly. No attempts to apprehend or interfere in any way, unless they're firing on your people. Understood?"

"Yes, sir."

"Get back to me within the hour," Brognola said before he cradled the receiver. He sympathized with the FBI brass, furious as they had to be at the deaths or disappearance of six agents and counting, frustrated at their inability to keep a tail on the various sleepers. It was doubly galling to the leaders of an organization known for its love of control in any given situation, and there was nothing Brognola could do about it.

As much as he hated the idea, their best hope of nailing the moles and Jasha Seriozha was to let the agents converge on their target—whatever that was. The sleepers already knew that they'd been shadowed. If the Bureau pushed it, they might scatter, go back underground and wait for revised orders from their handler. And in that case, Brognola presumed, they would be lashing out at multiple targets with no advance warning.

He wondered if the Bureau surveillance had blown it already, then dismissed the thought. There was nothing he could do about it now, no turning back the clock, so he'd press on and play the cards he held.

Right now it was the only game in town—and Brognola had raised the ante with a jackpot that included his best friend's life.

Quitman County, Georgia

IT HAD TAKEN four hours, but Millicent Bullard finally lost her federal tail. The agents were tenacious—she'd give them that—but they lacked imagination when it counted. She had stopped at the Columbus Metropolitan Airport, left her car in the long-term parking lot and rode the airport shuttle to the terminal. The agents had to scramble, keeping up, and she lost them in the terminal itself, bypassing the ticket counters while they argued with a city traffic cop outside, making for the car-rental kiosks instead. By the time her pursuers began searching the check-in and departure areas, she was out the back door and away in a new Ford Escort, her gear on the back seat behind her.

They'd give up eventually, maybe after calling reinforcements to the airport, sweeping the terminal from end to end, perhaps obtaining court orders to check the passenger lists on departing flights. She'd been forced to use a credit card for the rental—the agencies all wanted plastic nowadays, in case a customer didn't return the car—but it would be hours, she guessed, before federal agents thought to check the rental outlets. By that time she'd be out of Georgia and well on her way to the target.

Milly Bullard—née Milena Belayev, of Rostov—would've killed her federal shadows if it came to that, but evasion better served her purposes. The FBI was less likely to broadcast her likeness to local police along the route of travel if she embarrassed its agents, rather than eliminating them. In her experience, there were some things police couldn't forgive, much less forget.

But she was still ready to kill if anyone tried to stop her from answering her handler's call. Belayev had removed her 9 mm Makarov semiautomatic pistol from the duffel bag and made sure it was fully loaded, with a live round in the chamber, before she left the Avis parking lot. She had the pistol in her purse, the purse unzipped beside her on the Ford's front passenger seat. If she was stopped—for speeding, say—it would be only natural for her to reach inside the bag for her ID. Given that edge, her enemies would find her difficult to capture—alive, at any rate.

Belayev wasn't afraid to die, but she wanted it to count for something. She'd be happier taking out a hundred Americans than one or two traffic policemen. She wanted to leave a mark, be remembered as a hero of the glorious revolution by generations yet unborn. She was convinced that it had to be her destiny.

Belayev held her speed close to the limit as she drove southward through the red-clay country of southwestern Georgia, homing in on the Florida border and Tallahassee beyond it, Interstate Highway 10 running east from there to pick up I-75 for the long run down to Orlando. She watched for police cars the way any other motorist might do, no special paranoia in her attitude.

None visible, at least.

She didn't know the others she was on her way to meet, but that wasn't a problem. If her handler trusted them, they had to be loyal and able warriors of the revolution. She would welcome them as comrades and cooperate with them in any way she could. If they were privileged to die together, fighting side by side against the capitalist pigs, Belayev would consider it a fitting end to her existence.

And who knew? It might even be fun.

Raleigh, North Carolina

REFUELING TOOK the best part of an hour by the time they waited for the truck to service three more planes ahead of them. Bolan had long since learned to muzzle his impatience and accept delays that he couldn't avoid, but he was still aware of precious time escaping while they stood around the hangar waiting for the service crew to finish with the Cessna.

Galenka stood off to one side, catching up on cigarettes she'd missed while they were airborne. Barnum had staked out a corner for himself, watching the airport service team and picking at his artificial beard. He seemed to be upset by something, shooting harried glances at his two escorts and scowling as he did so, as if their proximity now made him ill at ease.

Bolan supposed the inmate's thoughts were turning to the climax of their mission and the knowledge that he'd be sent back to prison when they finished. Bolan didn't mind putting in a good word with Justice via Hal Brognola, but he knew it wouldn't count for much. Barnum was doing life for the peacetime equivalent of treason. Even if his sentence was commuted and he made parole someday, what sort of life could he expect to lead among the very people he'd betrayed? A change of name might help him for a while, but how long would it be before some enterprising tabloid journalist saw through his cover and revived the story?

Bolan shrugged it off and concentrated on the job that lay ahead. Before he thought about Burke Barnum's self-inflicted problems, he still had to deal with Seriozha's sleepers and the Russian spy himself, assuming they could get a handle on him this time.

"Five minutes," said their pilot, passing by in the direction of a nearby pop machine. Bolan was ready to be on his way. Whatever happened in Orlando, he preferred to face the music and get on with it.

Patient or not, the waiting sucked.

Barnum was suddenly beside him, speaking in a nervous-sounding voice, pitched low enough that Bolan had to strain to hear him. "I've been thinking about Jasha's target in Orlando."

"And?"

"It's just a thought."

"I'm listening," the Executioner replied.

"I mean, he had one guy in town already, right? But calling in six more, that's overkill for any normal target, don't you think? For seven guns he'd want something spectacular. That's Seriozha's style, and now he's got the grudge to settle, too. Besides, when you consider the publicity alone, it's like a bonus. How could he resist?"

"Is there a point to this?" Bolan asked.

"Yeah, there is." And Barnum spelled it out for him, two words that sent a chill down Bolan's spine. He thought about the crowds and automatic weapons blazing, frag grenades and plastique charges going off.

"You're guessing, right?"

"Of course I'm guessing," Barnum said. "I hope I'm wrong. If you can think of a more likely target in Orlando, I'll be glad to go with yours."

He couldn't think of anything more likely or more logical, however. It galled Bolan that he hadn't once considered it himself. He'd been shortsighted, a mistake his Russian adversary wouldn't make.

"We're set," the pilot told them, passing back the other way.

"Hang on a second," Bolan said. "I need to find a telephone."

"Around the north side of the hangar, there."

He didn't know if Brognola could help, especially considering the fact that Barnum's guess was only that—a guess, and nothing more. He could be wrong, in which case any move they made would help their adversaries, give them a clear shot at some alternative target. But if he didn't call...

Another scene of carnage flashed across his mind, and Bolan double-timed to find that telephone.

Orlando, Florida

JASHA SERIOZHA WASN'T a great drinker. When his comrades in Moscow had swilled vodka by the bucket, he shared a drink or two for courtesy's sake, forgoing the pleasures of morning-after nausea and splitting headaches as a practical matter. He had no scruples against drinking, or against much of anything else for that matter, betrayal of the revolution emphatically excepted. It was simply that he thought a man who voluntarily surrendered self-control had to be an idiot.

That said, he had enjoyed champagne with dinner at Orlando's finest seafood restaurant because he felt like celebrating. All the world would soon be witness to his masterstroke, a move so ruthless and audacious it was bound to stun America and her collaborators all around the world. He celebrated in the knowledge that his victory was already assured. Even if he should die this night, his memory would carry on, enshrined by warriors who came after him.

He hoped Tasya Galenka would be present when his sleeper struck. It would be fitting if she were on hand to see his triumph—and to pay in blood for her betrayal of the sacred ideology they'd once served together, side by side. If she brought the American traitor along, so much the better. Duplicity should always be repaid in full measure, as an example to potential traitors in the future.

And besides, it would be Seriozha's pleasure to kill them both. Was there a better way to spend what might be the final hours of his life than settling scores?

Celebration or no, Seriozha quit drinking after his second glass of champagne. It was enough to lift his spirits, without dulling his wits. He needed all his faculties, as he prepared to join his soldiers on the firing line. This action was his masterpiece, and he would play an active role if it was feasible.

His planning all came down to this. He had considered other targets—thought of summoning his moles to Washington, D.C., at one point—but he'd finally decided that an unofficial target might serve best to damage what Americans considered their identity, their soul.

And now he'd found it.

This night he would make history. His name, when published, would be instantly reviled by millions who took their cues from the corporate media. Their opinions meant less than nothing to Seriozha; he welcomed their scorn as high praise. For those who recognized and understood his purpose, no public condemnation would matter. The men and women who counted would recognize his heroism on sight.

And when America reacted, lashing out at Mother Russia in a fit of rage, the traitors who had seized control in Moscow would be faced with drastic choices. They could fight like Russians or prostrate themselves like spineless beggars, pleading for mercy. In the latter event, Seriozha had no doubt they would provoke an uprising to sweep the filth from power and restore a measure of the glory sacrificed in recent years.

It was his hope. It was his dream.

How many soldiers have a chance to make their dreams come true?

Not many, Seriozha realized. In fact, for all he knew, this night could prove to be unique in all of history. A lesser man might've been angry or depressed at knowing he wouldn't live to see the next day's headlines, but Seriozha was beyond such petty considerations. He was standing on the brink of victory, and there was little that his enemies could do to cheat him of his triumph. If they tried…well, he looked forward to the struggle.

He'd been working toward this moment all his life.

The Russian paid his check and stepped out into soft, warm dusk. The night lay waiting for him, ripe with promise.

In his mind, he could already hear the screams.

CHAPTER SIXTEEN

Orlando, Florida

Bolan's mood darkened as he pulled their borrowed federal Ford into the main parking lot of the Walt Disney World resort complex. The parking area itself was small-town size; in front of him, behind walls and fences, lay forty-three square miles of concentrated tourist attractions—four separate theme parks and room to ramble in between, complete with a movie studio, hotels, waterways and an internal highway network. Thousands of tourists were on-site at any given time, enjoying attractions valued in the billions of dollars.

And somewhere inside, if Barnum's guess was correct, seven terrorists were circulating through the crowds, perhaps accompanied by their handler. Armed and ready to unleash destruction at a moment's notice, they might wait for Seriozha's signal or run amok at will, on a whim. All Bolan and Galenka had to do was track down the seven and neutralize them all before they started killing women, children, anyone within their reach.

Bolan had checked out the brochures, briefly. With

signs to help, he reckoned he could find his way between Epcot, the Magic Kingdom, Disney-MGM Studios and the Animal Kingdom—but where in the insular fantasy world should they start? What would prevent one sleeper from shooting up Dinoland, U.S.A., while another struck at Epcot's Future World or Mickey's Toontown Fair? How could he and Galenka hope to corral and take down seven guns—or eight, if Seriozha was present and ready to fight?

It seemed hopeless, but Bolan squelched that thought before it could take root and blossom. The only sure defeat lay in not trying, giving up before he tried. Defeatism had never been a part of Bolan's personality, and he could ill afford it now.

They locked the car and moved toward the entrance where tickets were sold. Bolan shelled out cash for three of the cheapest activity booklets available, absolutely uninterested in the relative value of the promotional wizardry that preoccupied standard-issue tourists. The money was irrelevant. If Barnum's guess was wrong, they had already wasted vital time and were about to waste much more. If he was right, tickets and the formalities of commerce would become irrelevant with the first gunshot or explosion, making it each soldier for himself.

Hal Brognola had offered reinforcements after Bolan phoned him from Raleigh with Barnum's guess at the Orlando target, but Bolan had opted for caution. By the time he'd called in, all six sleepers had managed to ditch their FBI surveillance, meaning that they could be anywhere within three hundred miles of their respective starting points. For all he knew, the mass movement of moles had been designed by

Seriozha to divert and concentrate reactive forces in Orlando, while the terrorists lashed out at other targets scattered far and wide across the Southern states.

Maybe...and maybe not.

An FBI Hostage Rescue Team was airborne from Miami, headed north, but they would stop short of invading Disney World unless the worst-case scenario came true and violence ensued. Until then, Bolan and Galenka were on their own.

They stopped a few yards past the entry gates and huddled one last time. Equipped only with side arms and compact walkie-talkies, they had already agreed to separate and scan the crowds for faces they'd memorized from seven driver's license photographs Brognola had collected and faxed to Orlando, waiting for them on arrival at the airport. It wasn't quite like looking for a needle in a haystack, more like searching for one particular needle in a tub containing tens of thousands. They could bypass children, young adults, the elderly and any nonwhite visitors to Disney World, which still left several thousand faces to scrutinize.

"We're short on time," Bolan remarked, stating the obvious. "First confirmed sighting, get on the air and stay in touch. No intervention without backup unless it's essential."

"I'd feel better with a gun," Barnum said.

"You're lucky to have the two-way," Bolan told him. They'd decided it couldn't hurt to let Barnum hunt on his own at this point, but arming him was out of the question. "Just report back if you spot anyone."

"You're the boss," Barnum groused.

"Don't forget it. Let's move!"

Frontierland, Magic Kingdom

OLEG ROMOCHKA MOVED along the mock Old West street like any other tourist, smiling at the costumed characters who passed him on the sidewalk, chuckling appreciatively at their movie-script dialogue. Coonskin caps and Stetsons were the dominant headgear in Frontierland, moccasins and cowboy boots in roughly equal favor among the park's employees. Romochka, for his part, wore a lightweight raincoat to cover the AKS assault rifle slung beneath his right arm, pockets heavy with spare magazines and RGD-5 fragmentation grenades.

It was going to be a hot time in the old town tonight.

He'd separated from the others ten minutes earlier, the seven of them fanning out to different points around the Magic Kingdom theme park. It had been decided they should start the killing there, in more or less coordinated fashion, then disperse as feasible and spread carnage throughout Disney World at large. Romochka checked his watch and found six minutes still to go before the fireworks started.

He was looking forward to the show.

Construction on the giant park had started back in February 1967, nearly all the basic work completed before Romochka had assumed his deep-cover post in Orlando twelve years later. Disney World had been his primary target from day one—a whimsical choice, in his initial view, but one that evolved over time into a target of substance, providing him with thousands of potential victims on any given day. He'd visited the complex half a dozen times per year on average, clipping newspaper reports and taping television broadcasts that described additions to the several theme parks, staying up-to-date with Epcot and the rest as they evolved.

Romochka almost felt as if the park were his, to some extent. After this night, its name and his would be forever linked in history. Whenever Disney World was mentioned in the future, he would be remembered for his gift of blood and pain.

Four minutes.

He was ambling past a saloon that sold only soft drinks, when he saw the woman watching him. She stood across the street, staring with such intensity it raised the small hairs on his nape. Romochka wasn't worried even then, however—not until she palmed a little two-way radio and started speaking urgently into the night.

Trouble, he thought, and slipped a hand inside the pocket of his raincoat, where he'd slit the lining with a razor for swift access to the AKS. Romochka thumbed off the rifle's safety and slipped his index finger through the trigger guard. He moved along the sidewalk, trying to be casual, and felt the woman watching him. Dawdling at a polished shop window, he glimpsed her reflection, keeping pace with him across the street.

It wasn't time yet, but how long could he wait? The woman had to be on to him. Why else would she be trailing him that way? Whom was she talking to? How many more were watching him right then?

Romochka felt his pulse throbbing behind his eyes,

heard the sound of his own heartbeat in his ears. Though trying to relax, calm down, he felt each movement as if every step he took was stiff, unnatural. The woman's piercing scrutiny made him feel ill at ease, like a nervous stranger to his own body. If he didn't counteract the feeling soon—

A group of faux pioneers passed by on his right, fringe dangling from their buckskin costumes, muskets cradled in their arms. Romochka turned as they passed, glancing across at the woman who trailed him. Her eyes met and held his, flashing a challenge he couldn't ignore.

Who was she?

No matter. Her windbreaker had fallen open far enough for Romochka to glimpse the edge of a shoulder harness she was wearing, almost certainly a holster. She was armed, which told him everything he had to know. Private security, police or FBI—in any case, she was his enemy.

Romochka raised his AKS and fired a burst across the crowded street.

Adventureland, Magic Kingdom

BURKE BARNUM WAS moving past the dock where tourists stood in line to board some kind of jungle boat ride on a manmade river when his walkie-talkie sputtered in his pocket. Palming it, he raised it to his ear—the volume was deliberately set low—and heard Galenka say she'd sighted Otis Reynolds in Frontierland, some two hundred yards from where he stood.

They had agreed to keep in touch, but Barnum had no weapons. Short of drawing fire to keep the subject busy and distracted from his escorts, there was nothing he could do to help them bag the mole. Unless...

The tour guide for the jungle river cruise was dressed like someone from a 1930s Tarzan movie, complete with pith helmet and khaki shorts. He also wore a small revolver on his hip, presumably loaded with blanks, for use at the journey's high point, when a mechanical hippo or crocodile surged from the water to "menace" the boat. Barnum had seen the show at California's Disneyland when he was twelve; it never changed. The actor's gun was harmless, but a stranger wouldn't necessarily know that if it was shoved against his ribs or pressed to the back of his head.

Barnum veered toward the dock, jumping the line and ignoring bleats of protest from children and adults alike. He plastered a smile on his face, glad-handing the startled jungle guide as he launched into his spiel.

"I'm afraid we've got a small emergency," he said. "There's a rhino loose on the midway."

"Excuse me?" The actor looked baffled.

"No cause for concern," Barnum told him. "I just need to borrow your piece for a minute."

"Hey, now—!"

The jungle guide began to protest, but his holster was empty by the time he reached it, Barnum sprinting off into the crowd with fake gun in hand. He tucked it out of sight beneath his windbreaker at once, slowing his pace after he'd covered fifty yards and put a few hundred people between himself and the dock.

Barnum was halfway to Frontierland, with no police or security personnel in sight, when he passed a familiar face headed in the opposite direction. He remembered the photo he'd studied and matched a name to the face: Thomas Atkins, from Baton Rouge. Barnum had the walkie-talkie in hand when he realized his call would only distract Galenka and Belasko from Reynolds, their previous target.

I can do this! Barnum told himself, reversing directions and falling in step behind Atkins. He jogged to catch up, closing the gap unnoticed, careful not to flash his blank-loaded pistol as he shoved it against the sleeper's lower spine.

"No sudden moves," he said. "We're going to the lavatory, just ahead and to your right."

"You're making a mistake," Atkins said. He'd rehearsed the Southern drawl to perfection.

"We'll discuss it in the crapper," Barnum said. "Get moving!"

Atkins did as he was told, making no move with either hand to reach inside his unseasonable overcoat. Barnum guided him toward the public men's room and through the entrance, glancing around to see if they had company. One pair of legs was visible in a toilet stall halfway down, but Barnum couldn't wait.

"All right," he said, "let's have the piece."

"You got it, friend," Atkins replied—and spun, swinging an elbow toward Barnum's face.

Barnum was quick enough to dodge the blow, seeing Atkins grapple underneath his coat for an automatic rifle on a shoulder sling. Panicked, Barnum raised his faux revolver and triggered three quick shots into the sleeper's face, blinding him momentarily with hot powder and cotton wadding. He took advantage of the moment with a swift kick to the sleeper's groin that doubled Atkins over, followed by a rising knee to crush his adversary's nose.

Atkins fell backward, striking his head on a nearby urinal, and sprawled at Barnum's feet. He offered no resistance as Barnum tore his coat off and relieved him of his AKS assault rifle, then lifted a pistol from his belt. Across the room, those feet had disappeared in the middle toilet stall, a frightened tourist striving for invisibility.

Barnum stood over the sleeper and considered letting him live. It was a toss-up until he thought about the prospect of hidden explosive charges and the damage a trained guerrilla could do among helpless civilians, even if her were left unarmed.

"You lose," he told the semiconscious enemy and fired a pistol shot into the downed man's forehead. Moving toward the exit, he called back to the tourist on the toilet, "As you were down there!"

Burke Barnum was smiling as he left the men's room, jogging toward a rendezvous with danger in Frontierland.

Liberty Square, Magic Kingdom

THE FIRST SOUND of gunfire made Jasha Seriozha smile—until he checked his watch. He hadn't been sure where the killing would start, but the time had been fixed in advance. None of his soldiers should've started firing yet, three minutes early, unless they'd been challenged by someone in authority. Premature firing meant their cover was blown, but it also meant Seriozha might have a chance to kill his two enemies.

Galenka and Barnum. He wasn't obsessed with

them, would never admit such a weakness to himself or anyone else, but killing either one of them would please him greatly. Killing both would damn near make his day.

Seriozha carried all three pistols—his Polish Radom semiautomatic and the matched Smith & Wessons he'd lifted from the dead FBI agents back in Arizona. All three were fully loaded, with spare magazines stashed in his pockets. He could kill thirty-three people without reloading, but random fire into a crowd wasn't Seriozha's style. Not yet, anyway. Not unless he was cornered and left with no choice.

From the direction of the first gunshots, he placed them in Frontierland. That meant either Romochka or Belayev had been sighted, perhaps both. Pistol shots punctuated the distinctive rat-tat-tat of a Kalashnikov, as Seriozha started jogging southward from Liberty Square toward the source of the noise.

It had amused him for a moment, standing among the collected symbols of American freedom, harboring the secret knowledge that they'd soon be stained with blood, perhaps swept away forever, if an unforgiving White House and Congress blamed the traitors in Moscow for Seriozha's bold initiative. A bitter realist, he doubted whether it would go that far, but as long as one die-hard believer like himself survived, the people's revolution would continue.

Moving through the crowd, Seriozha enjoyed sampling their fear. The rattling sound of not so distant gunshots continued, some tourists passing them off as normal sound effects from Frontierland, while others quickly understood that Davy Crockett and Wyatt Earp hadn't been armed with automatic weapons.

Here and there, children were already crying; some of their parents were looking frantically for the nearest exit, while others seemed more curious than alarmed.

Americans, he thought. So naïve and unprepared for most emergencies. Complacent to the core, they were their own worst enemies. Seriozha appreciated that in an adversary.

It made them so much easier to kill.

Some of them noticed Seriozha as he passed them in the crowd, recoiling from his predatory smile. One careless teenager collided with him, turned on Seriozha with an angry face and seemed about to challenge him, when he thought better of it and retreated, mouthing, "Sorry, man."

Sorry indeed. Such spineless creatures deserved whatever was done to them. It might be too late to conquer them, make them toiling vassals of Mother Russia, but it was not too late to spill their blood.

Seriozha was running by the time he reached the entrance to Frontierland, shoving those who blocked his path away to either side. It struck him that he hadn't felt this good in years.

Frontierland, Magic Kingdom

THE FIRST SHORT BURST of automatic fire was high and wide, giving Galenka time to duck and roll behind a wooden barrel with a trash can set inside. The barrel wouldn't stop AK rounds, but she thought the inner oil drum filled with litter might, if she was lucky.

Then again, she didn't plan to wait and let the shooter have it all his way.

Reynolds squeezed off another burst, and two civilians went down screaming in the middle of the street. As long as they were making noise, Galenka knew they were alive, but there was no time for her to consider their condition, much less offer them first aid. Their best chance for survival lay with her eliminating Reynolds soon, before he had a chance to spread more carnage through the crowd.

People were running every which way, panicked, as she edged around the barrel, angling for a shot. The Gyurza pistol was a risky choice for fighting in a crowd, but she could only use the tools at hand. Her enemy's Kalashnikov was clearly a much greater threat to innocent bystanders than Galenka's pistol, but she still had no clear shot and balked at firing wildly through the crowd.

Ducking and dodging, Reynolds did it for her, triggering another, longer burst that cleared a momentary lane of fire between them, dropping three more tourists in their tracks. Galenka couldn't tell if these were dead or only wounded, and she didn't stop to think about it as she found her mark. She didn't risk a double tap, but squeezed off one round from a range of twenty feet and saw her target stagger, blood spilling from a wound to his left shoulder.

It was a solid hit, but not enough to knock him down. Firing the AKS one-handed, Reynolds lurched off down the street, leaving a trail of moaning, wailing victims in his wake. Galenka waited for the man to turn and run, then started after him, hurdling the bodies of the fallen in pursuit.

Wounded or not, Reynolds was strong enough to run as if his life depended on it. Twice he spun and fired short bursts behind him, forcing Galenka to duck and dodge the spray of 7.62 mm bullets. She dared not return fire on the run, while Reynolds wove a zigzag pattern through the ranks of startled tourists, themselves fleeing at random with no apparent cover in mind.

A child of three or four ran in front of Galenka and nearly brought her tumbling down. She veered off course in time, thereby colliding with the tiny runner's panic-stricken mother. Jarring impact separated them and sent a lancing pain through Galenka's left arm.

She left the tearful woman stumbling after her elusive child and kept on in pursuit of Otis Reynolds. He surprised her a moment later, veering off course from the middle of the street toward the entrance of a simulated jail and marshal's office. Unfazed by the irony, Galenka followed him and dropped into a crouch beside the door where he had disappeared. A burst of fire and strangled outcry from within told her that he'd disposed of the resident "marshal" on duty that night.

Galenka didn't know if the mock jail had a back door, but she didn't feel like giving Reynolds time to look for one. She was about to rush the open door and take her chances, when another AK opened fire *behind her,* chipping jagged patterns in the jail's facade and driving her to ground.

MILENA BELAYEV didn't recognize the woman with the pistol, but she knew an enemy when she saw one and her response was automatic. Drawing the AKS rifle from her It's a Small World shopping bag, she raked the frontier marshal's office with a hasty burst—and missed.

Belayev knew she'd missed her mark, although the woman dropped, because there was no spray of blood to indicate a hit. With half a dozen rounds of military ammunition, even a flesh wound should be bleeding profusely, but the woman was intact and wriggling around to face Belayev, leveling a pistol in both hands.

Belayev fired again, just as her adversary squeezed off two quick shots. She felt one of the bullets sizzle past her face, heard it smash glass somewhere behind her, but relief at the near miss was tempered by frustration as her own rounds missed again, chipping concrete and taking bites out of the jail's simulated log wall.

Belayev knew she couldn't give the bitch another chance to make the shot. Dodging, she grabbed a teenage tourist on the run and spun him in front of her, using him as a human shield. He struggled briefly, until she gouged her fingernails into his throat and hissed a warning to him, standing close enough that he could feel her breath and lips against his ear. Reaching around his slender body, Belayev fired another burst at her target, but the younger woman was moving, scuttling along the sidewalk to her left, spoiling the shot.

This time Belayev cursed in Russian and the young man, startled, asked her, "What?"

"Shut up!" she snapped at him, turning his body with her own to track the enemy. A short burst from her AKS scattered some tourists who were slow to find a hiding place, but still her adversary ducked and dodged.

"Hold still, dammit!"

"I'm trying!" the boy sobbed.

"Not you, stupid!"

"I'm sorry! Jesus!"

"He can't help you!"

Losing sight of her target, Belayev took a short step backward, smashed the muzzle of her AKS against the young man's skull and dropped him to the pavement in a heap. It would've pleased her more to shoot him, but she needed every round of ammunition she possessed to stop the woman who eluded her, ducking in and out of sight along the street of shops.

Belayev started after her, anger overriding caution as she took up the pursuit. Her time might be better spent spraying the crowd with bullets, inflicting maximum death and destruction as planned, but the bitch's defiance galled her. This one had to die, above all else, before Belayev could proceed with her mission.

Where were the others? Why did they not help her?

She was halfway across the street when her enemy popped into view, craning around an old-fashioned lamppost and aiming her pistol two-handed. Belayev unleashed a burst from her rifle, the Kalashnikov's racket loud in her ears, eclipsing the other woman's pistol shot. She couldn't hear it, but Belayev felt the bullet drill beneath her ribs and punch her spinning backward, tumbling to the ground.

It hurt like hell, but she recovered swiftly, driven by equal parts of fury, fear and savage determination.

Belayev had prepared herself to die this night, but not this way, not groveling in the street like a drunkard with her weapon out of reach.

She lurched after the AKS, scooped it up as she regained her feet and turned to face her enemy. The other woman's pistol cracked again, and this time there was blunt force without pain, the impact lifting her, plucking Belayev off her feet and dropping her to the sidewalk on her back.

She was suddenly numb, hands twitching uselessly as they lost purchase on the AKS rifle, letting it slip from her grasp. She couldn't see the stars above her, washed out by the theme park's bright lights, but she knew they were up there. Milena Belayev wondered if they were disgusted with her, the stars that directed her fate, repulsed by her ultimate failure.

Slowly, softly she closed her eyes and claimed the final darkness as her own.

Main Street, U.S.A.

BOLAN WAS ON HIS WAY from Disney's version of *Our Town* to the battleground of Frontierland, responding to Galenka's radio distress call, when he saw one of Seriozha's moles emerging from the doorway of a 1950s-era malt shop. George Jamison wore a knee-length raincoat over an open-collared sport shirt and navy slacks, with runners on his feet. The lenses of his wire-rimmed glasses caught the street light for a moment, flashing brilliantly before he turned his head to sip the milk shake he was carrying.

Faint sounds of automatic gunfire echoed from Frontierland. Bolan stiffened at the noise but kept his eyes on Jamison. The Russian dropped his milk shake, splashing chocolate on his shoes and cuffs without concern. He drew the right side of his raincoat back to bare an AKS assault rifle slung muzzle down beneath his arm.

Bolan responded instinctively, drawing his Beretta and dropping into a crouch on the sidewalk, facing his target over gun sights from a range of twenty yards. He called to Jamison, using the sleeper's name, and heard a woman scream at first sight of the weapons.

"Drop the rifle, Jamison!"

He had no reason to believe his adversary would comply, but Bolan hesitated to start firing on the crowded street unless there was no choice. Jamison took the choice away from Bolan as he spun, dropping to one knee on the pavement, and unleashed a stream of death from his Kalashnikov.

Bolan held his fire as he hit the deck to save himself, unwilling to jeopardize bystanders with wild rounds fired in haste. Somewhere behind him, the Russian's bullets found an innocent target, dropping the body across Bolan's outstretched legs. He kicked free of the dead or dying man and rolled away as Jamison tried again, his next burst stinging Bolan's neck and scalp with slivers of concrete.

The guy was good, no doubt about it, but his nerves weren't made of steel. He broke for cover while Bolan was angling for a clear shot, deliberately strafing the crowd as tourists ran pell-mell to escape his field of fire. Bolan watched bodies fall, silently cursing and holding the Beretta rock-steady while he waited for his chance.

It came as Jamison cleared an ornate street lamp, no one between them for a heartbeat or two. Bolan fired once, twice and saw his man stagger, right foot slipping out from under Jamison, dropping him heavily onto his side. Even then, though, the Russian rebounded, kicking with both heels and scooting along on his backside toward the cover of a barbershop's doorway. Bolan fired again before he got there, but the slugs chipped wood and masonry, missing flesh.

Up and moving before his target was fairly out of sight, Bolan closed the gap between them on a diagonal, running in a crouch across the street. Jamison saw him coming through the shop's window, sidearming a grenade that wobbled through the air before it landed, bouncing, in the middle of Main Street, U.S.A.

Bolan kissed the pavement again, trusting physics to save him. An explosion uncontained and undirected normally went upward, sending its shrapnel along for the ride. Jamison's frag grenade was no exception, scarring the street with a flash while its killer payload peppered shop fronts and tourists still running for cover.

Ears ringing from the blast, Bolan scrambled to his feet and pressed on. From twenty feet he glimpsed Jamison through the window, kneeling as he drew another grenade from his pocket, tugging the safety pin free. Bolan fired through the glass, three quick rounds, their impact obscured by a fast-spreading spiderweb of cracks. At least one bullet found its target, though, for Jamison slumped backward, fumbling the grenade into his lap. Its blast, a moment later, sprayed the street with bits and pieces of the mole who couldn't pull himself together.

All the king's horses and all the king's men, Bolan thought, turning away from the blood-smeared doorway, double-timing up Main Street toward the sounds of combat raging in Frontierland.

CHAPTER SEVENTEEN

Frontierland, Magic Kingdom

Tasya Galenka turned back toward the marshal's office after finishing Millicent Bullard with her second shot. It had been touch-and-go but she was still alive, shaken but otherwise uninjured. If her luck was holding, Otis Reynolds waited for her in the frontier jail, ready to face her in a showdown for his life.

It felt like something from a Western movie, and she almost glanced around to see if there were cameras mounted on the rooftops to record the moment for posterity. It would've boosted ratings on the television nightly news, but viewers would be forced to get along with after-action shots of bodies scattered on the street. Right now, with uninjured civilians either gone to ground or fleeing out of range, Galenka had the street to herself.

She edged along the sidewalk, thankful that the make-believe marshal's office had no windows on her side of the door. Reynolds, assuming he was still inside and hadn't scampered out a back door she was unaware of, wouldn't be aware of her approach. He would be ready with his AKS, though, to kill anyone who ventured through the open door.

Galenka hoped his shoulder wound was bleeding steadily, but she couldn't count on finding him dead or unconscious in the office. Instead, she'd have to do it the hard way, going in alone to confront him and finish it, before he rallied and tried to fight his way clear.

As if to punctuate that thought, she heard an explosion—grenade?—from somewhere behind her. It wasn't close enough to be Adventureland. What lay beyond, farther south?

Main Street, U.S.A. Belasko's hunting ground.

Galenka had barely answered her own question when a second blast echoed through the park. She flinched involuntarily, imagining Belasko flattened and torn raw by shrapnel, then forced the grisly image from her mind. She had a job to do, and stalling only made it worse.

She edged toward the open doorway of the marshal's office, duckwalking along the sidewalk. Behind her, she heard slapping footsteps, a man's voice shouting, "Hey, you! Stop right there!" She swiveled toward the sound, still crouching, and found a uniformed security guard gaping at her across the battlefield strewed with bodies, a revolver trembling in his fist.

Galenka didn't hesitate. She had no time for explanations and she wouldn't let some underpaid rent-a-cop shoot her in the back. She aimed and fired in one fluid motion, saw his left leg buckle as the kneecap exploded and his fingers splayed to send the six-gun flying. Galenka instantly dismissed him, ignoring his cries of pain as she turned back to her primary target.

Getting through the door would be a risky proposition. There'd been ample time for Reynolds, wounded as he was, to find cover inside and prepare for her rush. She'd be an easy target coming through the door, unless…

Galenka rose and ran across the street to the spot where Millicent Bullard had fallen, taking care to avoid line-of-sight from the doorway of the marshal's office. Bullard was small, almost petite, but it was still a strain to lift her deadweight from the pavement and shrug her into a fireman's carry, Galenka lifting with her legs as she stood with the corpse draped over her shoulder.

She staggered back across the street, incapable of running now. When she stood against the wall, Galenka eased the body off her shoulder, ignoring the warm blood that soaked through her jacket and blouse. She held Bullard's slack body upright with muscle and will, edging her closer to the open door. It would be awkward and risky—might even increase her odds of getting shot if she flubbed it—but Galenka couldn't think of any other way to breach the office and live long enough for a quick shot at Reynolds. She'd feel stupid if the bastard was already gone, but not as much so as if he blew her head off.

Three more shuffling steps. Two. One. She posed beside the door, sucked in a breath and shoved Bullard's corpse through the doorway, upright, already tumbling as she released her supporting grip. The AKS cut loose immediately, bullets tearing into unresisting flesh, propelling Bullard through a jerky little dance before she fell.

Galenka was inside by that time, squeezing off in rapid-fire at Otis Reynolds where he crouched behind a wooden desk. The wood was solid, but it wasn't armored steel. The Gyurza P-9's rounds cut through it with solid thwacking sounds, like the blows of a hatchet, lifting Reynolds and slamming him back against the nearest wall. He hung there for a moment, crucified, then slithered toward a seated posture on the floor.

Two down, she thought. How many left to go?

SERIOZHA RECKONED his soldiers were dying, and it made him proud. Not on a personal level, although in a sense they were dying for him. Rather, he was proud to be part of a movement so strong, so compelling, that even a decade or more after its official "collapse" it could still motivate sacrifice. He was proud to be part of a cause that commanded such loyalty, such singularity of purpose.

And he enjoyed the action, too.

Seriozha had waited more than thirty years for this moment, the literal climax of his life, and he was determined to make the most of it. Approaching the border of Frontierland, he moved against the stream of tourists and employees fleeing gunfire in the park devoted to America's Wild West heritage. It struck him as ironic and supremely fitting that his death blow should be struck in such a place, where history and fantasy combined to venerate a past composed more of violent legend than fact. He had become a player and director of the melodrama that was daily

American life, ringing down the curtain on an era of self-satisfied complacency.

More gunfire, dead ahead. Seriozha picked up his pace, shoving aside those who were too confused or too frightened to clear a path for him. Man, woman or child—it made no difference as he bulled his way through the crush of sweaty, terrified humanity. Repelled and excited by the contact all at once, he longed to open fire on them but kept his weapons out of sight, waiting for the perfect moment to reveal himself.

At last he stood before the tall gate leading to his destination. Two or three more steps and he would be inside, a mind-warping transit to a mythical past that was now the bloody present, with grim portent for the future. Smiling, he stepped forward—and stopped as a voice behind him called out his name.

"Seriozha!"

The Russian turned, scanning the street. He barely recognized Burke Barnum, even after having seen him in the wig and beard, nearly strangling him in Chicago. It was more than the disguise that threw him off, though, for this Barnum was armed. He carried a Kalashnikov assault rifle and had a pistol wedged under his belt.

Seriozha saw the first shots coming, ducked and rolled as the AKS rattled off a 3- or 4-round burst. He came up with the Radom automatic in his hand, returning fire, but he was hasty and his shots missed by at least a yard. It startled him to hear his spent brass tinkling on the pavement, even as Barnum swung his rifle around for another try.

Seriozha bolted through the gate, running blindly

toward the rustic heart of Frontierland. It shamed him, but he didn't want to die this way, gunned down by a fugitive from justice who was once his paid informant, killed before he could witness the triumph of his sleepers. He needed cover, a chance to turn and fight Barnum on something close to equal terms.

Even running for his life, Seriozha had to laugh aloud at that: himself on equal terms with a spineless traitor who'd sold his homeland out for cash. Not entirely spineless, it now appeared, but still no fighting man in any recognized sense of the term. All those years in the Army, and this night marked the first time he'd ever fired a shot in anger. There was bitter irony in that, as well, but Seriozha had no time to appreciate it.

Dodging down the mock frontier street, he sought a place to turn and make his stand against the monster he'd created.

BOLAN WAS NEAR the northern exit from Adventureland, following the sounds of battle toward Frontierland, when he met another of the Russian sleepers. Franklin Watts was a man of average size, a trifle heavy for his build, whose thinning sandy hair had mostly given up to gray in middle age. He didn't look the least bit like a terrorist—except for the Kalashnikov assault rifle he held as he emerged from the concealment of a hedge to Bolan's left, some thirty yards ahead.

He saw Bolan immediately, took note of the pistol he carried and responded with a burst of automatic fire he didn't stop to aim. It was a near miss, even so, one of his bullets clipping his adversary's jacket, low and to the left, before he ducked back under cover with a snarl. Bolan refrained from firing back since he had no idea what lay behind the hedge or who might be endangered when his rounds cut through the shrubbery.

It could've felt surreal, chasing a clinical psychologist turned homicidal maniac through Disney World, but Bolan's mind was focused on the practical mechanics of the kill. He didn't care what mask the sleeper had been wearing for the past two decades. Watts—or whatever his name was—had abandoned his disguise and shown his true face to the world. He was a predator who had to be eliminated for the good of everyone around him, and the sooner Bolan did the job, the better it would be for all concerned.

He crossed the road, watching for any hint of movement in the bushes where his enemy had disappeared. It was the perfect time to drop him, but his adversary didn't fire. Encouraged, Bolan found the place where Watts had done his disappearing act and shouldered through, letting his pistol lead the way. He was in time to see Watts running toward some kind of medium-sized utility shed, fifty yards and fading as he sprinted for cover.

This time Bolan had a clear field of fire and nothing to lose. He braced his Beretta in a two-handed grip and chased Watts with a 3-round burst of autofire. Downrange, the runner wobbled in midstride, then went down on his face, but he rebounded instantly and scrambled for the cover of the shed, dragging his AKS along behind him by its shoulder strap.

Wounded but still alive and capable of fighting back. Bolan knew that could make his enemy more dangerous, instead of less so. Cornered rats would charge an enemy ten times their size, and they weren't motivated by fanatical devotion to a cause. He had his work cut out for him, and there was no time like the present to proceed.

Nearing the shed, Bolan slowed to listen, tracking any sounds that might betray his enemy. The shed was padlocked; Watts was hiding somewhere on the other side, concealed from Bolan by the prefab building's bulk. They could play ring-around-the-rosy all night long, chasing each other back and forth, but Bolan didn't have the time or patience for protracted games. He froze in place a moment, then began to circle counterclockwise, moving stealthily around the metal shed.

Halfway around he heard a scuffling near the corner, just in front of him. The sounds were coming closer by the second; he could hear the sleeper's heavy breathing now, pain and exertion causing him to pant. Holding his stance, Bolan stared down the barrel of his side arm, waiting for the mole to show himself.

A moment later, Watts emerged from cover, staggering. The left side of his shirt and trench coat were soaked through with blood, the product of a penetrating wound from back to front. He gaped at Bolan for a moment in surprise, recoiling just enough to swing up his rifle one-handed, finger on the trigger.

Bolan got there first, firing a double tap that stitched six rounds across the sleeper's heaving chest. Watts slumped against the east wall of the shed, relaxed his grip on the Kalashnikov to let it dangle at his side, legs folding as he crumpled to the earth. He wasn't snarling now, his face gone slack, eyes glazing even as he toppled facedown on the grass.

Bolan had lost count of his rounds expended, so he ditched the magazine and snapped a fresh one into place. From what he heard now, weapons hammering across Frontierland to the north, he'd be needing every round he had before the night was through.

EVGENII KHOKLOV RAISED his AKS and sighted on a group of tourists crouched for cover in an alleyway beside the Prairie Belle saloon. They didn't see him coming, huddled as they were behind a Dumpster, thinking they were covered from the street. In fact, they should have checked behind them when they chose their refuge—or perhaps continued on their way, fleeing Frontierland and the park itself.

Too late.

Khoklov fired into them, rewarded with the slap of bullets meeting flesh. One of his targets tried to run, lurching around the garbage bin, but he didn't travel far. A second burst lifted the man and dropped him lifeless to the pavement.

Perfect.

Khoklov felt no qualms about killing civilians. Back in Myrtle Beach, there'd been a military target on his list, but he was satisfied to do his handler's bidding as required. The main thing was an opportunity to kill Americans, after he'd waited all those years for word to make his move.

It wasn't quite what he'd imagined, but, then, nothing ever was.

Khoklov was moving toward Main Street, when a figure stepped into the alley's mouth ahead of him.

From the person's size and shape in silhouette, the length of hair, he knew it was a woman. Why she would approach the alley after hearing gunfire was beyond him, but he didn't mind accommodating one more death wish while he had the chance.

Khoklov was shouldering his rifle when the woman dropped into a crouch and aimed a pistol, triggering two shots in rapid fire from twenty feet. One bullet missed; the other struck Khoklov's left hip and knocked him backward, sat him down with stunning force that nearly made him drop his AKS.

Gasping with pain, he fired a wild burst toward the bitch who'd wounded him, then wriggled for the cover of the garbage Dumpster. There were bodies in his way, blood on the ground that mixed with his now, and his left leg wouldn't function as he shoved and dragged himself across the pavement. Khoklov flinched as another shot ripped past him, clipping the heel from his work boot, then rolled out of the shooter's sight.

It cost him nearly everything he had, in terms of strength and will, to turn and face the alley's mouth. His hands were clammy on the AKS, Khoklov squeezing until his knuckles ached to keep a solid grip. He'd been prepared for death this night, but blinding pain was something that he hadn't reckoned with. Unbidden tears left bright tracks on his cheeks, while Khoklov bit his tongue to keep from crying out aloud.

Footsteps.

The woman was approaching, closing in to make the kill. He heard her coming, but he didn't have the strength to rise and face her as he would've liked to do. Blood pooled beneath him, soaking through his pants, draining his life away with each beat of his heart.

Khoklov wondered if he would live to see the woman come around the corner, blundering into his rifle sights. His head was swimming from the pain and blood loss; he was slipping into shock, the signs apparent even in his present fuddled state. If Khoklov didn't move soon, he might never have another chance.

Summoning all that still remained of strength, determination, will, he threw himself into the middle of the alley, flopping like a fish across the pavement. All that mattered was the rifle, bucking in his hands as he held down the trigger, spraying armor-piercing rounds from left to right and back again. He cut a blazing swath across the alley—and the woman wasn't there.

It took a heartbeat for Khoklov to recognize his fatal error, and by then it was too late. The bitch lay prone, off to one side, against the wall of the saloon. He'd fired a yard or so above her head, not seeing her, and now his rifle's magazine was empty.

Khoklov cursed in Russian, fumbling for his Makarov, knowing he didn't have a hope in hell of reaching it before she fired. He stared into the muzzle of her weapon, saw it wink at him and closed his eyes before her bullet drilled a hole between them, slamming through his brain.

THE LAST MOLE nearly finished Bolan, coming up behind him as he cleared the gate to Frontierland. He didn't see the shooter coming, didn't even hear him, but a woman tourist crouched beside the gate as Bolan entered, saw the movement at his back and screamed in time to save him. Bolan didn't analyze it, barely even thought about it as he lunged into a shoulder roll and heard the swarm of bullets ripple through the space he'd occupied a second earlier.

The sleeper—Abel Decker—cursed in Russian as he missed, again in English as he saw his target swing around to face him, pistol rising into target acquisition. It was his turn to go acrobatic, taking three long strides before he threw himself behind a row of trash cans painted red, white and blue.

Bolan fired at the sleeper, his rounds chipping paint from the last can in line. A clean miss, and he scrambled for cover beside the gate, not knowing when his enemy would spring from cover for another try. The screaming woman had retreated, still wailing, her voice trailing off like an erratic siren as she ran away.

It could've been a standoff, but the sleeper after all these years lacked patience. Having thrown off his disguise at last, Decker was primed for action, couldn't bear to wait it out and see what happened next. He popped up twice from cover, triggering short bursts at Bolan, neither really coming close to contact, but they seemed to boost his nerve. Another momentary hesitation, then he came around the far end of the trash cans, firing from the hip as he advanced on Bolan's hiding place.

The storm of AKS fire chopped away at Bolan's gatepost, spraying jagged splinters as Decker advanced, closing the range from twenty yards to fifteen, then ten. He was close to point-blank range when the fast-moving bolt on his weapon locked open, pale smoke wafting from the empty chamber.

Bolan took advantage of the moment, craned around the bullet-scarred gatepost and triggered a 3-round burst from less than twenty feet away. He saw Decker lurch with the impact, clean hits at the center of mass, his body melting as the legs gave way. A heartbeat later, on his knees, the dying sleeper still tried for a fresh magazine, teeth clenched around his pain as he tried to postpone the inevitable.

Bolan put him down with another burst from the Beretta 93-R, punching Decker backward in a sprawl that left his legs bent underneath him, pinned by his weight. It would've been a painful pose, but he was long past feeling anything. Dead eyes, locked open, stared beyond the theme park lights as if they'd glimpsed the answer to a cosmic mystery.

How many shooters left? Bolan couldn't answer that one, but he still heard firing from somewhere ahead, inside Frontierland. He thought about the FBI's Hostage Rescue Team, surely inbound by now, and wondered if they'd been alerted to recognize Galenka and himself.

He put the problem out of mind and ran in the direction of the gunfire. He could only die once. Bolan would take the adversaries as they came.

BURKE BARNUM still wasn't sure how he'd lost Seriozha. One minute he'd been chasing the Russian along a stage-set kind of street in Frontierland, and the next Seriozha had ducked through the open doorway of a general store. Barnum ran to the nearest corner of the building, stopping well short of the store's broad windows, and crouched with the AKS ready in his hands. He hadn't stalled too long—a minute, maybe ninety seconds tops—before he got down on his belly and crawled underneath the window, to the doorway. Risking a peek around the jamb at last, he saw…an empty store.

Okay, so Seriozha could've been concealed behind the long display case in the middle of the room, shelves stocked with anything and everything a nineteenth-century housewife could ask for. That was why he'd sprayed the case with bullets, smashing glass and blowing out the flimsy wooden back of it before he went inside.

And found the place empty.

Somebody else could come back and clean up the mess. As for Barnum, he was too busy slipping out the back door Seriozha had thoughtfully left ajar. There was an alley back there for service personnel, no one in sight as Barnum cautiously stepped from the store. He knew Seriozha could've run in either direction, increasing his lead while Barnum worked up nerve enough to search the store, and now he was gone.

Dammit!

Barnum was trying in vain to pick a direction—left or right, south or north—when a gunshot made the decision for him. North it was. It might not be Seriozha, but at least Barnum knew he'd find some action waiting for him at the end of his next sprint.

In fact, he found more than he'd bargained for.

The sound of voices—make that one voice—drew him to an alley farther up the street. Approaching cautiously, he reached the alley's mouth, or one of them, and craned his neck around the corner for a look.

There were no less than half a dozen bodies in the alley, most of them sprawled around a modern garbage Dumpster, Frontierland's small concession to reality. Thirty feet in, a man was standing over one of those bodies, peering at the face and angling a pistol toward the fallen victim's head. Despite the darkness and the awkward angle, Barnum recognized Jasha Seriozha on his feet, Tasya Galenka on the ground at his feet.

Too late, he thought, and shouted, "You bastard!" as he raised the AKS to fire. Seriozha turned to face him as Barnum squeezed the rifle's trigger—and a sharp metallic click announced the hammer's impact on an empty chamber.

Seriozha laughed, a mocking noise that echoed through the alley like sound effects from a low-budget haunted-house movie. Barnum had time to curse himself for not searching Tom Atkins and picking up spare magazines, before Seriozha smiled at him and raised his pistol. Barnum dropped the AKS and groped for his Makarov, but the pistol snagged on something and foiled his quick draw.

Raging, determined not to meet death passively, Barnum charged snarling across the Russian's field of fire.

"YOU BASTARD!"

The shout—Burke Barnum's voice?—was followed by a moment of relative silence, tourist screams and sirens fading into background noise, before another shot rang out. Bolan fixed the probable point of origin in mind and ran for it, scanning the doorways and windows of Old West shops along Main Street as he passed. Any one of them might hide a sniper, but none emerged to threaten Bolan now.

He reached the alley's mouth and peered inside. Before the shooting started, it might've been the cleanest alley he'd ever seen—maybe the cleanest on Earth—but it had lately turned into a charnel house. Bodies and blood were everywhere, Tasya Galenka's among them—but at least she was moving, albeit fitfully. Nearby, Barnum and Jasha Seriozha were locked in hand-to-hand combat, fighting over the pistol Seriozha clutched in his right fist.

Bolan had no clear shot at the Russian, but he didn't need to rush it as long as Barnum held Seriozha's gun hand. Bolan was edging closer, angling for a shot, when the two men stumbled out of view behind the garbage Dumpster.

Another shot rang out almost immediately. Someone gasped, the sound eclipsed by two more shots in rapid fire. A moment later, Barnum staggered into view, one hand clutching his abdomen, blood streaming through his fingers, while the other flailed for a grip on the bin. He found one, muscles straining, trying to hold himself upright as his legs turned to rubber. It was a losing battle, and another moment saw him kneeling, slouched against the Dumpster.

Seriozha was next to emerge, looking rumpled but self-satisfied as he raised his side arm, aiming at the back of Barnum's head. A hint of movement stayed his hand at the last moment, Seriozha glancing up from his target to find Bolan facing him, no more than twenty feet distant, the Beretta leveled at his chest.

Unflappable, the Russian said, "I saw you in Chicago."

"I wish I'd seen you," Bolan replied.

"Here I am."

"Here *we* are."

"You seem to be—what is the phrase?—a little shorthanded."

"I'll take my chances," Bolan told him.

"As will I."

"The way it should be, yes?"

Bolan saw the flicker in Seriozha's eyes, preceding the movement of his hand. Seriozha was lifting his pistol when Bolan double-stroked the Beretta's sensitive trigger, firing two 3-round bursts. At that range, all six rounds hit their mark, Seriozha stiffening, lurching back in a clumsy moon walk before he collapsed on the pavement.

Bolan kept his adversary covered as he closed the distance between them. Kneeling first beside Barnum, he had to lean in close to hear the convict ask, "Is he done?"

"He's done."

Barnum smiled. "So, you did it."

"*We* did it."

The smile broadened a little, then froze. Barnum's eyes went glassy and he surrendered to gravity, sliding down the garbage bin's flat side to the ground. Bolan moved to crouch beside Tasya Galenka, noting her grimace of pain at his touch. Blood pooled beneath her, but no wound was visible.

"I didn't see him coming," she told Bolan through clenched teeth. "Stupid."

"Human," he said. "I need to see how bad you're hurt."

"Do it."

He turned her gently, trying to ignore her gasp of pain. There was a single entry wound below her right shoulder blade, where Seriozha had shot her in the back. It didn't sound like a sucking wound, but damage to the lung was still a possibility.

Sirens were louder now, inside the park itself. There would be suits and uniforms incoming, agents from the Bureau's Hostage Rescue Team and anybody else available once news of shots fired at the park began to make the rounds. They were about to have a crowd of nervous, trigger-happy cops for company.

"Help's on the way," he told Galenka. Bolan put his gun away and took his FBI credentials from an inside pocket, dangling them conspicuously from the breast pocket of his sport coat. "I need to get some help back here."

Galenka smiled at him despite the pain and said, "You won't forget me?"

"Not a chance."

He squeezed her trembling hand, then went to greet the cavalry.

EPILOGUE

Arlington National Cemetery

The graveside interlude was brief—no eulogy or loving testimonials, no prayers or hymns, no flowers on display. Attendance was minimal—no honor guard or other uniforms, no clergyman, no family or co-workers. A pair of grave diggers showed up to do the dirty work, idling beside their backhoe while two mourners spent a moment with the casket.

"Arlington," Brognola said. "Go figure."

"He was still a veteran," Bolan replied.

"He was a traitor."

"It's a loophole, I admit." But here they were. "He did all right the last few days."

"If you say so."

"You had to be there," Bolan said.

"No, thanks. I'll pass." Another silent moment passed before Brognola asked, "Did you have anything to say?"

Bolan had already considered it and come up empty. "I guess not."

"We're finished, then?"

"We're done."

"Lunch, then," Brognola said. "They've got a brand-new Cajun place in Arlington I want to try."

"Gumbo?"

"Maybe the jambalaya. I don't know yet."

"Here comes heartburn."

"Hey, we're celebrating, right?"

"We are."

They started toward the parking lot, moving past rows of grave markers. "Your comrade has her coming-out party tomorrow, I understand."

"Unless she has a setback," Bolan said.

Galenka's wound hadn't involved the lung, nor had the bullet broken any major bones. It was a lucky wound, if such a thing existed. Three nights in the hospital and she was cleared to head for home.

"The word I get," Brognola said, "she's up for a promotion when they get her back in Moscow. Job well done, and all that jazz."

"It was too messy for my taste," Bolan replied. He was inured to bloodshed, but the hunt for Jasha Seriozha and his sleepers had involved a painful number of civilian casualties. There were a dozen dead and twice that many wounded from the last firefight, in Florida.

"Messy's what you get, sometimes," Brognola said. "It could've been a damn sight worse."

That much was true, at least. None of the plastic explosives planted by the Russian moles at Disney World had detonated. All had been recovered and disarmed by state and federal bomb squad officers after the theme park was evacuated. If the plastique had exploded while the night's first panicked exodus was underway, they might've been counting fatalities in scores or hundreds.

"Still no progress with the other sleepers?" Bolan asked.

"They're sitting tight behind the Fifth Amendment," Brognola replied. "Not saying much of anything to anyone, including their attorneys. Background checks are going on through INS. We've got four of them pegged on false identities so far, and I expect we'll get them all before it's over."

"Then what?"

"That's the problem. With no fingerprints on file, the only charges that'll stick are weapons violations for their hardware and a few stray counts of fraud. I'm guessing they'll do time, but not too much."

"Conspiracy?" Bolan suggested.

"It won't stick. They never knew each other and we can't prove any link to Seriozha. Legally it takes at least two people to conspire."

"Can you deport them?"

"Maybe. State's discussing it with Moscow, anyway. The Russians are relieved to have this mess behind them, but they can't admit they ever planted sleepers in the first place. We can't prove the moles are Russian, only that they aren't who they pretend to be. We'd have to send them somewhere, but nobody wants them. It's catch-22 all over again."

Six sleepers in limbo. Bolan didn't like the sound of that, but at least they were exposed now, in custody. When they were freed again—if they survived that long—he took for granted that there'd be surveillance mounted over each of them as long as they remained in the United States.

"Covert repatriation, maybe," Bolan said.

"It's been discussed," Hal said. "We lock them up a while, let things cool down, maybe the Russians won't mind taking them off our hands, one or two at a time."

"What's the alternative?" Bolan knew the answer to that one before he asked the question.

"They could have accidents," Brognola said.

Wet work. Four men and two women who'd spent the past two decades as Americans, scheming all the while against the country they occupied, could be disposed of singly or en masse. A van could crash and burn while they were on their way to court. Too flashy? Prisoners were murdered in the U.S. every day—for drugs or money, in pursuit of sex, as a result of gang warfare, to settle private quarrels. If it was spread out over time, kept from the press, another six deaths would barely make a ripple.

"Count me out of that one," Bolan said.

"No sweat. It may not come to that." When they were halfway to the car, Brognola said, "Too bad about Barnum. The media, I mean."

There'd been no way to credit Barnum with his final actions, short of giving up the whole story and setting off a firestorm of publicity from Los Angeles to Capitol Hill. Instead, the FBI and U.S. Marshal's Service still blamed him for killing his escorts the day he'd "escaped" in Indiana, listing his whereabouts as unknown before he ran afoul of drug cartel gunmen in Florida. Officially there'd been no terrorist attack on Disney World, and Barnum's death was a "coincidence." It was the best Washington's whitewash artists could do on short notice, and allegations of conspiracy were already rife on the Internet, three Web sites dedicated to conflicting stories of "The Disney Cover-up."

It wasn't vindication, but Bolan had a hunch Burke Barnum would've smiled at that. If nothing else, a bit of mystery had been appended to his passing. It was more than Barnum would've got if he'd stayed put and simply withered in his cage.

Tasya Galenka would be flying out the following day or the one after, back to Moscow and debriefing with her supervisors. Bolan had no plans to see the Russian operative again before she left the States. He'd visited her once at the Miami hospital and heard the doctors say that she'd sustained no lasting damage. It was more than most of those who'd crossed their paths could claim, and he was satisfied.

She would go home without knowing his name or how to get in touch again for any reason. That was Bolan's life, the way he moved from day to day. He had connections here and there, but they were few and far between, buried as deeply as technology could manage in this modern age.

He saw the car now, baking in the midday sun. He was already thinking past the moment, through the dwindling afternoon with Brognola, wondering where the next mission would take him. Whom he'd have to kill.

"You've got some downtime coming if you want it," said Brognola. Bolan wondered when he'd started reading minds.

"It couldn't hurt."

"My thoughts exactly. Nothing wrong with R and R."

Rest and Recuperation never lasted, though. It was a cheat, setting him up for another life-or-death confrontation—and the next one after that—until one day he didn't make it back.

Not yet, he thought. And said to Brognola, "Cajun? You're sure?"

"I'm positive. With beer, of course."

"Okay."

He walked on through the sunshine with his oldest living friend. There were worse things in life than heartburn, after all.

But they would have to wait.

Skydark Spawn

Available in
March 2003
at your favorite retail outlet.

In the relatively untouched area of what was once Niagara Falls, Ryan and his fellow wayfarers find the pastoral farmland under the despotic control of a twisted baron and his slave-breeding farm. Ryan, Mildred and Krysty are captured by the baron's sec men and pawned into the cruel frenzy of their leader's grotesque desires. JB, Jak and Doc enlist the aid of outlanders to organize a counterstrike—but rescue may come too late for them all.

Or order your copy now by sending your name, address, zip or postal code, along with a check or money order (please do not send cash) for $6.50 for each book ordered ($7.99 in Canada), plus 75¢ postage and handling ($1.00 in Canada), payable to Gold Eagle Books, to:

In the U.S.
Gold Eagle Books
3010 Walden Ave.
P.O. Box 9077
Buffalo, NY 14269-9077

In Canada
Gold Eagle Books
P.O. Box 636
Fort Erie, Ontario
L2A 5X3

Please specify book title with order.
Canadian residents add applicable federal and provincial taxes.

GDL61